# THE RAT REVEREND CLANCY AND THE SEVEN HEAVENLY VIRTUES

## DAVID L. CARTER

APOCRYPHILE
PRESS

Apocryphile Press
PO Box 255
Hannacroix, NY 12087
www.apocryphilepress.com

Copyright © 2024 by David L. Carter
Printed in the United States of America
ISBN 978-1-958061-67-1 | paper
ISBN 978-1-958061-68-8 | ePub

Please join our mailing list at
www.apocryphilepress.com/free
We'll keep you uptodate on all our new releases,
and we'll also send you a FREE BOOK. Visit us today!

*This one is dedicated to my loving Mom,*
*a woman of all the virtues!*

# CONTENTS

# TEMPERANTIA

"I 'VE NEVER BEEN SO excited in my life!!" Clancy declared to himself. But that was just characteristic over-statement, for Clancy was by nature given to enthusiasm. But it was true that he could hardly contain himself when he overheard the news. After what felt like an eternity following the departure of his beloved Reverend Silas DeBassompierre, Th.D. to accept a lectureship position at Harvard Divinity School, St. Aloysius Episcopal Church in Morehead City, North Carolina had finally called a new rector. And Clancy was eager to see what he was like.

It was a shame, Clancy lamented to himself, that he and the new rector would never enjoy a collaborative ministry, just as it had been a shame that Clancy and Reverend DeBassompierre had likewise never established a collegial professional relation-ship, even though they had the experience of Christian ministry in common. But unfortunately providence had ordained that Reverend DeBassompierre and the new rector called to replace him were human beings, while Clancy was a rat. It was on account of their difference in species that Reverend DeBassom-pierre had never known that Reverend Clancy even existed, though Clancy had observed the human clergyman at close range for most of his adult life. He had furtively regarded him from a hiding place behind the enormous set of bookshelves along the western wall of the Rector's office, along with other strategic locations throughout the church building, such as the narrow space beneath the console of the Hammond Organ in the sanctuary. By observing the handsome, youngish and erudite human rector, Clancy had learned the rudiments of Christian faith and the practice of the ministries of Word and Sacrament.

Given such a positive example, it was not surprising that, not long after the passing into eternity of his dear Great-Aunt November, who had raised him in the cellar of St. Aloysius, Clancy experienced, in a numinous nocturnal vision, his own call to ordained priesthood. He then established, by the Grace of God and the prompting of the Holy Ghost, a mission to the suburban wildlife that inhabited the general area surrounding St. Aloysius Church. Clancy called his faith community "St. Aloysius Jr. Church for All God's Creatures Great and Small." Quickly—almost miraculously, it seemed to him—there came to be gathered together a small but devoted and thriving cadre of members drawn from a variety of species, from invertebrate to mammal. Every Sunday at 10am, while the humans of the mother church gathered indoors to attend to the liturgy presided over by the Reverend DeBassompierre, the Rat Reverend Clancy held services for his own little flock in the backyard of the church, preaching and offering a diverse species of communion from atop the vermicomposter that stood at the edge of the community garden. Pastoring a church—particularly one with a congregation made up of creatures as diverse in background and temperament as were the members of St. Aloysius Jr.—was not always easy, God knows, but it was the light of Clancy's life and he would not abandon his calling for all the world. So it was ironic that his beloved mentor had found parish ministry, apart from administering the sacraments, incredibly trying. The Reverend DeBassompierre had left much of the pastoral care duties to his capable administrative assistant, Grace Holbach, who, Clancy had to admit, handled them with good sense and aplomb. But now there was going to be a new Rector in charge. Clancy wondered how things would change, if at all.

And so on the Monday morning that the new rector was due to arrive, Clancy awakened bright and early, in fact even before sunrise, made his way up to the administrative suite of the church building from the cellar, and tucked himself behind the bookcases. And there he waited eagerly until the sound of automobile tires crunching over the unpaved gravel parking lot heralded the arrival of a new chapter.

☙❦❧

"...AND here, last but not least, is your office..." said Grace. "It isn't much, but Silas made the best of it, and there's plenty of room for whatever you might want to bring in to make it your own. We left the desk in front of the window...Silas liked to face the door...but of course you can rearrange things as you like..."

"Wonderful." The voice of the new rector was soft and low, yet firm—and to Clancy's utter astonishment, indubitably female. So surprised was he that he could not resist poking his snout around the corner of the bookcase to take a quick look. And indeed, there she was, the newly called rector of St. Aloysius Episcopal Church, clearly a female human despite her short hair and more than average height. "I think I'll leave the desk as it is, at least for now...I, too, prefer to face what's coming. But this is certainly a lovely view of the woods..." And she spread out her arms before the large window behind the desk that overlooked the backyard—a playground, a small fenced-in graveyard, and the community garden as well as the woods beyond. Clancy stared at her broad figure, monolithic and dark against the daylight admitted through the window. Her expansive gesture gave him an odd, dwindling sensation. He reached for his tail and began to gnaw at the tip, a nervous habit left behind from an unstable infancy.

Grace walked around the desk to stand beside the new rector, and this gave Clancy the opportunity to compare the two women, albeit from behind. Grace was slightly smaller in many ways, several inches shorter, at least, and not as broad in the hips, dressed as usual in blouse and slacks that were, if not close fitting, certainly conformed to her shape. The new rector, however, was wrapped in flowing garments reminiscent of the Reverend DeBassompierre's liturgical vestments, but the shawls and flowing skirts in which the new rector was swathed were filmy and pastel-patterned rather than heavy and embroidered, and they accentuated not only her broad figure but the relative smallness of her head, with its close-cropped, limp and rather seaweed-colored hair. She was one of the most unusual looking human beings that Clancy had ever seen. A starker contrast to the rather stark figure of the Reverend DeBassompierre was hard to imagine.

"Yes, it is a nice view, isn't it?" said Grace. "It's a shame though, that the garden's so weedy. I just haven't had the time to do much with it since Silas left..."

"Of course you haven't," said the new Rector. "I don't know how you've managed to keep it up at all, with all that's fallen onto your plate. Well, that's all over now. I understand that you're used to taking on more than the diocese is paying you for, but let me assure you, those days are over. Of course, you'll continue the pastoral care that you've been providing... word from the bishop is that you have a real gift... but I will not allow your time and talent to be taken for granted."

"I appreciate that, Reverend Grey," said Grace.

"Please," said the new Reverend. "Call me Jean."

"All right," said Grace. "Jean. Jean... just let me know if you have anything special in mind you'd like for me to include in the bulletin for this week's service. I've got to get started on that right away. If I don't knock it out on Monday, something always comes up later in the week and I'm scrambling to get it done over the weekend."

"Don't let me keep you, then. I'll just start unpacking. And as for Sunday's service... I think, to mark the occasion of my very first service as rector... why, I think I'd like to hold an outdoor eucharist! In the presence of that wonderful garden—so full of promise—like this church! What do you think, Grace?"

"Why not?" said Grace, not without some hesitation. She did not want to discourage her apparently congenial new boss, but Grace knew very well that the bulk of the congregation would grumble at best at the idea of an outdoor service. She shrugged her shoulders internally, and left the new Rector—Jean—to get settled.

৩%৩

OH, Lord! Behind the bookshelves, Clancy nearly bit the tip of his tail off. An outdoor service! What in the world! He peered out from behind the corner of the bookshelves to watch the new reverend, in her flowing garments, assume the Reverend DeBassompierre's old leather cushioned swivel chair, and then lean back and sigh with all too human self-satisfaction. An outdoor service—in the area behind the building—for the humans! It just seemed...out of order. And, of course, it meant that his own service could not be held. Resentment began to take shape and sharpen in Clancy's heart like an icicle. *Reverend DeBassompierre would never do this!* he said to himself. Reverend DeBassompierre did things the way they were supposed to be done.

Clancy withdrew into the narrow dark space between the back of the still empty bookshelves and the western wall of the rector's office and curled into a ball. He felt as freshly bereft as he had on the day that Reverend DeBassompierre left for Harvard. So he closed his eyes tightly in the darkness and brought to mind an image of the Reverend DeBassompierre, tall, handsome, solemn, yet resplendent in his crisp white cassock and his bright red stole with the Chi-Rho embroidered upon it in golden thread—so austere, and so much less distracting than this old woman with all her patterns and colors. *Oh, Reverend DeBassompierre!* he lamented, *why have you forsaken me?*

☙❧

THE ANIMALS OF ST. Aloysius Jr. were all wildly curious, many of them having observed the arrival of the new human rector that morning. "Looked like a female to me!" said Ometa the opossum on her way to scavenge some provisions from the dumpster of the grocery store up the boulevard. "Hard to tell, though, with humans sometimes."

"Oh, I don't think so," said Ottoline, a female pigeon who with her gentle and competent manner had become one of the rat reverend's most reliable lay pastoral assistants. "I've always found that the females of that species tend to be much more differentiated. But I suppose it's all subjective. At any rate, Reverend, what do you make of her?"

The rat reverend, and a few of his most active parishioners, were gathered around the composter that sat at the edge and nurtured the soil of the community garden. From the beginning, this edifice had served as the centerpiece of the outdoor worship space, housing a teeming colony of countless earthworms who were almost entirely the progeny of Hertz, an earthworm who was in fact the Reverend Clancy's first, if reluctant and largely agnostic convert to the Christian faith. Having been trodden into the sanctuary of St. Aloysius clinging to the muddy shoe of the Reverend DeBassompierre one evening not long after the sudden death of Clancy's Aunt November, Hertz had been discovered by Clancy in critical condition, and Clancy had placed him in the soil of the potted fern that hung suspended above Grace's desk in the administrative wing and nursed him back to health. By nature and—on account of his traumatic early experience—suspicious of authority, Hertz was nevertheless, in his grudging way, grateful to the rat for saving his skin, and with a show of grousing reluctance allowed the rat to use the sturdy composter as pulpit and altar.

"Oh, Ottoline!" said Clancy rather breathlessly, for he had just emerged from the cellar of the church building through a gnawed-off gap in the corner of the crawlspace door that was, with the passage of time, growing too snug for his girth. "I don't know what to say. She's nothing in the world like Reverend DeBassompierre... and she wants to hold the next Sunday service outside, right here by the garden! Can you believe that? She's got that great big beautiful sanctuary, but she wants to bring all those humans out here! I just don't understand it! What is she up to? This is where *we* have worship! What in the world are we going to do?"

The gathered creatures took in this information with a range of vocalizations expressive of alarm, sympathy, and even indignation. Only Hertz, who in spite of himself often found himself interested in the various turmoils of this community that he considered to be frivolous, expressed something like nonchalance. "What's the big deal?" he said in his gravelly insinuating manner. "It's *their* church! It's *their* churchyard. They can do whatever they want—they always do, anyway. Besides, that means you get the day off."

"I don't want the day off!" said Clancy, with a petulance uncharacteristic of his normally sprightly nature. "I want her to leave us alone!"

This sentiment, evincing an attitude towards the new female rector so opposite to his admiration for the former rector, struck everybody, even Clancy himself, as unchristlike. "I mean..." He endeavored to curb his vehemence. "I hate for us to miss *our* service. It's important that we gather for worship every single Sunday. It says so in the Bible." At least, he added to himself, he was pretty sure it did.

"But we don't have to miss nothing!" said a voice from above. The animals (including Hertz) who were gathered around the composter each looked up. And sure enough, descending in a graceful, tightening spiral from the bright blue sky, floated a cruciform figure, followed closely by a similar, if slightly smaller figure. They were Bertram and his sister Sudie Mae, a pair of buzzards who were devoted to the rat reverend Clancy, and who were founding members of the small but spirited St. Aloysius Jr. choir.

"Bertram! Sudie Mae!" Clancy greeted these two parishioners. "Lord! I'm glad y'all are here. There's big news. The new rector of the human church is here! And she's already changing everything! She wants to have this Sunday's service outside!"

"We heard," said Bertram, landing beside the composter, and thus compounding if not complementing the stench it exuded with his own pungent, acrid, somewhat putrescent odor. Sudie Mae settled as close as she could manage to the rodent, to whom she was fiercely devoted. "But Reverend, just 'cause the humans'll be outside doesn't mean we can't worship with them, does it? We'll just all have to be real careful not to let them know we're watching. Nothing against you, of course, Reverend, but I've always been curious how the humans praise the Lord. I mean, I know you've been studying them a long time and know what you're doing, but I just think it'd be interesting to hear what they have to say about Jesus. Might even be fun."

Clancy reached for his tail. What Bertram was saying stirred up a maelstrom of confused emotions within him. He understood, of course, Bertram's natural curiosity about the ways of the human race, and while the rat couldn't help but worry a little that his own homiletic and liturgical skills might compare unfavorably to those of this odd new female rector, on the whole he was fairly confident in his congregation's recognition that he was uniquely suited to address their non-human spiritual needs. Still, the impulse to shield himself from possible if unlikely rejection was strong. And there was also the question of discretion. The humans, after all, were notorious for overreaction to any perceived divergence from the ordinary. "I don't know..." he said, for lack of anything else to say.

"You know, I think Bertram's got a point," said Ottoline. "There's no reason that we couldn't worship along with the humans...as long as we're discrete. Now, it would be tricky for Magnus and his family to get too close...they *are* so large and so compelling..." Magnus was a buck deer with a spouse and three offspring, all of whom were regular parishioners of Clancy's community. "But they should be able to see fairly well from the edge of the woods without being too noticeable. And Bertram and Sudie Mae..." Ottoline addressed the two large and odiferous buzzards. "I think if you two perch right up on the apex of the roof, just by the belfry, none of the humans will get wind of your presence. Reverend, you're small enough to tuck yourself away just about anywhere, and as for the others who aren't here right now..." Ottoline tuned to her mate, Stephen, who had just fluttered down from the rooftop to join the conversation. "Steven and I will make sure they understand the situation and take the necessary steps to ensure all of our safety. Really, when you think about it, Reverend, it's not that much different than when they're inside. Even then we have to be on our guard."

One by one Clancy regarded the small group of variegated creatures that made up, in a certain sense, the informal inner circle of his church, those members who were most consistently involved and who had been with him from the beginning. Without them, he never could have managed with any equanimity the various storms and lulls of his early days in ministry. They had supported and challenged, and most importantly, loved him through it all. Perhaps that was why he now felt so inexplicably threatened. Of all of the animals, only he and

Hertz had ever observed the humans at worship within their cool and spacious sanctuary, only he and Hertz had ever heard the human choir sing accompanied by the whines and moans of the Hammond organ, only he and Hertz had ever heard the human Reverend DeBassompierre delivering one of his erudite sermons. Hertz had been unimpressed by it all, but Hertz was never very impressed with anything. And his recollection of that worm's dependable dissatisfaction had the paradoxical effect of heartening Clancy. "All right," he said. "Amen. This Sunday, we'll worship with the humans. And I know that I can count on everyone to be careful."

☙❧

As OTTOLINE HAD SUGGESTED, the buzzards and pigeons of the congregation, with their bird's-eye view of the surrounding area, were easily able to locate and inform the other regular members of the church. Bertram and Sudie Mae visited Magnus and his brood in a clearing deep in the woods where they made their usual habitat. Magnus, his spouse and three offspring were among the newest members of St. Aloysius Jr., but in their brief time had established themselves as important voices in the community. Hans, the middle buck, had in the past demonstrated, along with his fierce intelligence, a tendency toward a more than ordinary adolescent recklessness, which a burgeoning friendship with Hertz had served to channel and to tame. Magnus was very grateful for that and readily agreed to Bertram and Sudie Mae's request for the deer to conceal their presence at the forthcoming service on Sunday. "Thanks for the head's-up," said Magnus to the two buzzards. "I sure don't want to get any closer to all those humans than I have to. Wonder why they want to have their service outside? Seems like it would be more trouble than it's worth. Hope they don't make a habit of it."

"They probably will." Hans, having overheard the conversation, ambled over and, as was his wont, put in his two cents. "They take over everything, even if it they don't need it. We'll probably never be able to have our own church again."

"Hans." His father's remonstration was calm and weary with repetition. "Remember what you told me that the worm told you? That no one species is all bad, that there are plenty of decent humans?"

"I remember," said Hans. "But here they go again, Father, muscling in on our territory! It isn't fair!"

"All they want to do is worship God, just like we do," said Magnus. "We don't own the outdoors, son. We have to learn to share."

"So do they," said Hans balefully, and he stalked away muttering.

"Sorry," said Magnus to the buzzards. "He's still upset about our having to move from where they put that big road in through the marsh. But he's a good boy..."

"Sure he is!" agreed Bertram, always encouraging. "It's not easy being young." For, though young himself, Bertram, having had the responsibility of caring for his sister Sudie Mae since the death of their tyrannical daddy some time before, sometimes felt like a very old soul, full of hard-won wisdom.

❧

MEANWHILE OTTOLINE and Steven alerted some of the smaller, less conspicuous members of the community, and advised them that they could stay close to the action as long as they were quiet. This posed no real problem for most, in that they were naturally wary of humans and were accustomed to keeping a low profile in the presence of those unpredictable beings. A couple of devout middle aged squirrels named Horace and Mildy agreed that it would be best to observe from the trees, and promised to spread the word among the other squirrels who occasionally attended services. Ometa, the gregarious opossum, who was nocturnal and thus irregular in her attendance in any case, believed that she would sit this one out. "I don't take no chances when it comes to humans," she said. "They always look at us like we're the ugliest things they've ever seen, and my young'uns might get their feelings hurt."

"Understood," said Ottoline. "Well, we'll miss you, but it'll be a chance for you to get some extra rest."

And so it went. Ottoline, for her part, continued to feel fairly certain that the presence of the humans really wouldn't be all that disruptive, and she began to look forward to observing them at worship. She said as much to her spouse Steven, who agreed that it would be an interesting spectacle. "But we better keep an eye on the reverend," he said, and Ottoline was not a little alarmed, for it was unlike placid Steven to be alarmist.

"The reverend?" she said. "Why?"

Steven took his time responding, as if he were considering every single word before he uttered a peep. Ottoline, having become accustomed to his careful taciturnity over the years of their relationship, simply waited and looked up at the stars and the moon from inside the purely decorative belfry atop the church that she and Steven had long made their roost.

"He's scared of her," Steven said.

"What? Steven! Why on earth!?"

Steven paused, until Ottoline, her considerable patience at an end, poked him with her beak.

"I don't know," said Steven. "There's just something about her that he doesn't trust."

"Oh, dear," said Ottoline.

❧

JEAN GREY WAS careful to keep an eye on the very mercurial coastal weather forecast; however, by Friday morning she felt confident that the current sunny and mild conditions were likely to hold, and that it would be safe and acceptable to go ahead with her plan to hold the service in the area of the churchyard between the community garden and the fenced-in cemetery. Taking her cue from the Hebrew Scripture reading for the week, she would develop the motif of Exodus, of faith leading the church and the individual out towards the other, the liminal, the unknown, and thus explicate in her sermon, her inaugural speech, so to speak, the importance of maintaining a sense of mission, of moving out of the church into the world, to love and serve the neighbor.

Grace had well-founded concerns regarding the decision to hold the service outdoors that had nothing to do with the weather, but she did as the so far pleasant new rector bade her, and announced in the bulletin that the service was to be held behind the church, and that parishioners should dress accordingly. The choir would choose anthems and hymns to be sung acapella, and a folding card table from the fellowship hall would serve as the altar. It all seemed to Grace to be an awful lot of trouble to go to for no good reason that she could discern, but she held her tongue, for she was finding herself becoming fond of her new boss, quite beyond her expectations. Hopefully all would go well, and the inevitable grousing from the hardliners on the Vestry would be kept to a minimum and away from the notice of the new rector. But that was a lot to ask, from a congregation temperamentally resistant, for the most part, to anything out of the ordinary.

And here we go, said Grace to herself that afternoon, upon receiving a call from perhaps the most contentious and elderly of parishioners, whose avowed dislike of the former rector was already transforming into nostalgia. "At least that feckless DeBassompierre realized that I can't sit in the hot sun all morning with the medication I'm on!" old Mrs. Meilish declared with as much indignation as if she'd been asked to attend church nude.

"Well, I'll bring you communion in the afternoon, hon," said Grace. "And I'll be sure to let Reverend Grey know you're sorry to miss the service, and that you'll look forward to welcoming her next Sunday."

"Well... all right," the old lady said, not a little put out by having her problem solved so tidily. "I just hope we haven't made a mistake."

"We haven't," said Grace, silently praying that she was not lying.

❦

"OH, WHAT A BEAUTIFUL MORNING!" exclaimed the Reverend Jean Grey as her Subaru tires crunched onto and into the gravel parking lot of St. Aloysius Episcopal Church on Sunday while the morning stars still shone along the horizon to the west. "Following a beautiful night. Thank you, Creator, for clear skies and light winds. Now, if You please, don't let it get too warm too early!"

Stepping out of her automobile, the Rector stood for a moment and filled her lungs with a deep breath of the balmy coastal air. She spread out her arms in the filmy sleeves of her favorite caftan, and lifted her countenance, eyes closed, to the rising sun. She felt as fresh and invigorated as a leaping doe, and indeed, she thought she saw, as she opened her small blue eyes, one of those noble creatures, that she considered to be something of a spirit animal, dash off in the distance into a stretch of woods behind the church. This glimpse of natural beauty gave her spirit an additional lift. Jean Grey was not unaware that she was starting off on thin ice with many established parishioners. But such signs indicated that she was doing the right thing.

Grace, for her part, had not yet arrived at the church to assist with setup...but it was, of course, very early still, and it suited Jean Grey just fine, to begin the preparations for her inaugural service on her own, in the agreeable company of her own person. She entered the church, disabled the alarm, and before doing anything else, she stepped into the empty and silent and still rather dawn-dark sanctuary. She walked down the aisle like a virgin bride, and paused before the altar and closed her eyes and breathed deeply, intentionally, meditatively. There lingered in the sacred space the faint scent of decades of incense, candles and floral arrangements, the holy ghosts of countless liturgies. For a brief moment Jean Grey second-guessed her impulse to forego the sanctuary, but consoled herself that she would still be on holy ground. She would, in good time, make it clear to her members that in spite of her love of innovation and renewal, she did not come to abolish, but to fulfill. It was too late, at any rate, to turn back now. She gazed up at the crucifix suspended from the rafter above the altar and genuflected with real sincerity. She turned and swept out of the chapel. To save Grace as much trouble as possible, she set up the folding chairs behind the church.

IT WAS the unusual and highly disruptive and intermittent noise of chairs being dragged down the corridor above that section of the cellar where Clancy made his sleeping pallet of discarded choir robes that awakened Clancy from a turgid and distress-filled dream in which some gargantuan machine of human invention plowed up the community garden with relent-less rapacity.

"Stop it!" he cried aloud, jolting himself into waking consciousness. "Stop it right now!" But even as he came to his senses, the noise above continued. He stood straight up in his bedding, wide-eyed and ears pricked. He felt utterly disorien-tated, and for a few moments he could not remember his own name or species, much less that he was a reverend, and that it was another Sunday, and even more less that the new human rector had arrived and was planning to hold the service outside, which upset everything. It all came back to him soon enough, however, and he sank back into his bedding with a moan. For the first Sunday since almost the very beginning of his ministry, he would not be preaching or consecrating. He was relegated to the status of parishioner, and hidden parishioner at that, and it didn't feel good. Maybe I should just stay in bed, he said to himself sulkily. He closed his eyes and reached for the end of his tail, but try as he might, he just could not relax. He moaned again and crawled over to the crawlspace door, where a beam of daylight streamed through the gnawed-out corner that served as his portal to the outside world. Church isn't about me, he upbraided himself sternly. It's about the Lord.

And with not a little effort, he squeezed himself through to the outside.

FROM THE ORNAMENTAL ROOFTOP BELFRY, Ottoline and Steven observed with silent fascination as a blousy female human dragged a number of large flat objects from the emergency exit of the church building's education wing and unfolded them to stand in rows between the east edge of the community garden and the west edge for the church cemetery. As the sun rose higher and grew stronger it was easy to see that the human woman was becoming increasingly breathless and moving slowly, and her countenance, (so vividly expressive, like that of most humans and canines) conveyed an increasing consternation. "Heavens!" the pigeons heard her exclaim. "How did it warm up here so fast!" And she sank onto one of the chairs she had unfolded and fanned her pink face with a pale hand.

Meanwhile Clancy peered carefully around the cornerstone of the church building, so that he could observe the new rector as she commandeered a space that no rector before her time had ever paid much attention to, much less visited. Clancy felt freshly invaded, as if a flea were burrowing into his pelt. He was particularly irritated by the fact that the new rector was just sitting there, doing nothing but breathing, it seemed, before she finally stood up with a grunt and went back into the building, returning with a larger object that he recognized as the card table in the parish hall which was usually laden with various packs of playing cards and stacks of board games that had not been played since the last youth minister was let go years before on account of the fact that only a handful of teenagers had attended the church since the early 1980's. The new human rector unfolded the table to stand at some distance from the front row of chairs, then sat down again, as if to adjudge the effect. She got up immediately, and went back into the building to return with a clear plastic packing container. This held a large altar cloth with which she covered the card table. Again she sat, and then went into the building and again returned with a large ceramic goblet and a silver platter that she placed upon the altar cloth. Then she returned with a large clay pitcher and a loaf of unsliced bread, which she placed upon the platter.

That looks just like a subway sandwich, Clancy thought, appalled. He could not imagine a less holy communion than one that used as the Body of Christ a subway sandwich. Why wasn't she using the wafers?

The very thought of the tidy little round wafers, preferred by the former Reverend DeBassompierre as the communion element of choice, brought upon a wave of nostalgia that completely overtook Clancy's spirit until a familiar voice reached him from the emergency exit of the education building. There stood Grace, regarding the scene. "The acolytes are already in the vestry. You better go on in and get ready. I'll take care of things out here."

❧

FROM THEIR VANTAGE point at the edge of the roof overlooking the community garden, the two pigeons, Ottoline and Steven, could see that the animal community was more

than adequately represented on this occasion, albeit discreetly.
Bertram and Sudie Mae were concealed in the boughs of one of
the pines at the edge of the woods, but not invisible to the
pigeons, who were hardly surprised to see that they were in
attendance. Indeed the four of them, the buzzards and the
pigeons, along with one newcomer, a purple martin by the name
of Christopher P. Martin, comprised the choir of St. Aloysius Jr.
Reflecting upon this led Ottoline to remark *sotto voce* to Steven
that it would be interesting to discover how well those humans
could sing without the accompaniment of those odd sounds
that issued from that wooden box in the sanctuary when its
teeth were pressed. Christopher P. Martin, who spent his nights
in a decorative gourd that hung from the porch beam of a gift
shoppe across the boulevard, was nowhere to be seen, but then,
he was often late for most events, as he enjoyed a vibrant social
life beyond the congregation. Also concealed in the trees were
Horace and Mildy, the squirrel couple devoted to the rat
reverend on account of his pastoral care for them following the
tragic accidental death of their youngest offspring Timmy, the
victim of one of those proliferating vehicles that the humans
used to carry themselves along the roadways. Deeper in the
woods, visible to Ottoline and Steven largely as gleaming and
beautiful eyes, Magnus the buck deer and his mate and their
brood of three stood silent and watchful. Even Ometa, the irrepressible opossum, had decided to watch from behind one of
the gravestones, her litter of young clinging to her pelt. Hertz,
Ottoline suspected, was watching from one of the ventilation
slots in the casing of the composter, and of course the reverend
was there. Ottoline could sense, rather than see him, for he was
well-hidden around the corner of the building, and she could
see the reverend's special friend Percy, a reformed but yet still
streetwise wharf rat who now lived in the dumpster of the
convenience store beside the church, boldly perched on the
bottom edge of the ajar access door of that edifice.

By the time the Reverend Jean Grey, vested in what

Clancy recognized as Reverend DeBassompierre's old embroidered cassock and surplice, emerged, preceded by her
acolytes, from the emergency exit of the education wing of
the building to process down the makeshift aisle to stand
before the makeshift altar, the thirty or so folding chairs were
not quite half occupied, but as it was already five past the
hour, the liturgy must go on. Spreading her cassocked arms as
if to embrace the congregation, empty chairs and all, Jean
Grey smiled then—by pooching out her thin lips so that the
corners of her mouth lowered to form a curious pout that
was, with the help of her twinkling tiny blue eyes, still recog-
nizable as a smile. "The Lord be with you!" she greeted
them all.

"And also with you," came the dubious, perhaps even luke-
warm response from the congregation.

Nevertheless, she persisted. The tight, curious, upside-down
smile deepened, and she then continued with the benediction.
When that was accomplished, and the choir had performed at
her request three full verses of "Morning has Broken," she stood
aside during the readings of the Hebrew Scriptures, the psalm,
and the epistle, then she assumed her place before the
makeshift altar and read, in chant, the day's Gospel, taken from
Matthew. Then she spread out her arms out again so that in the
cassock her general shape, with her disproportionately small
head, resembled that of a dreidel, and lifted her face to the blue
sky above and commanded, as a preface to her homily, "Fear
Not!"

The response was, from the assembled humans, including
Grace, a discomfited silence followed by the distant drone of a
faraway aircraft that seemed to accentuate the incongruity of
the new rector's carefully chosen introductory statement.
Nevertheless, she persisted.

"Fear not!" she said again, albeit with not as much conviction as before. And, as the human congregation—along with a
host of intrigued animals—watched, she began to glide, like a

target in a track, in a line parallel to the first row of folding chairs, her skirts and cassock rippling in her wake.

"Beloved fellow followers of Christ!" she continued. "I stand before you this beautiful morning as the one that you have called to become your rector, following a process of intense scrutiny and careful discernment. Many of you have been and continue to be very involved in the process of calling your priest, many of you have stepped back from the process, and some have felt called to simply support the process with prayer, trusting your fellow members to steer the church in the direction most proper to all concerned." She closed her eyes, as if to consult some internal authority, and opened them after a moment to note that most of her listeners seemed ill at ease. She reminded herself that they were unaccustomed to *extempore* homiletics. She smiled, this time broadly, like a parent before an uncertain toddler about to take their first steps, so as to reassure them that she was not in the least dismayed by their understandable uncertainty.

"It would be foolish, and indeed disingenuous of me to make the claim that I, too, have not had my own doubts and fears regarding the opportunity to serve you as your fifth—and on top of that your first female—rector. Rarely are the matches between parish and priest made in heaven, as we all know very well. It would not be an exaggeration for me to say that there have been moments throughout our process of discernment, that have, for lack of a better term, terrified me. It is an awesome responsibility, after all, to presume to lead, to be first among equals, to speak for the Church, and to preside over the most holy of moments in the ministry of the Sacraments. Beginnings are often as full of terror as they are of joy; new babies, new careers, new ministries, new relationships, even new testaments—all of these can be frightening, and justly so, for beginnings signal the end of a status quo. But as we know, from our own scriptures as well as those of faiths throughout time and space, terror is an aspect of a greater glory. 'Fear not!'

is the salutation of the angels, those intellectual beings so present and yet so invisible to us under normal circumstances, when they manifest themselves to our limited senses. They have an awareness, I believe, that for us their unveiled appearance can be intimidating, just as our own proximity seems to intimidate those lesser creatures whom we might approach with the sincere intention simply to admire, the flora and fauna with which we share this planet in all of its diversity of life forms. But why, as rational creatures, with our own unique awareness of our being created in the image of God, should we feel fear in the face of God's messengers? Is it because, as Freud teaches us, that the human mind cannot handle too much reality... ?"

Here the female human reverend, moving so close to the front row of the ersatz folding chair pews that she could smell the arthritis creme rubbed into the knuckles of 96-year-old Mrs. Irene Macklin, St. Aloysius Sr.'s senior member, came to a standstill and paused. Her face assumed a faraway expression, as if she was hearing a voice from within or beyond.

"You see, my beloved community... what we fear most is what we need most... the challenge that comes of acknowledging the Other, in all of the Other's complexity. It is natural to wish to cling to the time-honored, the traditional, the familiar... and indeed, sometimes wise. But as followers of Christ, we are called to welcome the Stranger in our midst... whether that be the displaced refugee, the woman fleeing an abusive marriage, the LGBTQ teen cast out of their family circle, the prisoner who has served his or her time with no means of support on the outside, or even indeed..."—she smiled her peculiarly pursed and prim and yet genuinely cheerful upside down smile—"... even the newly appointed and relatively inexperienced new rector. For it is here... in the visible church, the kingdom of heaven on earth, as our Lord declared, that the Body of Christ is broken and the Blood of Christ is shed for ALL... all of God's children are welcome to partake in the

Heavenly Feast. And with that in mind, let us stand, join hands, and exchange God's peace, in preparation for our celebration of Holy Communion."

And with her cassocked arms outspread, she totally enveloped old Mrs. Irene Macklin, wheeled walker and all, within her flowing vestments. "God's Peace be with you!" Rev. Jean proclaimed.

Mrs. Macklin sank to her seat, trembling. Grace, who was seated to her right, patted her wizened and age-spotted forearm reassuringly. "And also with you," prompted Grace.

⚜

FROM AROUND THE corner of the foundation of the church building Clancy was watching restlessly, his nostrils and whiskers twitching as he followed the movements of the human rector as she arranged upon the makeshift altar before her the elements of the communion service. Her sermon had reassured him with its brevity relative to what he was accustomed to but scandalized him by what seemed to him to be its aimlessness, lacking the pointed erudition of one of Reverend DeBassompierre's homilies as well as what he considered to be the sharp scriptural focus of his own preaching. Why, she had barely mentioned Jesus at all! Angels were nice, of course, but Jesus was the point! As Reverend DeBassompierre had once said, if it hadn't been for Jesus, there would be no need for church whatsoever.

Clancy's attention was so taken up with disapproval of the new rector that even though he was looking straight at them as they approached, it did not register with him until the damage was done, that the enormous flock of seagulls approaching from the east and behind the altar was going to be a real problem.

⚜

"ON THE NIGHT before He died, He took bread, and broke it, saying to His disciples, take, eat, for this is My Body..."

So absorbed was the Reverend Jean Grey, her countenance lifted and her hands clutching the two halves of the loaf that she was consecrating, that she had no awareness of the increasing alarm of her congregation until they began to gasp, cry out, and rise from their seats, pointing and shouting. And by that point a flock not of her own, with sudden and raucous outcries after their own inhuman manner, descended upon her. It was not until she felt the first painful jab of a careless beak-tip, that she opened her eyes to behold, and that her ears registered the maelstrom of swooping and diving seabirds. Like a plague of gigantic screeching locusts, seagulls surrounded her, screaming, flapping their wings, jostling one another in mid-air to get at the consecrated bread of life that the Reverend Grey still clutched aloft.

Jean Grey had never been so terrified in her six full decades. With a gasp and a shriek of her own, she instinctively, self-protectively, flung the body of Christ as far away from herself to the ground as she could manage, to be devoured by greedy, vociferous gulls. Continuing to cry out, she clutched up her vestments and disappeared around the corner of the church building, pursued by a contingent of the more aggressive birds who imagined that she might still have some bread in her grasp. Those members of the human congregation that hadn't already left for their vehicles watched it all with mouths agape, including Grace, who felt frozen to her seat. It wasn't until the woman sitting behind her, Mrs. Robert Meilish, Senior Warden of the Vestry, who had resisted hiring a female rector with all of her considerable but in the end ineffective powers of persuasion, leaned over to her and said, in a whisper that managed to convey unmistakable schadenfreude, "Poor woman. I knew this was a bad idea."

Grace knew better than to respond or even acknowledge the Senior Warden. She simply rose and walked away, leaving

Mrs. Robert Meilish to turn to Mr. Robert Meilish and roll her eyes knowingly and shake her head and purse her lips disapprovingly.

🌣

GRACE FOUND REV. JEAN GREY, as she knew she would, in the Women's Room, bent over one of the sinks rinsing her wounded hands and forearms, assiduously avoiding the sight of her own reflection in the mirror, her cassock hung on the clothing hook on the door.

"Jean." Grace stood at a respectful distance and crossed her arms over her chest. The wounded rector glanced up at the mirror to take in Grace's image as well as her own. Grace could see, reflected in the mirror, the older woman's troubled, determined expression, before she lowered it again and went back to rinsing the blood from her hands.

"Out, damned spot!" The rector said, and she smiled a grim, tight smile. "Lady Macbeth. I used to teach high school literature, you know. Maybe I'll go back to that."

"Oh, Jean..." said Grace.

"It's a sign, you know," said Jean Grey, quite calmly. "A warning sign. I should have known better. I've been hell-bent on going against the grain of this community, and it took Mother Nature to open my eyes. These things happen for a reason, Grace. God is not mocked. I went my own way without considering contingencies, and that always ends in tears. I believe in my heart that St. Aloysius is in need of renewal in order to survive, but the renewal I have to offer is simply not tenable. I think a congregation with this particular demographic needs a more...traditional presence at the helm, at least for now. I'll hand in my notice to the Bishop on Tuesday."

Grace could not suppress a groan. *Good God*, she thought, *it's like Silas in drag!* These clergy people. Are they really all the same? Do they all think every little thing that happens is a message from God just to them? "Jean," she said. "Give me a break. Everyone makes mistakes. God knows Silas made more than his share."

"I know that." The rector's eyes, or at least their reflection, met Grace's in the bathroom mirror. "God knows I do. But Grace, you should know as well as I do... men's mistakes are much more easily forgiven and forgotten. And to be honest—" Here her anodyne composure seemed to melt away, so that she slumped over the sink and sighed. "I don't want to face those people again. I'm so embarrassed." And she covered her face with her beak-pecked and bleeding but still elegant, slim hands.

"To hell with them!" said Grace. "They're never satisfied anyway. Like I always told Silas, you just have to do your own thing." And she took her new boss into her own maternal embrace, and an alliance was forged.

❦

THE SCENE of the attempted liturgy, now a wasteland of overturned folding chairs and scattered service leaflets, looked as if the Rapture had occurred. The coast being clear, at least for the time being, of human activity or observation, Clancy loped forward to where his own makeshift altar, which contained Hertz and his multitudes, stood at the edge of the community garden. Without thought, as if guided or prodded by the hand of Providence, he climbed atop the composter, that focal point of his church without walls, and stood on his hind legs with his forepaws raised, in what was his typical gesture of benediction. This was not an easy pose to hold, so after a moment he came to rest on all fours, his abdomen against the sun-warmed plastic of the composter lid, and allowed an unbidden contentment to course through him. As if in tandem with his physical flesh, his spirit warmed toward the clearly incompetent and disgraced female rector of the human church; for the first time since beginning his own ministry, he regarded himself as being, like his mentor the departed and deeply missed Reverend DeBassompierre, a seasoned professional. He knew what it was like to be a beginner in ministry; he could recall, now without undue chagrin, his own early missteps and mistakes, when he had allowed himself to be guided more by zeal than by prudence. Figuring out the difference between what the Lord wants with what seems exciting was never really easy. God's plan, it seemed, was something that could only be discovered by trial and error. One of the things you just had to get used to with God, Clancy figured, was God's tendency to be capricious. That's why humans, just like the rest of God's creatures, ought to have the benefit of the doubt.

*She'll figure it out*, Clancy said to himself, basking, as he so rarely allowed himself to do, in the warm open sunshine. *Lord knows I'd help her if I could.*

🕮

WHEN JEAN GREY had been searching for an apartment in town once her call to become the rector of St. Aloysius was finalized, several considerations prompted her eventual choice. Chief among these was the absolute necessity of a large and comfortable bathtub. At five feet ten inches and weighing slightly above average for her height, she found most modern bathtubs to be far too small to afford relaxation, and for Jean Grey, a bath was every bit as much about restoration as sanitation. As a Pisces, it was essential to her sense of well-being to experience full immersion as regularly as possible, and particularly when she was feeling raw or vulnerable or otherwise in need of comfort. A nice hot bubble bath never failed to restore her equanimity. For that reason she was willing to put up with some of the inconveniences of the attic studio she'd eventually settled upon; it galled her to pay what she considered to be an exorbitant rent for very little space on the whole, and the presence of the property owner just below her was far from ideal, but she'd fallen in love with the old claw-footed porcelain tub, which was long enough for her to stretch her legs and deep enough for her to slip beneath the surface and shut out the world for as long as she could hold her breath. And that is what she did following her first communion service, which had ended so phantasmagorically. She came home, she climbed the rickety outdoor stairs to the attic entrance, she turned on the ceiling fan, disrobed, drew her bath, stirred in her salts, and lowered herself slowly, luxuriously, into the steaming, fragrant cauldron, and marinated, eyes closed, in her reflections.

In retrospect, now that the initial shock and embarrassment had faded, she did not regret for a moment her impulse and decision to initiate herself and her ministry with a nontraditional service, with all of the opportunities and dangers that such a departure opened her up to. The descent of the gulls, as harrowing and disruptive as it had been, she could—and did—with one eye squinted so to speak, accept as an affirmation. That there were challenges to be faced that would appear on the surface to be formidable, but that would prove ultimately nurturing, seemed to be the message of those impertinent birds. As she gazed up at the cracks and stains on the ceiling in the safety and bliss of the steaming bath, she now recognized that the trick would be to learn how to gently yet firmly navigate her ship of elderly and dubious parishioners through the bracing waters of change.

*Next few Sundays*, she said to herself, blowing suds playfully from the palm of her hand, *everything by the rubric, just as they like. I'll even throw in the Athanasian Creed! Just to reassure everyone —myself included—that it isn't all going to be contention.*

## 2

# HUMANITAS

GRACE COULD NOT HELP BUT WONDER what old Silas would make of Jean Grey. Grace had texted Silas, almost immediately, the overall story of the Seagull Eucharist, but Silas, being Silas, had not responded to the text with anything other than an open mouth surprise emoji. Grace was dying to get his opinion, and so Friday afternoon after work she took a cold Bud Light onto her front porch along with her iPhone and called him on FaceTime. As the former rector, now assistant professor of Patristic Theology and Byzantine Studies, kept the camera lens of his own iPhone taped, all she could see of him was a grainy darkness.

"Now she wants to start what she's calling a 'pollination and honey ministry,'" said Grace. "You can imagine how *that's* going to go over."

"What in God's name is a 'pollination and honey ministry'?!" said the blank black screen that was the former rector. "I'm almost afraid to ask..."

"I know," said Grace, shaking her head. "It sounds almost filthy, doesn't it. But it just means she wants to keep beehives back around the old community garden. Bees! She really is out there. Don't get me wrong—I like her; and that's a relief, because, you know, I wasn't sure about her when they were interviewing—but I just don't think she knows what she's getting herself into. She wants to liven the place up, and I'm all for it, but you know better than anyone... you have to take it slow with these old school southern Episcopals. They're about fifty years behind the times..."

"Have you told her... how I was treated?"

Grace rolled her eyes to the heavens, with exasperation and affection for her still rather reflexively self-referential old boss. As a cisgendered, presumably but not definitely heterosexual Caucasian male priest, the Rev. Silas DeBassompierre, for all of his aloofness and his overly intellectual style of preaching and his often-misguided attempts to instill progressive values into his largely staid and elderly congregation, he'd had it easy. He would never experience the level of pushback that this middle-aged female rector was going to be obliged to endure. But you couldn't tell him that.

"I don't want to scare her," said Grace drily. "Not that I think she'd be scared. She's fragile, for sure, but she's also very sure of herself. It's almost funny. I wish I had her balls."

"So do I," said Silas in a rare spasm of self-awareness. "Well... more power to her. I wish her the best. Better her than me, as far as I'm concerned. And I guess a few bees can't hurt anything. Seagulls... bees... what will come along next, a cobra? It's like Noah's Ark..."

"God forbid!" said Grace. "Anyway, I have a feeling that yours truly is going to be the one picking up all the pieces."

"Some things never change," said her former boss.

"No!" shouted Hertz the earthworm. "No! NO! I'm not gonna stand for it! It's a takeover! It's an invasion! It's foul play! It's an ABOMINATION!"

The core membership of St. Aloysius Jr. gathered together

around the composter, casting glances at one another until the worm's angry outburst had subsided into inarticulate grumbling. "But Hertz!" said Clancy after a moment. "I don't understand! I thought you'd be real pleased!"

"Pleased!" cried the earthworm, once again erect and quivering with fury as he extended nearly his entire length from the ventilation slot of his composter casing. "PLEASED! Why in Ground's name should I be pleased!! Don't you know what this means, you birdbrain?"

Standing by, Ottoline's feathers ruffled, but she held her peace. She was used to the earthworm's bigotry, for he held a prejudice towards birds that he did not bother to hide, and it was always best to ignore his ignorant slurs. Plus, for once he seemed genuinely distressed.

"Why Hertz! It means you and your colony here will have some help!"

"HELP!" Hertz fell limp with exasperation, then immediately became stiff again. "I need help like I need another hole in my tip! There's not enough work to go around as it is! We hardly get enough scraps from those stingy humans to last us a week! And now they're bringing in another colony!? From Ground knows where?! It's a nightmare, you stupid rodent! It means... it means WAR!"

From Ottoline came an irrepressible warble of exasperation. "Good heavens!" she said. "Surely, Hertz, it can't be as dire as all that! I do understand that the close proximity of another composting colony must give you some cause for concern. But you must know that we'll do everything we can to keep you supplied with biodegradables so that your colony won't suffer. After all, that's what church is for, isn't it! To provide for one another in the breaches..."

"Pfft!" spat Hertz. "You say that now, but I know what's in that rat's noodle. He can't wait to go over there and run his mouth to them about God and Jesus and all that jazz. Never mind the fact that it's gonna leave me high and dry..."

"Hertz! That's not so!" Clancy faltered as he said this, however, for in fact he had been looking forward to approaching the newcomers with the saving message of the Gospel.

"Oh, give me a break!" Hertz said. "You can't fool me, even if you *do* fool yourself. Anyway, it's no use trying to get you to face reality. But just wait. If you think for one minute those humans are going to keep two colonies around here, you're crazy. I may be half blind, but even I can see from here, that new set up is a thousand times nicer than mine, bigger, roomier, and there's even a built-in moisture gauge. No, it's out with the old and in with the new, you know as well as I do how they are. Huh! I give it two days. That nutty new rector—or probably her slave Grace—will be out here to break down my casing and leave me and my colony here to dry up like a bunch of sticks. That is, if they're not stupid enough to try to dump us in with the new lot—which would really be trouble, because damned if I'm gonna work for another leader! Been there, done that, and not doing it again. So, the long and short of it is, you're not going to have old Hertz to kick around anymore... give me liberty, or give me death, or something like that..."

"Hertz!" squealed Clancy. "Hertz! Don't you talk that way! You know we're not going to let anything happen to you. You know we won't let anyone take you away! Hertz, haven't I always helped you when you needed it? I can take you inside to stay in that fern pot in the office right now if you want!"

"Pfft," said Hertz again. "Like that fern can hold me AND all my offspring! Even you have more brains than that! Face it, rat. I'm a goner. The least you could do is let me curl up and die with some dignity..."

"HERTZ!" cried Clancy. Unable to contain himself, he reached for his friend, who withdrew into his composter and said no more. "Oh, Lord!" As usual when he was at a loss, Clancy turned to Ottoline. "What are we going to do?"

"Reverend, I'm sure he'll calm down. In the meantime, I

suppose we'll just have to keep a close eye on him, in case he does try something foolish. I'll—"

"OW!"

All heads turned toward the fresh new structure whence a cry of outraged pain had sounded, and were astonished to observe Percy, the rat who lived in the dumpster of the convenience store beside the church, leap three times his own height into the air, and then gnaw at a spot near his tail as if rooting out a mite.

"Percy! What in the world?! Are you all right?"

"No, goddamn it!" said Percy rather crossly. "I just got stung by one of those stinking bees they put over here for some stupid reason!"

Silence descended as all the animals regarded Percy with dawning comprehension, then all gazed past him towards the new additions to the churchyard, those plain and yet mysterious upright boxes.

"Bees?" said Ottoline. "Percy... are you saying there are bees in that composter?"

"You bet your beak there are!" said Percy, still rubbing the site of his injury. "About a million of 'em, if you ask me. And if that's a composter they're all holed up in, it sure doesn't smell like one. Smells like a bunch of leftover pancakes to me, which is why I went over there to see what the hell was going on. And then one of those little bastards got me. Well, that's my luck. Now you know. Stay away from those things if you know what's good for you. CHRIST that hurts!"

"Bees!" said Clancy. "Bees! Well, praise the Lord. Now, that's a relief, isn't it, Hertz! We've got bees in the neighborhood now, and not another set of worms. You don't have anything to worry about. I told, you, Hertz, the Lord will look after you, just trust and believe..."

The earthworm was indeed relieved; but it was not his policy to look on the sunny side. "Bees!" he grumbled. "That's even worse."

"*Why?*" said Ottoline with genuine, if exasperated concern.

"Because they sting!" said Hertz with a vehemence that nevertheless lacked conviction, for as a worm who rarely left the interior of his composter, there was only a minuscule chance that he would ever be stung. "And besides, they're stupid. Just fly around making everyone nervous. I can't stand them." And so saying, he withdrew from the discussion into the muck of his own chamber, and coiled up into a tight, self-soothing cone, and only away from the eyes of his friends did he admit to himself that he felt spared a fate worse than death.

"I MUST SAY, I don't understand," said Ottoline. "Why on earth would the humans introduce bees to the churchyard? They stand to get stung every bit as much as the rest of us, if we're not careful."

"Honey," said Ometa the opossum. "Don't you know that? Humans like it just as much as bears do, and only bees can make it. The humans try, but they know they don't have the touch. I've seen it before. There's a place way down the highway inland where there's one of them great big fenced up places they call a farm, where in one corner they keep a whole bunch of beehives in a wall of boxes about as wide as this church. The humans wrap themselves up in all this white stuff —even their faces!—and go in there and spray the bees with some sort of clouds and grab the drawers out of the boxes and pour honey off 'em into buckets. Then they hightail it back to their trucks. They pour it all over some of the things they eat, and even into stuff they drink. There's a restaurant down near the waterfront where there's always a bunch a little bottles shaped like little bear cubs with honey stuck inside. Tasty stuff, but sticky, and it'll make you right thirsty. Reckon that's what they're gonna do here. Spray 'em and take their stuff. Y'all know how them humans are..."

"Typical," said Hans, that young buck deer whose contempt for the human race knew no bounds. "Thieves and murderers... all of them. Even the so-called Christians."

"Hans!" exclaimed Clancy, but he too was appalled by Ometa's revelation. "Oh, the poor bees! We've got to help them!"

"Help 'em!" Ometa's hissing vocalization was aghast. "Help 'em do what? Reverend, I'm telling you, Hertz ain't lying. They're mean critters and'll sting you just as soon as look at you. Best thing to do is stay away from 'em and let the humans do as they please. It ain't that big a deal."

"But..." Clancy was astonished at the opossum's callousness. "We can't just stand by and watch them get killed!"

"They don't get killed. You mean by the cloudy stuff? That just knocks 'em out a while. No, the humans don't kill 'em...then they'd just have to go find more to make the honey. No, they just try to make 'em so dizzy they won't sting. Pretty smart, if you ask me, and I'm not one to have much good to say about them humans myself."

"Oh," Clancy was at once relieved and somewhat disappointed. What a witness it could have been, for the Lord and for the Church, if somehow they could have succeeded in saving the bees from certain extinction. Now, however, it was clear that the new inhabitants of the churchyard were going to be more dangerous than endangered. "Well..." he said. "I guess I'll go over and invite them to church."

"Over my dead body!" said his fellow rat Percy. "I know you, pal, and you won't take a hint. One sting's enough for me, but you're a glutton for punishment. Just look at this!" And Percy used his snout to edge up a patch of fur to reveal an angry swollen mound of flesh with a barb still ensconced in the center. Curling his lean body into an ouroboros, he bared his orange incisors and tweezed the barb out. "One down, thanks to yours truly, but there's plenty more over there ready to die for their stupid queen."

"Die?" said Ottoline.

"Sure!" said Percy. "Don't you know? They die when they sting anyone, but they don't care. All they care about is guarding their Queen. Pretty dumb, if you ask me. But pretty sweet, if you're the Queen. Isn't that right, Ometa? They die if they sting?"

Ometa vocalized her agreement, and Clancy reached for his tail and began to gnaw the end thoughtfully. Here was a pastoral dilemma he had not been expecting. To approach these creatures with the Gospel would be not only to endanger himself, but them as well!

*Oh, Lord,* he said to himself. *Why does following you have to be so confusing sometimes?!*

⚜

"DON'T GET ME WRONG, I think it's a great idea, Jean," said Grace, standing before the rector's desk, eager to get back to her own and complete a discussion board for her Pastoral Counseling Certification program. "But I don't think the Vestry will go for it. You know how they are...or maybe you don't. Silas had a hell of a time getting them to approve and fund the community garden, and he only managed because we had a refugee family at the time that took care of everything. And since then, they've never allowed for a dime of the budget to cover any of the outlay. It's a shame, really..."

"Yes it is," said Reverend Jean Grey. "Shortsighted, to say the least. At any rate, happily, neither vestry approval nor budget outlay will be necessary. It is written into my contract that I have sufficient latitude to pilot any outreach ministry that I wish so long as it does not create an undue burden on the facility, and as for budget, I have it on good authority that the pollination-honey initiative invariably pays for itself within one growing season. And in the meantime, the setup can come directly out of my salary. It's fairly inexpensive, and after all,

Grace, I'm a successful business owner with a hefty investment income. I'm not in ministry for the money, as if there were much to be had. I'm here to—" She patted her secretary's hand across the desk, for they were conferring in her office. "—to follow the Way."

"But Jean," said Grace. "Who's going to do all the work?" And here Grace raised an eyebrow pointedly, for she was not eager to be stung.

"Ah!" Jean Grey narrowed her small bright blue eyes with childlike exuberance. "That's what I wanted to talk to you about. It occurred to me last night, while I was at the YWCA doing my laps—you know, I do some of my best thinking while swimming—it occurred to me that the perfect person to help me get the pollination-honey ministry off the ground, so to speak, is someone very close to you...as close as can be, at least at one point in time..."

Grace was bewildered by this characteristically roundabout reference, until comprehension dawned. "Tommy?" she exclaimed. "Are you kidding me?"

"Not at all!" Jean Grey grinned. "I think it would be perfect —if, that is to say, he takes an interest. It is of course entirely up to him. But I imagine that he might find the prospect interesting, in light of his culinary career interests. According to my dear, dear friend in the Bay area, the cultivation of honey is a highly sought-after skill in the burgeoning field of natural ingredients and locally sourced cuisine. It would be a very valuable addition to Tommy's resume. And the work is not that time intensive. There's a good bit involved in setup and harvesting, but apart from that, why, we simply let nature take her course. Now, there is certainly no pressure. If Tommy isn't interested in the project I can certainly look elsewhere. My dear friend in the Bay Area supplied me with a list of local contacts. I just thought it would be fun for Tommy to have first refusal. What do you think?"

Grace's heart filled with an odd and surprising amalgamation of nostalgia for Silas and gratitude for this thoroughly womanly, refreshingly extroverted new rector. For all of his diffidence and rigidity, Silas had genuinely loved Grace and by extension Tommy, but it would never have crossed his mind that the resources of the church could be put to helping Tommy in any way. "I think it's a great idea," she said when she could. "I think he'll be thrilled."

"Wonderful," said Jean Grey. "Unto an land of milk and honey! Exodus 3, verse 8!"

BEHIND THE BOOKCASE, Clancy listened to this remarkable and illuminating exchange with growing interest. So this was what was behind the sudden arrival of the hive and its inhabitants! Of course, it was another ill-conceived innovation of the new rector, this Jean Grey. Clancy ground his teeth. Once again the human female was trespassing against him. While he reminded himself that the church and the land upon which it rested was the Lord's only, in spite of the claims of human or non-human, he could not help but feel proprietary towards the rear church-yard, which after all seldom ever saw a human apart from Grace until this woman came along to turn everything topsy-turvy. Typical, he said to himself, remind himself not a little of Hertz. Just like a human... they never learn.

Of course, that aspect of himself that was least influenced by Hertz's contempt for all things human was inwardly intrigued. So Ometa was right, and the bees were here to make honey, which would then be taken by Tommy, a human with whom Clancy only had occasional contact, and that of course at a safe distance. Clancy knew that the Reverend DeBassom-pierre had regarded the young man with a grudgingly avuncular fondness. Maybe Jean Grey wasn't being entirely foolish after all. Still, the presence of the beehive in his churchyard, both proximate yet unapproachable, was a thorn in Clancy's proverbial side. It reminded him of when the cat Macrina, at the time a stray before being taken in by the Reverend DeBassompierre, used to watch Clancy hold his first few church services from where she'd crouched balefully underneath the bottom of the slide of the dilapidated church playground. Clancy's evangelical zeal and his natural rodent's terror of the feline species had been violently in conflict until he finally made up his mind to risk martyrdom for the church. In the case of Macrina he'd eventually won a friend, if not a convert, but this bee situation was different. If provoked by an approach, the bees themselves would be the ones to die upon their swords. It was a real catch-22.

"I've always wanted to keep bees," Jean Grey was confiding. "I've always felt a connection. I come from a tiny town in the Sandhills region of this state called Beeville. Have you heard of it?"

"No," admitted Grace.

"Few have. There isn't much to distinguish it beyond its rather whimsical name. I suppose on that account I've always felt deeply drawn to bees—especially honeybees! They seem to me to incarnate and signify a kind of cheerful industry that I find so very inspiring. I have a very ancient and rare honeybee amulet from the Old Kingdom that I picked up in Egypt from a bazaar vendor when I was on a jaunt there in my mid-thirties. I'll show it to you soon. It's one of my most treasured talismans." Her small blue eyes closed for a moment as if she were consulting some inner mentor, and Grace, sensing a shift in the conversation from professional to personal, took a seat and waited.

Jean Grey spoke with her eyes closed, as if in therapy. "Beeville did have some charm... your typical small southern town, close knit community, surrounded by picturesque countryside. Racism so thick you could cut it with a knife, of course, alongside extraordinary income inequality, and of course there were many, many buried secrets. The church that dominated the town was, of course, the First Baptist." Here she opened her eyes, and she sighed loud and long. "My family was very involved in that church. My father was a deacon for much of his adult life, and my mother taught Sunday School for many years. It should have been a place of safety and nurture for me... but there were very unhealthy dynamics at play." She opened her eyes and glanced towards the bookshelves behind which Clancy crouched, listening avidly, as if to look away from some interior scene. "The pastor while I was growing up was a predator. He took advantage of me, and likely many other young people in the church. I know this sort of personal information can be difficult to hear... but it was a significant and formative experience, and had a lasting impact upon my psyche... a negative impact that I have managed, with therapy and support... and time... and privilege, to turn into a positive tool for ministry. I am averse to pastoral manipulation in any form, for any reason. Which is *not* to say I cannot be guilty of it. But I am, I hope, self-aware enough to avoid it, and apologize for it when I fail." She leaned forward and glanced at Grace's expression. "You don't mind my sharing... but we should be aware of one another's... growing edges, if we are to minister together..."

"I don't mind," said Grace. She placed her hand over the tightly clasped hands of the new rector.

"Thank you, dear," said Jean Grey. "It is so important that these matters be out in the open—between friends."

"It is important," agreed Grace.

Behind the bookcase, Clancy felt very small. He was very careful to stay still and quiet, as if to disturb the silence that followed Grace's last words would be to disturb somehow the very balance of the cosmos. Something had happened between the two women, so subtle that Clancy could not put his claw on it, but it was as if they had both been changed in some invisible yet significant way. A warm and not altogether comfortable sensation passed through Clancy from the tips of his ears to the end of his tail, as if his own core had been touched. He felt a longing very different from the longing for the Reverend DeBassompierre's presence. He felt at once alone and deeply connected.

*Lord...* he said to himself. *What's happening to me?!*

SHE KNEW she was not pulling her weight; at least, she was aware of her own inadequacy in the same vague sense in which she was aware of anything beyond her duties. She was only troubled by this niggling anxiety in moments of stillness in her cell at the end of the day. And it always dissipated as if it had never existed during the torpor of slumber or the resumption of activity. It wasn't even identifiable to her as anxiety per se, but simply as the none-too-pleasant sense of her own uniqueness, her deficiency in relation to the others like herself. She was not as swift as the others, not as sure, not as productive. This she knew even more intimately than she knew her name, for she had no name that she knew of. But she knew she was a worker, that she belonged to that particular subcategory within her species. She was a worker, not a drone, and she certainly was no Queen, for there can be only one Queen, who was not herself and to whom all consideration was to be directed, rather than to the individual needs of the worker's self. Her function was to do what she was told by the delegates of the Queen to maintain the working order of the colony, whether that was foraging for pollen, cleaning cells or sometimes tending to larvae. She shared these duties with dozens of other workers like herself, and by virtue of these duties she belonged to the colony. Her activities, her memories, her very being itself was inextricably associated with her identity as a worker. Nothing mattered for the worker apart from the fulfillment of obligations.  Never could she have conceived of anything else, much less of falling short... until she fell short.

It all began with the simple observation, upon returning to

the hive after a long afternoon of pollen gathering. She noted that all other workers had preceded her; furthermore, their leg-sacs were all more bountifully laden than her own with the dust of life.

*I am last*, she found herself noticing. And, following upon that perception, another: *I have less.* Whence came the *I*, a referent she did not recall ever before being conscious of? She did not know. It was as if, by becoming aware of her distinction from the other workers, inextricable from her inferiority to them, she became simultaneously knowledgeable of a signifier for her individuality—*I. I am last, I have less.* Once conceived of thus, *I* was not to be forgotten. It accompanied her from that moment on throughout her days. She had no initial emotions or concerns regarding herself and her comparative inferiority, these were simply facts to be noted alongside the facts of her duties and the means by which they must be accomplished in order for her existence to continue. But as the time passed, it became clear to her that the consciousness of her *I* had an impact upon the performance of her duties, and not one that was salutary. Like an invisible weight, this self-awareness had an increasingly retarding effect upon her activities. Having become aware of herself as a distinct subject, she became aware of a universe of particularities apart from duty, the Queen, the hive, the self. There was a lot to take in besides pollen. This proved terrifically distracting.

And yet she found it all obscurely exciting, in spite of the sense of inferiority and the associated sense of peril. Rooted as it was in deficiency, the self-awareness was, to her, nevertheless enlivening. She was always last. She always gathered least. She was different from the others, and this made her feel paradoxically more aware of them as individuals. And she became aware that more and more were hatched every day, joining the throng. It seemed to her to be inevitable that she would, in her inferiority, prove expendable. She began to imagine her possible futures. She would be left on her own, and on its own no bee survived for long. Her consciousness became dominated at times by an unfamiliar and highly unpleasant sensation. Dread.

This was not constant. It came and went. When it came, it was usually upon returning to the hive after a period of foraging for pollen: she was always last, she always had least, and she would retire to her cell certain that this would be the last time she would find it unoccupied by some younger, more efficient worker. She would lapse into dormancy only after a period of fretful despair, during which some aspect of her consciousness which had the strange capacity to observe her inner states as if they were outer states would marvel at the intensity of what she was experiencing, even though there was no real alteration in her conditions. If this dread was the price she was to pay for the admittedly exciting and marvelous sense of self that she had somehow developed, she wasn't sure it was worth it.

At other times, however, she would not have traded her new self-awareness for anything in the world... not even to be Queen. Last, least, plagued at times with the most insupportable anxiety, it seemed on the whole to her to be worthwhile to be herself. Whoever that was... she realized that she wasn't quite sure.

ॐ

SUNDAY WAS, of course, always a thrilling day (more or less) for Clancy, but he was always particularly excited when the morning proved temperate and pretty, for that made a difference in attendance. And this was one of the loveliest days to come along in weeks, breaking a spell of damp and grey coastal weather. Early in the morning, Clancy squeezed through the gnawed-out corner of his crawlspace door, and after blinking in the sudden unexpected brilliance of the sunshine, regarded the rear churchyard with more than usual delight. Oh! What a pretty day! Dew still sparkled on the blades of grass and the sky was a cheerful bright blue. Everything seemed to be freshly

washed and brightly awake, as if overnight the world had under-
gone a gentle and thorough cleaning. Clancy skittered over to
the warm, odiferous shade of the composter to wait for his
congregation to gather.

Inside the composter, at once indignant and chagrined,
Hertz writhed a little, uncomfortable in his own skin. He had
not spoken to a soul, not even to any of his own kind, since
discovering these few days before that his livelihood was not
necessarily in jeopardy after all. Upon Percy's revelation that
that brand new and undeniably superior structure contained
bees and not rival worms, he had withdrawn into his executive
chamber and lapsed into a kind of psychic torpor. He could
not help but acknowledge to himself, in a kind of stunned,
inchoate way, that the prospect of competition with a new
colony had been truly harrowing. It had stirred up for him all
manner of turmoil and insecurity, the residue of the instability
and betrayal of his early life before he'd arrived by sheer dumb
luck in the chapel of St. Aloysius and the tender mercies of
the reverend rat. So now it appeared that, even after all this
time spent establishing and leading and maintaining his very
own colony, he was by no means safe. He must never lose
sight of that, he reminded himself. The world could turn
against him and his at any random point. And what the
reprieve of the beehive seemed to reveal, was that he could
always by mistaken. That in fact, his current situation was
very different from that of his youth, when he'd been at the
mercy of elders in his colony who really cared nothing about
him as an individual. For, although the rodent and his congregation might be deluded by all the crazy human claptrap they
chose to believe, in the end they did care about him. They
might not be able to prevent the destruction of all that he'd
accomplished, but they would have tried, had it been necessary. This was a painful and reluctant admission for the worm
to make to himself. He did not relish the thought of being
beholden to non-worms. But it was clear now, more than ever,

that self-sufficiency, like so much else that he valued about himself, was a fleeting thing.

The distant sound of the bells of the Presbyterian Church down the boulevard melodiously overcame the reflections of both worm and rat. Clancy glanced around to make sure that the coast was clear of humans, then mounted the composter and assumed the posture of benediction.

"The Lord be with you!" Clancy proclaimed when the congregation was assembled in a loose semicircle made up of a variety of creatures before his "altar."

"And also with you!" came the chirped, growled, hissed, warbled response. From there, as always, according to rubric, the service proceeded, from collect, to the Lessons warbled charmingly by Ottoline in her rich, deep, maternal tones, to the homily prepared and delivered by Clancy, which this Sunday he considered to be among his finest, inspired as it was by one of his favorite episodes from the Life of Christ, the exorcism of the Gerasene Demoniac. So vivid to his mind's eye was the dramatic scene he was describing for his audience that it was some time before it dawned on him that their normally polite if not rapt attention was not upon him at all. What signaled to him their distraction was, paradoxically enough, an uncommon stillness and silence. It was as if every single member of his beloved community had by some mysterious spell been turned to stone. He paused in the middle of his description of the mad dash of the swine driven to squealing frenzy by the sudden sense of evil within and among them and peered rather sternly at the gathering before him.

No one vocalized so much as a peep; no one stirred so much as a whisker. Everyone's attention seemed to be fixed, not upon their reverend, but upon the front of the composter itself. Clancy looked down, expecting to see Hertz poking out of the casing, up to one of his tricks. But all that the rat saw was the slight bobbing movement of one of the gladiolus blossoms that Sudie Mae had just that morning placed before the composter/lectern/altar as part of the floral offering. Sudie Mae had just recently appointed herself, with Clancy's enthusiastic approval, as chair of the St. Aloysius Jr. Altar Guild, after she'd observed Grace arranging the humans' floral tribute before the card table altar just before the new human rector's first disastrous Eucharist.

"Praise the Lord, Sudie Mae!" Clancy had said when she'd shyly approached him with her idea. "I think that's a wonderful ministry for you. You have such a good eye for what's attractive and appealing. I can't wait to see what you come up with." And indeed, Sudie Mae's arrangements, comprised primarily of gleanings from shopping center shrubbery and landscaping, were lavish and clashingly colorful. They certainly drew the eye, and thus had to be dismantled immediately following each service. But it wasn't with appreciation that all the members of St. Aloysius Jr. were regarding the bouquet now. It was with apprehension, for themselves and for their rector. For the gladiolus was bobbing up and down because it was being investigated by a bee, which had just darted over from the hive while Clancy had been transported beyond situational awareness by the vivid mental pictures suggested to him by his own sermon.

"What's everybody looking at?" he asked, not a little peeved. He clutched the edge of the composter lid and bent down so that his snout came perilously close to the bobbing blossom. "Reverend! Look out!" Ottoline cried, and at that the bee, apparently sensing a threat, or perhaps having gathered its fill, emerged from the gladiolus, circumnavigated around it and then darted off. The entire congregation gave a collective vocalization of relief. Clancy went on with his sermon feeling vaguely upstaged.

During fellowship hour Sudie Mae approached the Reverend, filled with a delectably austere spirit of renunciation. "I don't reckon the flowers at the altar are a good idea right now, Reverend."

"I guess not, Sudie Mae," said Clancy. "It's a shame. You

really did a good job of beautifying our worship space. I'm sorry it just didn't work out."

"It's all right, reverend," said Sudie Mae. "Beauty don't matter. It's Jesus that matters."

Though he would not have put it quite that way, Clancy understood. Sudie Mae was enjoying her renunciation. "Amen," he affirmed.

⚜

OF COURSE, she had no idea what she'd started. She'd simply spotted, from the distance of the hive, the inviting spray of blossom at the foot of the composter, and had flown over to investigate, as was her nature. Being by that point not much more than a bunch of rapidly desiccating petals, the gladiolus blossom did not have much to offer, so she'd soon lost interest in it after a brief investigation, and only then noticed that there was an uncommon amount of different creatures gathered together in the immediate vicinity—birds, squirrels, a couple of rats, an opossum, and at a slight distance, five deer, a couple of raccoons, and there was even a curious anole clinging to the air conditioning unit. The novelty of the scene was at once interesting and alarming, and, raising her altitude just a few feet, she circled about the area, just in order to take it all in and assure herself that she was not in any danger. Which motion clearly further alarmed most of the gathered animals, who had frozen already at her approach. Paralysis or frenzy being the usual response of creatures outside of her species to her presence, she didn't feel anything about that. Turning to the east, she spotted a heretofore uninvestigated clump of clover near the edge of the woods, and she dashed her way over to it, and when she was finished there she flew all the way across the boulevard to the shopping center, where it turned out the landscaper had planted a fresh rosebush in the bed of soil over which the tall road sign towered. As she gathered her pollen, she found herself wondering about the gathering of different creatures back in the churchyard. What were they up to? Why were they together? To see so many different species in one place without being under duress was unheard of to even the most cosmopolitan of creatures, and to one as sheltered as she had always been it just seemed unnatural. At the same time, she felt a sliver of regret at having been the agent of their fright. It left her with the sense that she'd left some ineffable damage in her wake. She would like to go back more discreetly and see if the group was still there. But she had work to do, she was already behind, so she gathered as much as she could from the strip mall shrubbery and returned to the hive last, but for once not least, and retired to her cell and dreamed of fields of innumerable varieties of flowers as far as her inward compound eye could see.

THE FOLLOWING MORNING, she, along with the other workers, awakened and took off from the hive in search of fresh stores of that golden dust and clear sweet nectar of life, and whether this daily departure was driven by habit, or by instinct, or by inner or outer compulsion she never thought to wonder. It was just something that she and most of the others had done for as long as she could remember, just as, for as long as she could remember the Queen, Her requirements and Her comforts were to be served in all that she, a daughter and dependent of that figure, endeavored. The Queen was the reason and the origin of her existence. She was aware of this without having any particular feeling associated with it, it was a fact of life, like her body itself. Only now, after observing with some consciousness and closeness the activity of these creatures congregated around the composter, did it dawn on her that the Queen was not the center of existence for all creatures. This awareness engendered a subtle sense of something completely unfamiliar to her: equality. And along with this, and what seemed to be inextricable from it, a burgeoning curiosity. What did these other creatures, so massive and ground-bound and rather slow, it seemed, in relation to her, do all the time with themselves? What was the object of their behaviors? These questions, as if they had a life of their own within her, began to unsettle her in moments of rest, as if they were blossoms yet unexplored. At last, one afternoon on her way back to the hive, richly laden with dust and nectar, she happened to pass above the composter, and saw one of the large rodents crouched in its shadow in a relaxed attitude. Sensing an opportunity for the satisfaction of a vague but compelling desire, she descended to land right in front of him.

Clancy, startled beyond measure, leaped like a flea almost three times his length up into the air, with a shriek as if a thorn had pierced his flesh. As he landed, he instinctively hunched to protect his soft plump underbelly and distressingly prominent testicles, and so fell forwards, forcing the bee to become airborne lest she be squashed. Clancy tentatively unhunched and, seeing that there was no longer any threat before him, began to glorify God out of sheer relief. "Thank the Lord!" exclaimed the rat, "I'm mighty jumpy today! I guess I've been working too hard lately."

It was true that, following the arrival of the beehive, and the subsequent uptick in the human presence in the area behind the church, which was normally sacrosanct to the animals, his own flock had been uncommonly fretful, and he'd been obliged to constantly reassure them when he was hard put to find any reassurance for himself. Frequent human proximity to his domain could be highly nerve-wracking. Even though it was usually just Tommy, a known quantity to be sure, his presence for hours at a time during the occasional evening was inhibiting. Clancy was accustomed to the freedom to conference or simply chew the fat with Ottoline or whoever else happened to come along in the cool of the evening, and with Tommy in his strange white protective garments puttering about the beehive almost every weekday evening no one felt free to be themselves. Clancy had the uncomfortable sense that something essential to the cohesiveness of the community was being compromised, as if, with the arrival of the beehive, and perhaps even with the arrival of the new lady rector, an era had ended.

"Oh!" the bee heard the rat exclaim. Standing upright and drawing his paws together against the soft white fur of his chest in that classic posture of prayer, he began to beseech the Almighty. "Guide me, Lord, and strengthen me! Things around here are changing so fast! First this new lady rector, and now a beehive, and Tommy out here all the time—I just can't keep up! Lord, I believe I might need a vacation before long. But where in the world would I go?!"

Dimly recognizing the rodent's vocalizations as being conversational in nature, the bee grew all the more intrigued. Conversation, at least on a very basic and impersonal level, was nothing new to her. It was necessary, after all, to maintain order in the hive. But who or what was the furry creature talking to? She could see, after all, in all directions, and there was no one around but herself. The need to make sense of the situation was overwhelming. She descended again to land directly before the rat. "What are you talking about?" she said, blunt on account of her utter innocence.

Once again, Clancy leaped into the air as if he'd actually been stung. Even though the tiny being had merely, if unexpectedly, asked him a simple question, which he could understand, his instinctual tendency to associate these tiny striped creatures with intense physical pain was strong, and he scampered backwards in a panic with such force that he actually jostled the composter, alarming Hertz out of an afternoon drowse.

"What are you saying?" the bee buzzed again. "I don't understand." And as if she perhaps thought that coming closer to the creature before her might facilitate communication, she became slightly airborne and made a graceful arc towards him.

"No!" the rat shrieked. "Please! Don't sting! It's not worth it! I promise! We won't hurt you. We don't want any trouble!" And so saying, he clasped his claws together against his pale furred chest, a posture very much like that of prayer, but a signifier of retreat and surrender in this context.

"Sting?" buzzed the relatively harmless looking creature inquiringly. She knew, of course, what it meant to sting, she'd seen it happen plenty of times—for instance, not too long before when another furry creature rather similar to this one had approached the hive too cavalierly. Another worker had immediately responded. Protection of the hive was yet another duty of her class, one which meant, of course, the loss of life. It was an aspect of her condition which she now, with her burgeoning sense of self-and-other, hoped she could avoid. "You aren't close," she said.

This response, which came as a relief in that it did not seem hostile, nonetheless made no sense to Clancy. "Do what?" he said.

The bee, for her part, did not understand the rat's response. The two strangers found themselves at an impasse. It was not until another voice, low and at once sharp and textured like gravel, emerged crepuscularly from the interior of the composter, that the silence was broken.

"What the Ground is going on out here!?"

"Hertz!" Clancy, still clutching his paws to his chest, responded breathlessly. "Hertz! Don't come out! Stay in! There's a bee right in front of the composter! And I think it's upset!"

"A what?" Hertz's tip emerged from one of the ventilation slots in the casing in spite of (or perhaps because of) the rat's hysterical warning.

"Hertz!!!" Clancy shrieked. "Oh, Lord, watch out!"

The worm, whose sight was rudimentary even up close, saw merely a speck on the ground before the rat. He extended himself as far as he could to get a better look. "What did I tell you! There goes the neighborhood." With his ability to withdraw back into safety in an instant, Hertz felt no real concern that he might be stung, and so he seized the opportunity to assert his dominance.

"Hertz!"

The bee did not need to move a muscle to regard Hertz carefully with her compound eyes' magnificent vision. She saw a slim, rather slimy protuberance from the strange greenish hive-like structure before her. She recognized it as an earthbound invertebrate, no threat whatsoever. But what was it doing in that hive?

"Hertz!" the rodent cried. "Watch out! Get back in! It'll sting! Oh, Lord!" He wrung his paws as if they were attempting to remove one another and directly addressed the bee. "Please... don't do it. It's not worth it. You'll hurt yourself for no reason. I promise. I won't bother you, and neither will Hertz. He's just joking. We won't go anywhere near your hive, and I'll make sure all the church members know not to..."

The bee remained motionless on the dusty ground before the rat, so Clancy surmised it was at least paying attention. He went on, pleadingly: "It's a big churchyard, after all, and there's plenty of room for everyone, and there's no reason for us to have any problems. The only time that there really might be any misunderstanding is on Sunday mornings and maybe a few other days every now and then when we have services. Just tell your friends that that's when they may notice a lot of different creatures over here around the composter, because we all get together to sing and pray and worship the Lord, because we have what's called a church. A church is a group of creatures... usually humans, actually, but not always... who get together to help each other because we all believe that we are creatures of God, and that Jesus came to save us just like He came to save His own kind. So, you'll see a little crowd on Sunday mornings. And you'll probably hear us too, because like I said, we sing. But that's all. I know that one of our newer members, a rat like me, named Percy...maybe got too close to your hive last Sunday, and one of your friends had to sting him, and I'm so sorry for your loss, and I promise it won't happen again. Percy didn't know that you all were there, he saw the hive and he thought it might be another composter, we all did. He didn't mean to bother y'all. We're really very peaceful here at St. Aloysius Jr., and I just hope you understand, and that we can share the churchyard, because we really don't have anywhere else to gather..."

As always when he was anxious, silence was a challenge for Clancy, and so when the bee did not respond it was difficult for him to bear. He took in a deep breath, and was prepared to reiterate all that he had just explained, for he knew quite well that he'd been talking in nervous circles and probably hadn't made much sense. But something in the bee's stillness held Clancy spellbound.

The bee's stillness at the moment was the stillness of fascination. It was true that she had only the vaguest idea of what the rodent was going on about, but to be addressed so very directly, at such length, and with what many would recognize as deference, was the most unique of experiences for her, who had theretofore really only taken orders. Certainly, Clancy's reassurances were unnecessary, for she did not perceive a threat to herself at all, from either rat or worm. It was no more in her mind to sting either of them than to fly into the sun. What was in her mind was an entirely novel impulse, which filled her at once with excitement and trepidation. She wanted to express herself, to make herself known to these unfamiliar creatures. She wanted to establish that she was capable of self-disclosure. Of course, this desire was largely inchoate. She could not have put it into words. But what she could put into words was her sense of identity, of distinct individuality.

"I am last," she said forthrightly. "I have less."

Clancy was so bewildered by this response that for a moment he imagined that he only imagined that the bee had spoken. He glanced up at Hertz, who, for once in his life, seemed likewise unsure. "I beg your pardon?" said Clancy.

The bee, sensing the rat's perplexity, felt yet another new sensation. She felt embarrassed. She was aware that she was communicating poorly, that she could do no other, that she had no skill and no appreciable experience when it came to cross-species communication. She wanted to make herself known. However, she was so little known to herself that she could only present a negative definition. She felt an immediate urge to fly away, to escape this sense of having failed. But just as immediately she realized that these states of feeling in relation to events could not be escaped. She would continue to feel bad whether she stayed or went. There was no reason not to keep trying. But what should she say? What did she and these other creatures have in common that she could acknowledge?

"I am here," she said.

Clancy was still very puzzled, but at least here was something that he could respond to. And so, with his usual effortless cheer, now that his anxiety about being stung and thus becoming the agent of death for this little creature had been dispelled like a morning fog, he said encouragingly, "You sure are! And I'm so happy to see it. You have to forgive me for being so jumpy, but I've just always heard that bees don't like to be bothered, and that if you get stung you aren't the only one that gets hurt, and here at St. Aloysius Jr. we believe in nonviolence. We don't want *anyone* to get hurt, for any reason at all."

Here Clancy paused to gauge whether or not he was being understood by the little creature. He still had his paws drawn against his chest, and in a conscious signal of relaxation, he fell to all fours. The bee, so small and still—and to be frank, rather alien in aspect—still rather intimidated him. With a quick backward glance up at Hertz for reassurance, he once again attempted to engage the bee. "What's your name?" he inquired.

She understood the question, and in understanding, understood that she had no answer. Having never been addressed as an individual by another individual, she did not have a name, and she had only a vague idea of what one was, a designation that set one apart, she supposed, like *Queen*.

"No name," she said simply. She regarded the furry creature before her as he became visibly aghast, his whiskers and ears erecting.

"You have to have a name!" the rodent cried. "Everybody has one!" Clancy turned to Hertz, as if he expected the worm to confirm the obviousness of this fact. "Hertz! She says she doesn't have a name! That can't be true!"

Hertz, who had a far better sense of how cheaply regarded individuals could be within invertebrate colonies, especially ones that operate along rigidly hierarchical and authoritarian lines, was not a bit surprised. The colony of his origin had been very much like that, and in fact, until coming to the church, and having his complaint about his physical injuries misunderstood by Clancy to be his introduction, he had only been known to others of his species as "A Son of Crawley."

"If she says she doesn't have a name, she doesn't have a name," said the worm. "Not everybody has had it as easy as you."

"Everyone should have a NAME!" Clancy's indignation shoved aside Hertz's blasé response. He could not bear the thought that a child and creature of the Living God would have no way to refer to themselves. He crouched so that his snout was on a level with the bee, and for the first time since the bee had arrived, the rat felt absolutely no fear of being stung. "Friend, are you sure you don't have a name?"

The bee had never heard—much less been the subject of—a debate. Bees did not debate. She followed the brief dialogue between rat and worm with interest if not understanding. This was an exchange between equals, free-flowing, containing contradiction. This was not the command and assent she was accustomed to. She had no answer for the rat, however, apart from the answer previously given, so she remained silent.

"Well, I can't stand it." The rodent raised himself up to his hind paws as if to signal his indignation corporeally. "You deserve a name. Everyone deserves a name, and especially you, because you have been a good neighbor and haven't stung me. You deserve a nice name, too, and not something ugly. I'm going to give you a name right now. This is an emergency. You have to have a name so that you can say who you are. Now, what would you like to be called...?"

"Better speak up," said Hertz to the bee. "Or he'll come up with something goofy. Trust me."

"Stop it, Hertz!" said Clancy with uncharacteristic sharpness. "You know I wouldn't give any of God's creatures a bad name. I'll name her whatever she wants to be named." He tuned back to the bee. "Is there a name you like?"

The bee knew of only one term that she could conceive of as being what the rat was referring to as a name, and that was Queen, which certainly did not suit her. She was no Queen. She discovered, to her surprise, that she was rather glad of this, for all that the Queen was very important. No, she was just a worker, but of course there were countless other workers, so it did not seem to make sense that worker was a name. It was beginning to seem that a name was entirely unique to one's self, like the hexagonal cell to which she retired at the end of her working day, something boundaried and containing. Her cell was to her a place of rest, of sanctuary. Maybe her name would be like that in some sense. But of course, her cell was contingent upon her work. Would her name have a price, so to speak? It became important to know.

"What do I have to do?" she said.

"Do!?" Clancy's voice rose like a spark. "You don't have to do anything to have a name! Good Lord! Names are a nonhuman right! Every single one of God's creatures deserves a name, no matter what. Why, even the Devil himself has a name, and I think it's a pretty one, too—it's Lucifer! You don't even have to be good or love God to have a name, it's just something you have like you have your own body. Now, most of us get our names when we're born, from our parents, but it sounds like you might have missed out on that, so like I said, I'm going to give you a name right this minute. But I don't want to name you anything you don't like, so let's think about this real hard. A lot of times your name comes from someone else in your family... like for me, I was named after my Aunt November's daddy. Clancy was his middle name. And in the Church, a lot of times we like to use names that are in the bible. I think we should do that. There are so many pretty names in the Bible, and you're pretty yourself, so you should have a pretty biblical name. Now, some names can be given to males or females or anything in between, and it doesn't matter. But most names aren't like that, especially in the Bible. And there aren't as many female names in the bible that I've heard, but let's see: there's Mary, that's the name of Jesus' mother and also of a couple of his friends... There's Eve, she's the first human lady, that all the humans in the whole world come from... There's Sarah, she's a lady who was married to a man named Abraham, and she started a great big family called the Jews... And then there's one named Esther, she was a great Queen—"

"No," said the bee.

"No? Okay... if you don't like those, that's okay, I can think of some more... Let's see, there's Bathsheba... She was supposed to be real, real pretty, and there's Veronica, she was another friend of Jesus, and she washed his face for him when he was carrying his cross..."

Clancy went on to mention Deborah, Rachel, Hepzibah, Elizabeth and Martha, but the bee did not really take note of these, for something about the name Veronica, the verve and music of it, had stuck with the little creature. "Veronica," she repeated, in her fuzzy way.

"Oh!" Clancy said. "You like that one? I like it too. I don't know too much about her, though, other than she washed Jesus' face, but I'm sure she was real special just to do that. Is that the one you want?"

"Veronica," the bee repeated.

"Oh, good," said Clancy. "That was easy. Praise the Lord. Well, then, with the power vested in me, as a minister of the Gospel of our Lord and Savior Jesus Christ, I now pronounce you Veronica. Amen!"

And so it was accomplished. Instantly, upon the rat's proclamation, the signifier "Veronica" became inextricably united to the little bee's sense of uniqueness. For the very first time in her life, she reflected upon her state without recourse to a comparative adjective or a descriptor. The *I* that was last, and least, or was tired, or anxious, or curious, was Veronica.

"Welcome to St. Aloysius Church, Veronica," said Clancy.

"You're in for it now," said Hertz.

❦

CLANCY WOULD HAVE LIKED to spend the remainder of the afternoon getting to know Veronica and acquainting her more fully with himself and his concept of the Gospel, but almost as soon as she received her name she said that she was late and must leave.

Clancy did not want to appear overeager, but his disappointment was evident in the wheedling tone of his voice. "Oh, that's too bad. What are you late for, Veronica?"

Veronica, in spite of her vague sense of peril, felt a little thrill at the sound of her own new name. "Work," she said. "I have to finish my work."

"Oh—" said Clancy. He always felt a bit chagrined when reminded that he was blessed among animals, in that most of his basic needs for food and shelter, were provided for by virtue of his habitat among humans, and that other creatures did not share his amount of leisure. "Well, I don't want to hold you up.

But Veronica, before you go... will you join us for church on Sunday Morning? Only if you want to, of course..."

"Church?" Veronica buzzed inquiringly.

"Yes! Like I said, we meet every Sunday, to worship the Lord, and sing, and pray, and I preach, and then we share communion, which is like a little snack that I can turn into the body of Christ. We start when the bells of that great big Pres-byterian Church down the boulevard ring. I know that everyone will be real happy to meet you, and of course, if you want to bring any of your friends, we'd love to have them as well."

Veronica had every intention of returning, to this spot and to this funny, furry creature, who had confirmed for her, in the most profound way, the fact of her own individuality. But the idea of sharing this experience with those of her kind struck her as totally unthinkable. If all the workers came to know themselves as something beyond their assigned role, what would ensue? Knowing herself, she suddenly realized, was something she wanted to keep to herself. It was going to cost her somehow. She could feel it. And on this account, she wanted to cherish and savor it in secret.

"I will come back," she said, and off she went.

🕸️

ONE COULDN'T BE certain at this early stage, of course, but the Reverend Jean Grey believed that the pollination-honey ministry was getting off to a marvelous start. Often during breaks in her working day she liked to stand at the window behind her rector's desk and look out over the rear churchyard's variegated little landscape, the fenced-in little graveyard, the unused and dilapidated playset, and the community garden, at the far end of which stood, like a monument to responsible stewardship, her current pride and joy—the beehive.

Of course, from the distance from which she observed the

hive, it was unremarkable: a plain white columnar structure. But within, she knew, it was a world of light and life unto itself. Once the colony had settled in, Tommy had shown her pictures on his phone of the glistening golden honeycombs, and these images filled Jean Grey with satisfaction. "Pretty rad, huh," Tommy had remarked and Jean Grey had agreed wholeheartedly. "'Rad' indeed!—a radical statement of how one small church, by taking the course of sustainable small-scale community-based agriculture, could make a beautiful difference.

Tommy's clear investment in the project was also immensely gratifying, further bolstering her confidence in her own pastoral instincts. At first he'd been unsure of the relevance of the project to his own goals, but as soon as the equipment and the bees themselves arrived, he'd allowed himself to become enthusiastic. And now, even though the setup stage was accomplished, and there was very little need for human oversight or intervention in the workings of the colony until it became time to harvest the honey, Tommy continued to visit the churchyard daily to marvel at what he'd wrought. One afternoon he'd arranged with his culinary arts instructor to have the entire class visit as a field trip, and it gave Jean Grey no end of pleasure to lead a group of young people around the church and then share with them details about the initiative. This was, apart from the honey, precisely the outcome she'd hoped for—something that would help the church distinguish itself as something new and different in traditional garb. Her vision was being wonderfully realized. Heaven be praised!

Now if only she could do something about this recalcitrant, reactionary vestry... They were to a person so suspicious and stiff-necked and resistant to even the most gradual change! No wonder the former rector had apparently developed a drinking problem!

VERONICA RETURNED to the hive with woefully little pollen and nectar to show for the time she'd supposedly spent foraging, but with a secret knowledge that meant more to her than her work. Still, it would not be wise for her to continue to come up so short every day. If anything, her newfound sense of inviolate self was stoking a renewed, of not wholly new will to thrive, which would entail a satisfactory degree of usefulness to the colony. For how could she survive without the colony? The fact that she had come upon the knowledge of a life beyond the life she'd always known and a self more substantial than her utility to the Queen did not mean, in the end, that she was not a bee like other bees. She could not afford to fail, now that she had something—herself—to lose.

"YES, FRIENDS..." Clancy affected a greater sheepishness than he truly felt, "I know I probably say this every Sunday Service, but today really is a very special and unique day. We have a special visitor. She's new to the neighborhood, and new to the church, and I know we're all going to do everything we can to help her feel welcome. Before I introduce her, though, I need to tell you all one thing. When you see her, you might be a little nervous at first, because we've all been warned to stay away from anyone who might sting. But she's not going to sting. She knows that no one here is going to hurt her, and so she's not going to hurt anyone here. I want us all to remember that we all have things that we do to protect ourselves... but it's just that hers is a little more obvious. That's why I've asked her to wait until I've had a chance to prepare you all before she comes over to join us, So now... let me introduce everybody to Veronica. Veronica? You can come out now!"

With a buzzing hop from where she'd concealed herself in the corner of the window of the rector's office, Veronica landed on the ground between the rat and the other animals, all of whom, having been duly prepared, restrained their instinct to flee. "Welcome to St. Aloysius Church of All God's Creatures Great and Small, Veronica!" Clancy prompted.

The congregation dutifully echoed the welcome in their distinctive chorus of growls, hisses, chirps and coos.

Veronica, for whom an acknowledgement of her sheer presence by even one individual was a novelty, was completely at a loss as to how to respond to an entire group's welcoming. She could find no words. It was not until Sudie Mae, who, remembering her own first time attending these services, and how awkward and out of place she'd felt even with her beloved big brother Bertram by her side, stepped out of her own position in the choir and bounded over to the tiny creature standing alone on the ground. "Come with me," she said in her gruff but warm voice. "You don't have to stand here all by yourself. The Reverend's going to start preaching now, so you can listen with us over here, and after the service I'll introduce you to everyone. Okay?"

Veronica's silence, and the fact that she followed Sudie Mae to where the choir stood by the composter, was her assent. From there she observed, and to some degree participated in, her very first worship service. The rat, chattering away, the center of attention, was in a way analogous to the Queen—*that* she could understand. There would be no 'church' without him. And yet there was very little about him of the Queen's imperiousness. The rat was not a figure to inspire deference; rather, he seemed to provide a point of reference. As he preached from atop the composter, Veronica's sense of the other creatures was that they regarded him with respect, but also with not a little indulgence. Only the great female bird who'd taken Veronica under her wing, so to speak, seemed to be listening uncritically to the rodent. Just observing Clancy, the sparkle in his little black eyes, the breathless energy of his high-pitched vocalizations, the effervescent innocent glee he communicated, reminded Veronica of a flower in bloom. There was about him a quality of generosity that was wholly absent from the Queen, who was nevertheless the source of life for her workers.

When the service ended with the recessional hymn and the fellowship hour began, Veronica followed the lead of Sudie Mae and was greeted by a number of the more outgoing creatures, each of whom approached her with an evident determination not to betray their instinctual aversion to her. "Welcome to St. Aloysius Jr., Veronica," said Ottoline. "I'm Ottoline, and this is my spouse, Steven. We look forward to getting to know you."

Veronica was only beginning to know herself! So once again she was at a loss. It still seemed extraordinary that another creature would be curious about her. And yet, the same sentiment was expressed, with apparent sincerity, by each member that approached her that morning. She was asked all sorts of questions, mostly about how she spent her days, if the other bees were going to attend the church as well, etc. The question that she found most perplexing, however, was Clancy's inquiry as to what she thought of the service. For never before had her personal opinion been solicited.

But she recognized that she ought to say something. But what? What was there to say about an experience so totally unfamiliar and seemingly without purpose? The random gathering of creatures, as peaceful as it had proven to be, still seemed to her somewhat like asking for trouble. Things were bound to go wrong at some point with so many differences in one place. The secure homogeneity of the hive was alarmingly absent. And yet, it was all right.

So that's what she said, making a brief arc before the rodent's eyes. "It was all right."

Clancy couldn't deny to himself that this seemed to be faint praise, but it would be ungracious not to appear gratified. "Oh, good," he said. "I hope you'll come join us next week if you can. I try to make every liturgy something special. Some things change and some things stay the same... different songs, you know and different readings from the Bible, and of course I always try to have a brand-new sermon every single week. But the communion service is always the same... just like you saw this time, everyone brings whatever it is that they like to eat, and I turn it into the body of Christ. And then after that, we always have fellowship. Every now and then we have a service that doesn't happen on Sunday... those are special services to remember important things that happened to Jesus, like when He was born, and when He died, and when He rose up to Heaven. And we have special events for special times for members in the church, like when they decide to give their lives to Jesus—that's Baptism—or when they decide to give their lives to another creature—that's Holy Matrimony, and of course when they go to be with the Lord—that's a funeral. I want my members to know that the church is here for them all the time... not just on Sunday! So you can find me here anytime you might need me, Veronica, hear? This is your spiritual home."

Here Veronica began to experience yet another inner state entirely new to her: conflicting interests. What the rat was describing sounded interesting, but also time intensive. Although she now possessed the transcendent freedom of her own consciousness and identity, she was still bound to the hive and obligated to serving it. How could she possibly devote any more time than she already had to this new and apparently nonproductive community?

"Veronica?" said Clancy, with some concern, for his sense was that the bee seemed overwhelmed. "Oh, Lord!" he said after a moment's reflection. "I'm being too pushy again. It's just that I'm so excited that we're going to be friends. But don't feel like you have come back if you don't want to. I know you all are real busy. But you're welcome any time. I mean that. I believe that the Lord has led you to us for a reason."

Veronica had no idea who or what the Lord was, but she hoped he was not as demanding as her Queen.

It was at this point that Sudie Mae made her way toward the composter, as fellowship hour was wrapping up quickly so that there would not be too conspicuous a gathering when the human church services ended and that congregation began to make its way outside.

"Well, here's Sudie Mae!" said Clancy, grateful that one of the more introverted of his core members seemed to be going beyond her comfort zone to make the newest little member feel welcome. "You've met Veronica, haven't you?"

"Yes." Sudie Mae acknowledged the bee with a nod of her beak. "Hey there, honey. Reverend, I was thinking, since we know Veronica ain't gonna sting us, would it be all right for me to start bringing flowers again? I know it wasn't much, but I sure do miss it. I enjoyed hunting for just the right colors, and putting them all together..."

Clancy had forgotten all about Sudie Mae's erstwhile ministry. He drew a breath to declare that he thought it would be just lovely for Sudie Mae to resurrect the custom of bringing a floral offering. But before he could speak, Veronica, for whom self-expression and movement were almost inextricable, signaled decisive objection with a mid-air arc that seemed to trace a pronounced frown.

"You don't think Sudie Mae should bring any more offerings, Veronica? But why not? After all, when you think about it, that's what brought you to the church in the first place! Why, without Sudie Mae's flower ministry, you wouldn't be with us right now! Don't you think if Sudie Mae keeps bringing flowers for the Lord, it might even bring some of your friends to church, too?"

"No."

The rat and the buzzard looked at one another quizzically, then back at the bee. "Why not?" inquired Sudie Mae straightforwardly.

"They aren't me," said Veronica. "They sting."

"Can't you tell them not to?" asked Sudie Mae quite reasonably.

"No," Veronica said, and in being obliged to explain her situation to the rat and the buzzard, she explained it to herself. "I'm not the queen. She makes all the decisions. We just do what she says."

"Oh!" Clancy looked across the courtyard, to the other end of the community garden, where the hive stood, a pale tidy structure that betrayed nothing at the moment of the teeming yet regimented life within. "Well, maybe you could talk with her. Or..." He felt a thrill of incipient fear. "Or if you think she'd listen to me...?"

"She doesn't listen to anyone," said Veronica. "She's the Queen." And, in relating the immutability of her relations within the hive, she was reminded of the precariousness of her own position within it, and off she darted, to disappear into its workings once more.

"Oh, Lord..." said Clancy. "I guess I was being too pushy again. I hope she comes back to church. I think she needs us. I really do. It sounds like that Queen of hers is not very nice."

Sudie Mae could not bear for her reverend to imagine for a moment that he had fallen short in any way. "I'm sure she'll be back," said the young buzzard, for whom the rat reverend's gentle style of leadership was a balm for the spiritual chafing of her own rigid upbringing by a tyrannical father. "She's just shy."

❧

FOR VERONICA, when the inevitable descended, it nevertheless came as a painful shock. She returned, at dusk, as usual, from a less than competitive forage, less bountifully laden than any of her colleagues, to find that her cell was inhabited by a freshly lain egg. The fact of her inferiority had been noted, and measures had been taken. Her constant if at times submerged dread surfaced like a boil, and burst. It was rather a relief, of sorts. It was finished. There was no more to be done, no more anxiety and anticipation to endure. Only her demise remained, and she imagined that it would not tarry. In the meantime, she was not unsurprised to find herself at peace with herself. It was not as bad as she'd anticipated, losing her place... for after all, here she was, still existing, at least for the time being. Being definitively outcast, she noted, by no means diminished her sense of self. But now what was she going to do?

It hardly bore reflection. She gathered her wits, took off, and covered the short but eternal distance to the composter.

❦

As was their habitus at the setting of the sun, the Rat Reverend and Ottoline, perhaps the closest thing he had to a pastoral associate or deacon, were standing in the shadows of the composter, discussing the business of the parish. Clancy was animatedly describing his plan for a guided retreat when out of the dusk a speck emerged and seemed to advance toward them, until it drew close enough to reveal itself to be Veronica. Clancy could not contain his joy. "Veronica!" he cried. "Praise the Lord! We've missed you at church!"

In Clancy's words was a none-to-subtle, if loving edge of reproval, but Veronica was oblivious. It was reassuring to hear the syllables of her own name. She landed on the dusty ground before the rat and the bird, who regarded her with shared amazement. "I'm out," she said.

Clancy and Ottoline exchanged a glance. The rat reverend, ever prone to worse case scenarios despite his essential optimism, felt his bowels lurch with regret. "You're out? Well, you sure are, and I'm glad to see it. I was afraid we might not have made you feel welcome, and I was just saying to Ottoline, I hope that Veronica isn't upset with us. But if you aren't comfortable coming to church, I sure don't want to put any pressure on you, just know that if you change your mind you are always welcome, and—"

"Reverend," Ottoline intervened, for she sensed, not for the first or last time, that the rodent was missing signals. "I don't think... Veronica, are you in some sort of difficulties?"

Veronica only knew that she was on her own. "I'm on my own," she therefore said.

Ottoline's maternal as well as her burgeoning pastoral instincts were activated. The bee's statement, benign on the surface, and delivered with her characteristic buzzing matter-of-factness, was nonetheless indicative of real distress. "On your own... do you mean, there's a problem in the hive?"

"No," said Veronica. "I've been replaced."

"Replaced!" cried Clancy. A brief glance from Ottoline, however, silenced him before he could go on. "Do you mean, you can't go back?"

"I'm on my own," Veronica said again, with remarkable complacency.

"Oh, dear," said Ottoline. "I'm so sorry."

Clancy, though bewildered, could not contain his indignation. "You mean you've been put out of your hive? How dare they! What in the world! How can they do that!"

"I'm slow," Veronica said.

"Do what!" Clancy was so incensed that not even Ottoline's' silent imploring glances could deter him. "You are not slow! You are the quickest little thing I've ever seen! Don't you believe that for one minute! Do you hear me?!"

Ottoline was always reluctant to proceed pastorally without the Reverend's go-ahead, but it was getting late and it seemed to her that it would not be safe or healthful for a bee to be out in the open after dark. "Veronica," she said. "Is there something we can do for you?"

"I don't know," said the bee.

❃

THE QUESTION IMMEDIATELY BECAME, for Clancy and Ottoline, as well as for Veronica herself, what is a bee without a hive? What is her purpose... and perhaps more importantly, how is she to survive? Veronica could not envision a future. She only knew that she knew nothing when it came to making her own decisions. It was not long, however, before Ottoline, who had raised many a brood from egg to adulthood and beyond, recognized this, and took matters under her own wings.

"First," she stated, "we have to find you shelter. You certainly can't remain out in the open; no one can. Now, I'm not sure what sort of habitation would be most suitable, but in the short term, at least for tonight, why don't we have you stay in the belfry, where Steven and I sleep. There's plenty of space, and since you won't have any trouble accessing the rooftop, there should be no problem. You can stay as long as you like."

Veronica had the impulse to express gratitude, but not the words. She simply remained still.

"Another thing," Ottoline went on, "there's the matter of sustenance. Obviously, you know what your nutritional requirements are, so I imagine you know how to provide for yourself. But if there's anything Steven or I, or I'm sure anyone in the church can do to contribute to your welfare, we would be happy to do so. Can you think of any other immediate needs?"

Veronica only knew that she did not know what to ask for.

Ottoline's breast filled with the cool night air and a sense of wonder. The little bee's silence struck her as being rather poignant. Of course! Veronica was no newly hatched creature, but a mature adult, with a previous sense of belonging and purpose that had been utterly shattered.

"Never mind," said the pigeon. "Let me show you to your lodgings for now. Good night, Reverend. See you tomorrow."

"Good night, Ottoline. Night night, Veronica," Clancy said.

Veronica did not know how to respond other than by following the pigeon to the ornamental belfry, which, like herself, had no real purpose, at least not the one for which it was designed.

·  ·  ·

SAFE FOR THE night in the round enclosure with the two pigeons snoozing nearby, a wide-awake Veronica made a conscious decision to consider her brand new situation in life carefully. She was now officially, inexorably replaced. She knew with the certainty of innate survival instinct that if she attempted a return to the hive, she would be driven away, and with an impersonal vehemence on the part of her former colleagues that would know no mercy. Her Queen Mother, and her fellow worker siblings, the only society she had ever known apart from this strange new and uncertain one, would perceive her as a disturbance at best and a threat at worst. She was more than dead to them.

Her mind was seized by this perception of the irrevocable. Never before had she really imagined that there might be life after banishment. And yet, here she was, alive, breathing, still capable of flight and thought, and presumably she would be for some time to come. The future seemed to loom before her consciousness like an endless abyss. What was a bee without a hive? What was she? The question seemed at once necessary and futile.

She cast her mind back as far as it would go... to the larval stage. She remembered being small, blind, singular, yet aware that she was being tended to and provided, from time to time, with a sweet substance that soothed her sense of need. Following these earliest impressions, she remembered the stages of growth, of emerging sense impressions, of metamorphoses, as she progressed from larva to pupa and from there to her current form. There was activity beyond the increasingly cramped enclosure that she was filling with her growing self, and as sound and vision sharpened, restlessness overtook her, and she emerged from the six-sided cell of her nativity and joined the colony proper. There were others all around her very much like her, and she could observe what they did. It was all very straightforward and easy to understand, and there was no discussion or conversation beyond simple directives. She, like numberless others, was to leave the hive regularly and return with all the pollen and nectar she could find, which would be her contribution to the life of the colony and the price of her own ticket to life. And that was her past—altogether simple, until that realization dawned, that she was a poor performer.

Which had led to this. A life as perplexing and as open-ended as her former life had been ordered and comprehensible. She was not sure now what to do when the morning came. But, looking back, it seemed that the inevitable result of her coming to a sense of self was exactly this indeterminate future. She could never go back to being a servant of the Queen Mother, in which each and every moment, past, present and future, was dedicated to another's will.

But never to go back to the hive! Never to experience again that industrious, golden symmetry! She recalled her snug hexagonal chamber with real and visceral longing. Here, in the belfry, in the company of the pigeons, there was so much space, so to think of this as an enclosure was impossible. This was no place for a bee to be. And yet, to return to the hive would be to return to nonbeing. Impersonal, inhospitable of her deficiency and self-knowledge it may have been, but the hive was the only home she'd ever known. Her thorax tightened. She'd been replaced, and survived, but the sense of dread remained. Why?

৩৶৫

"GOOD GRIEF," muttered Hertz. "What is it now?"

Veronica might not know much about how the church was organized, but she'd seen enough to gather that when one had questions, the rat reverend seemed to be the person to ask. When she arrived, however, the fuzzy creature was not there, and Veronica, unaware that he'd crawled back into his cellar for the night, vocalized, as volubly as she could manage, his name and title. Several times she repeated this summons, but there was no response. Until, from within the composter casing,

Hertz's still small gravelly voice emerged, followed by his blunt and featureless yet somehow expressive-of-perturbation, tip. "Oh, it's the stinger," he said. "Don't come any closer, understand? The rat's gone to bed. Come back tomorrow."

"I'm scared," Veronica said. So irrepressible was this unexpected sense of loss and peril that her expression of it could not be contained, the worm's dismissiveness notwithstanding.

"Oh, my Ground!" cried Hertz, and without being conscious of his action, he extended himself further through the casing, as if to get a better look. "Are you kidding me? You could take down a bear with that thing sticking out of your behind. What have you got to be scared of? No one's going to mess with you. Ground knows I wish *I* had your equipment! Things would be different around here, that's for sure."

Veronica found the worm's response, as well as his presence, so bewildering that for a moment she forgot her distress. What did he mean? She considered it for a moment, in her rudimentary way, and came to the realization that he did not realize that she'd lost her place. "I'm out," she said.

"What the hell does that mean?"

"I'm on my own," she repeated.

Hertz felt something deeply unsettling pass through his entire length from tip to tail. In the warmth and the muck of his enclosure, his skin prickled as if he'd been hooked and cast into freezing water. His own experience of expulsion from the colony of his birth, never forgotten and never to be forgiven, his knowledge of the implacably hierarchical, exclusive nature of invertebrate colonies, recognized a fellow exile. "Welcome to the club, sister," he said wearily. "That's life in the real world."

Once again, Veronica was startled out of her own distress by the worm's response. From the rat, from the pigeons, she'd received a welcome, and that was one thing. But this worm, who now drooped against the casing of his enclosure as if he'd released some inner tension, was different. He knew where she was coming from. She felt a sudden inward illumination and expanse, as if she'd once again hatched from the egg. In encountering this worm, whose words and posture reflected her own sense of being outcast from her own kind, she became curious about an individuality apart from her own. Who was this, and what had he experienced? "Who are you?" she said.

"Around here, I'm called Hertz," he said. "If that's what you mean. I'm the only one with any real clue around here, just so you know, the only one who isn't all gaga over this God and Jesus business. That rat spends too much time inside listening to humans if you ask me, and the rest of these weirdoes spend too much time listening to him. Maybe they know something I don't know and maybe they don't, I'll never understand what difference it makes either way. As far as I'm concerned there's no point in worrying about what you can't see. But just between you and me, if you really are in a pinch, you've come to the right place. That rat may be crazy, but he'll help you out if he can. Just don't let him think he's saved you. He'll never let you live it down."

As Veronica listened, fascinated, Hertz grumbled on and on, dangling his tip from the ventilation slot in the composter casing and sharing himself with all the copiousness of a bladder voiding. The worm, Veronica realized, needed someone to relate to. And for the first time in her life Veronica experienced the thrill and assurance of being indispensable.

## ❧ 3 ❧

## CARITAS

H E SUFFERED ALL SORTS of physical complaints and ailments, and had for as long as he could remember. But there was nothing worse, he told himself, than not being able to sleep when the time for sleep had come. It was the last straw as far as he was concerned. He could not take much more aggravation. Life had dealt him a number of sorry tricks in the course of his existence, from an apparently congenital sensitivity to heat that generated nervousness and headaches, to a marked limp resulting from a fall from a poplar tree as a young cub and a general slowness when it came to motor skills. For these reasons he had become more and more isolated as the years went by, and this tendency to keep to himself had been exacerbated recently by his solitary trek north from his original home in a swampy area to the south in search of a more temperate—that is to say, cooler—climate. And for a good while he thought he'd found it in this national forest bordering the coastal city, but as the autumn lengthened without much indication that cooler winter temperatures would ever arrive, he began to wonder if he ought to keep moving north. At the same time, the discomfort caused by the lingering heat, interfering with his ability to hibernate and thus restore some measure of vitality, made the very idea of a long journey horrible. There was no prospect of relief, and there was nothing for it but to endure as best he could. But what a nightmare, what a pain in the ass, what an insult. "Why me!" he roared, so loud that the sound reverberated throughout the forest. But he did not care who heard him, he was irritated beyond that. Let them shoot him, if they wanted to, the humans in their ridiculously unconvincing camouflage wrappings with their cowardly firearms. He was sick and tired of having to worry about them anyway. He was sick and tired of everything. Giving up on rest, he emerged grumbling and growling from his makeshift den and plodded towards the edge of the woods with no destination in mind, impelled only by that nagging, exhausting restlessness that comes of insomnia and heat. He had the small, vague, stubborn hope that a stroll out in the open, long or short, might serve to discharge some of his miserable fidgetiness so that he might be able to rest a little afterwards. But he knew he better not count on it. Counting on anything only led, in his experience, to disappointment. Life was far from just. It always had been.

As he rambled and grumbled, he remembered. He remembered growing up in the bosom of a large and rough and tumble family, dominated by his mama bear mother, and yet always feeling, on account of his unobtrusive yet disabling differences, rather scorned and pitied, or at least relegated to the margins. He was never without a sense of the injustice of life, even as he recognized his advantages—his size, his intelligence in spite of his troubles, his warm if not quite understanding extended family, and the fact that as a bear, he had few natural predators apart from the human race. But being and feeling privileged are two very different things. He'd tried, he'd really tried, to adopt the attitude of his parents, siblings and extended clan, that life was for enjoying and suffering for avoiding when avoidable and enduring with patience and humor when endurable. But he'd never been able to understand why he should have to suffer at all. It seemed so pointless, and this pointlessness further aggravated him. "Oh, Brian's my big ole sorehead," his mother would always say of him with exasperated affection, and so blithely dismiss, it seemed to him, all of his persistent troubles. "He never has gotten over that tumble he took when he was just a cub. I think it did something to his nerves." And with that understanding, she did her best to comfort him when he was distressed. But even her comforts were, in their own way, distressing. He knew that he was a burden upon his family. So he'd left their warmth behind with the even more cloying heat of the southern wilds, and missed them terribly. He felt quite sure that they did not miss him, though they might think they did.

So preoccupied was he with introspection and reverie, that he wandered much closer to the edge of the woods than he intended, so close that he could see, through what was obviously a manmade clearing, one of their buildings, larger than many in the area, and in the space between the building and the tree line a curious landscape, consisting of a flat plot of land dotted with upright stone slabs, an odd plastic structure in sun-faded primary colors, and a fenced-in garden, at one border of which stood a solid green boxy container. To one side of the container, as if cooling in its shadow, Brian could see a couple of birds, a squirrel, and of all things, a rat. He gazed for a while at this curious gathering, which seemed to be remarkably intimate and peaceful. Filled with a sudden, painful sense of wistful longing, he trundled away before they noticed him. He did not stop until he came to the railroad tracks.

SUDIE MAE COULDN'T GET BACK to sleep. Bertram had lately been spending more time than usual or necessary ostensibly scavenging. He always returned with a bellyful of good and dead meat to share with his sister, but after supper he'd taken off again, saying he had to visit a friend, and Sudie Mae knew what that meant. She knew well that her brother was more than a little eager to mate and start a family, and although in the wake of his broken engagement with a vulture named Donna he'd sworn that he could never love again, Sudie Mae hadn't for a moment believed that would last. And there was a telltale sparkle in his red-rimmed eyes over the past few weeks that suggested a secret happiness. She supposed she should be happy for her brother. And she was, in a way...but oh, how she wished things could just stay the same. As a member of St. Aloysius Jr., as a part of the choir, as the senior and only creature on the Altar Guild, she felt, for the first time in her life, reasonably secure. Sharing the roost with her big brother, the only member of their fractious family that she'd ever trusted, had been an inextricable strand of this security. But now it was beginning to look as if she would soon be on her own. Since the death of their father, Sudie Mae and Bertram had lived together. What in the world would living on her own be like?

Perhaps on account of the strange and novel and perhaps preparatory experience of being on her own in the roost overnight, she'd slept fitfully and dreamt wildly of endless flights over rough seas, with nowhere in sight to land and rest. She woke up to the just as novel and even more unpleasant experience of having to gather a breakfast for herself, something that in the recent past Bertram had always provided. Off she went to the waterfront, where there was always a dead fish or two to be found, and returned to the roost for a nap. But she soon found that she was still far too restless to rest. It was only mid-morning, and she knew that if she went to the church, the Reverend would more than likely not be inside, as he spent most weekdays hiding in the office of the human rector, which he considered an essential aspect of his theological education.

She thought about visiting Ottoline, but as kind as the elder pigeon could be counted on to be, Sudie Mae did not want anyone's sympathy. She left her roost, took to the sky, and flew in circles, as if scouting for carcasses. After a while she became self-conscious, knowing that a circling bird of her size was always conspicuous to ground dwellers, and she did not feel like being eyeballed. She took off to the west and soon executed a swift descent. She had not consciously planned on it, but she realized she was returning to a familiar path—for in her troubled youth she'd discovered a place where she could be alone and sort things out. She touched down on the ties of the railroad tracks, and in that narrow clearing she felt inconspicuous and safe. She walked and walked, and the plodding movement, so devoid of the thrill of flight, but with its own calming effect, restored to her a sense of her own agency. So Bertram was in love again, and life would surely change. Well, she would simply have to get used to it. Things could be worse, she knew. She could still be stuck with her daddy.

Her father. The mild feeling of acceptance shattered when his memory crossed her mind, so tyrannical, so downright mean had he been, and most especially towards her, as the most recalcitrant of his daughters. Sudie Mae had hated her father, and largely on account of the fact that he could only be bothered to hate her when she defied him. And in the end, it was Bertram's defiance, and not hers, that really got to the old buzzard. Patriarchal to the core, he'd deplored Sudie Mae's independence of spirit in comparison to her mother and sisters, but in the end he didn't really care. While she could whip him up into a rage in which he would abuse her to the point of near unconsciousness, after his passion was spent he hardly gave her a second thought. His unexpected death, coming as it had on the heels of his banishment of Bertram for taking up with the Church, was as much of a slap in the face to Sudie Mae as it was a relief. No longer would he abuse and disdain her... and he would never,

ever care. Her own eventual participation in the life of St. Aloysius Jr. was as much out of spite toward her father as it was out
of regard for the cute little rat reverend. At least in the beginning. All other species were, as far as her father was concerned,
better off dead. Sudie Mae didn't know why her father had been
such a miserable and hateful old cuss, and tried not to give a
damn. But sometimes it was hard not to wish things had been
different.

On she plodded, under what was now a noonday sun. The
rails on each side of her path, though pitted with rust, shone
with a burnished reflection. The psychic pressure of the
memory of her father lifted somewhat, and she began to think
of Clancy, of Clancy's God, of the promises that the rat
reverend so often made in the name of that God, that every
single creature was special, and loved, and cared for. Not for a
moment did Sudie Mae doubt the sincerity of the faith of her
dear reverend, but deep down inside she could not help but
question the possibility of his impossibly good god and His
Heavenly Father. She neither saw nor felt any evidence of this
mysterious person. Clancy believed and behaved with such
conviction that she figured she was just too selfish to see. But
now, here, in the hidden sunny silent solitude of the railway
clearing, she thought she could imagine something along those
lines. Here on the tracks she could almost believe that she was
somehow being looked after. Even though she was all by herself.

And so it was like a smack in the beak when she happened
to look up again, to see, in the very great distance, a figure,
unmistakably animate, moving slowly, haltingly, towards her. It
was too far off for her to see what sort of creature it was, but
what did that matter? The cruel and frustrating fact was that
she was not alone just as she had come to recognize her alone-
ness as something of a gift. Her previous sense of contentment
shattered like an egg that has toppled from the nest to the
ground. She quickened her pace and spread her great wings
with every intention of taking off and never returning to this

godforsaken place that just a moment before had been so god-suggestive. But just as she became airborne, she could hear, proceeding from that distant but approaching figure, vocalizations that she realized were intelligible. "Why me?!" It growled, or rather roared, and from the unguarded volume of this outburst Sudie Mae could tell that the creature had no awareness of her own presence. The creature was expressing itself to itself, just as she had been doing. She did not wonder... she just knew, that it had come to the tracks for the same reason that she had... to be alone.

Sudie Mae didn't decide to draw in her wings. She just did. Just knowing that the creature whom she perceived did not perceive her washed away her own sense that her own solitude had been breached. She felt a strange inviolability. In an astonishing emotional about-face, she was glad. As the distant creature grew nearer, staggering forward between the rails of the tracks, it became clear to Sudie Mae that it was a bear, a full-grown bear, quite big, ferocious in aspect on account of its obvious distress, but that ferocity was oddly unalarming, in that the ferocity seemed inwardly directed, essentially. The restless, clumsy gait, the pained, grumbling vocalizations, all this struck a chord in Sudie Mae. She was touched.

*This is one grouchy bear!* she thought to herself. *I wonder what his problem is?* And again, without making any conscious decision to do so, she came to a halt. She stood on the train track, her wings drawn in, her neck extended upwards and her countenance facing forward as the oncoming bear slowly and clumsily approached like a wounded animal. She stood and waited, and for what reason, she had no notion. It was as if there was nothing else she could do.

Naturally, the closer the bear came, the larger it seemed. And the more oblivious it obviously was to anything apart from its own obvious distress. It grizzled, it growled, it staggered and from time to time shook its head spasmodically as if to disperse a cloud of importunate flying insects. Sudie Mae watched its approach without feeling any apprehension. If anything, she realized, she felt she ought to see what was the matter with the gigantic but plainly suffering creature and try if possible to help it. She spread her wings and executed a low flying arc to land on the tracks just a few lengths from the staggering bear.

Sudie Mae's sudden proximity could not but break through the bear's misery to alert him to her presence, and he came to a stumbling halt and grizzled and snuffled his snout from side to side and then lowered it in her direction. His relatively small eyes were bleary and irritated, and he did not see at first that the figure now before him was really just a bird, small in comparison to him and certainly no physical threat. Still, her nearness was aggravation enough that he took a deep breath and loosened his jaw and emitted a lengthy, vociferous, and bellowing roar. The objective of this outburst was to scare off anything that got in his way, and the great noise did set Sudie Mae's heart racing. But she recognized it for what it was: sheer bluster.

And again, without making any conscious decision to do so, she stepped closer toward the great creature, stood on a tie between the tracks with her wings drawn in, and extended her retracted neck as the oncoming bear clumsily continued his approach, staggering on hind limbs like a wounded or drunken human. She stood and waited. And for what, she had no clear idea. It was as if there was nothing else she could do.

The closer the bear came, naturally, the bigger it seemed. And the clearer it became that it was oblivious to anything apart from its own distress. It grizzled, it growled, it staggered and from time to time shook its head violently, again as if to dispel an invisible but nonetheless noxious cloud, or a swarm of gnats or fleas. There was nothing plaguing this tormented creature that Sudie Mae could see. But clearly it was suffering. She extended her wings, just in case it became necessary to make a fly for it, and opened her beak and said, "Hey! Are you all right?"

The bear came to a sudden halt, roared, and gazed all around with its small eyes that were bleary with fatigue, and managed not to glance down to notice the sizable but by no means tall bird before him. He once again staggered forward and would have trod upon her if she had not leaped up into the air. That got his attention. She landed on a thick maple stump on the low bank of earth to the left of the tracks. The bear stopped again and looked at her with bald, aggrieved hostility, and recognized her for what she was—a buzzard, the most inauspicious of birds. And indeed, her posture upon the stump, hunched and staring at him, seemed to portend death. It was this sinister aspect of her appearance that overrode any impulse he had to lunge at her to make her depart. He nearly forgot his discomfort in the deep dread he suddenly conceived. And for a long moment the two creatures regarded one another warily. In that moment of encounter, each represented to the other a danger. And yet neither felt an impulse to escape. The sunshine seemed to intensify, as if that heavenly body was focusing its attention upon this scenario.

"Hey," said Sudie Mae again.

The bear froze, despite the heat. This was the first time that another creature had spoken to him since he'd left his family and the wetlands to the south. It took him a moment to even absorb the reality that the bold buzzard before him had issued her version of a salutation. That one syllable began to needle his consciousness like a burr in his pelt. He responded, therefore, with a vehemence to match his discomfort. "What do *you* want!" he roared. "I'm not dead *yet!*"

Sudie Mae's claws, her beak, and her heart all clenched with a furious hurt. It was always the same, everywhere she went, nothing but disrespect and stupid assumptions about her, just because of her species. It was enough to make a buzzard want to start eating live flesh! But she would die herself before she gave this beast or any other the satisfaction of thinking it mattered to her what they thought.

"Well, maybe you will be soon. You're sure acting like something's wrong with you, stumbling around and shaking and talking to yourself. I was just trying to see if you needed help. You don't have to be so ugly to me."

The bear blinked as if the nonexistent fleas swarming his head were now getting in his eyes. As a result, the bleariness of his vision reduced a bit, and he could see the creature before him a bit more clarity, a buzzard to be sure, with all of the balefulness of feature that buzzards possess by nature. But this one, female, while hideous to him, had a certain archness of expression that hinted of intelligence. He felt dimly sorry that he'd insulted her, but swamping that chagrin was his overall discomfort, which, in the unexpected presence of another, he couldn't deny expression.

"*Everything's* wrong with me! I'm sick. I'm sick because I can't sleep. It's too damn hot! It's not supposed to be this hot this time of year. And it's driving me crazy!!!" The bear vocalized this last sentence in a choked, anguished roar. Sudie Mae perceived real suffering, but she was still angry.

"That's no reason to be nasty. What you said was mean, and I don't appreciate it. And it's no wonder you're hot, running around on the railroad tracks in the middle of the day. Why don't you go where there's some shade?"

The bear was incensed. "Where do you think I've *been*!" he bellowed. "Shade doesn't make any difference when it's this hot! And it's not even supposed to *be* this hot anymore! Something's wrong with the world, and if you don't know that, you're just..."

The bear bit off the last word of his retort, for it dawned upon him suddenly that the creature with whom was disputing was female, and so his vociferation was unseemly. His upbringing, undertaken as it had been by his good-natured but nononsense mother, had been indulgent, but for all of that it was expected that one would always behave respectfully or suffer the consequences. One did not contradict one's elders, and one must not exploit one's advantages, whether of size, gender, or intelligence, over other creatures. "It's not like I can just take to the skies," he muttered petulantly.

Sudie Mae did not bother to respond. It was not lost on her that, now that she had allowed herself to become an object of attention and thus distraction for the discomfited bear, the whinging quality was becoming absent from his vocalizations, he was holding himself more steadily erect, and he was no longer panting, as he had been just minutes before as he staggered down the tracks. She opened her beak to point this out, thought better of it, and so shut her beak firmly and cocked her head thoughtfully. She regarded the bear now with quite considerable interest. In perceiving the change in its demeanor, she perceived the effect of her own presence. Clearly the bear was still in distress, but at the moment, he did not seem to realize it. Sudie Mae, in spite of what the bear might think, understood very well that her advice to seek the shade had not been helpful. But her attention had been. It dawned on her also that the conversation had relieved her own rotten mood.

"You know," she said, suddenly filled with a Clancy-esque zeal, "When I'm feeling down in the beak and like I just can't take much more, I just try to remember that God loves me, and that He never gives us anything to bear—I mean, to deal with—that we can't handle. I tell myself that the trials and tribulations that we're given are to make us stronger. It's not always easy, but God will always help us if we pray. All you have to do is ask, and you will receive! That's what Jesus says in the Gospels!"

Sudie Mae was not unaware that much of what she was saying was what she had heard, on various occasions, from the mouth of the rat reverend, and that she herself had never really, in the grip of her own suffering, managed to buck herself up with thoughts of God. But that didn't mean that none of it was valid. She regarded the bear while it peered at her from beneath its furrowed and agitated brow, and began to feel a bit foolish. But only a bit—not enough to deter her from what she now perceived as a golden opportunity to please the reverend.

"Are you nuts?" the bear said. "What are you talking about? What's love got to do with it?"

"No, I'm not nuts," she said. "I'm just trying to help you out. I can tell you don't feel good. I can't do anything about the heat, but I do know that if there's anything that can help when you're feeling bad, it's to be around someone who knows what it's like. And I do. And I also know that when we feel bad, we can't always think straight to figure out a way to feel better. So I think that you should come with me, and I'll introduce you to my pastor. He's real good at helping other creatures, and he might just know how to help you."

The bear regarded Sudie Mae. In her forthrightness and assurance he was reminded of his indulgent but ultimately indomitable mother, who had always taken his special needs into account without catering to his tendency towards hopeless helplessness. He took a moment—during which he might have noticed, but in fact did not, that he was relatively free from discomfort—to closely regard the creature before him. He'd seen buzzards before, of course—but not as close-up as this one, and he was aware of their grisly habits and unsavory reputation. But this female specimen, while harsh in aspect, did not come across as sinister. Sure, she didn't have the petite prettiness of a songbird or the graceful beauty of an egret. But about those red-rimmed eyes and that strong curved beak and dark plumage there was something at once compelling and fine. Never before had it occurred to him that buzzards had feelings, too. Of course they did! Who would want to be a buzzard? Especially a female one? And yet, for all of her disadvantages, here one was, offering what she thought of as help. It was possible that she was up to something, but what could a buzzard do to a bear? He decided he had nothing to lose.

"Where's this 'pastor' then?" he growled.

"Right this way," said Sudie Mae, and she hopped off the stump and began to make her way, with her ungainly yet purposeful stride, towards the edge of the woods. "I'm Sudie

Mae," she said chattily, her spirits light with the assurance that she was going to please the reverend. "You?"

It had been so long since he'd been addressed by name that the bear took a moment to respond. "Brian," he said, rather forlornly.

"Pleased to make your acquaintance, Brian," said Sudie Mae.

❧

STEVEN AND OTTOLINE happened to be perched on the power line that connected the church to the utility poles along the boulevard when Sudie Mae emerged from the woods on foot followed closely by—and it took Ottoline a moment to believe her own eyes—an enormous, lumbering brown bear. "Good gracious!" she cried. "Steven! What on earth!"

Steven had been snoozing, but at the sound of his spouse's alarm, his eyes opened and he sprung into action. A bear emerging from the woods into human territory in broad daylight was cause for alarm, to be sure. It was unprecedented but no precedent was needed to establish that the proximity of a bear would send any human that saw it into a panic. "Uh-oh," he said in his laconic fashion, and he took off. Ottoline was right behind him.

"Sudie Mae!" Steven landed right in front of the buzzard. "You know you got a bear on your tail?"

"Hey, Steven!" Sudie Mae seemed to effect an attitude of nonchalance, as if no creature any more remarkable than a squirrel accompanied her. "This is Brian. He's not feeling good... you can probably tell... so I thought I'd bring him to see the reverend. Brian, this is Steven. He's a member of the church I was telling you about, and he sings in the choir with me, too."

The bear, rather by inertia than initiative, staggered up to stand beside Sudie Mae and peered down at Steven. Steven knew there was no time for polite introductions. "Get back!" he cried, as loud as his low voice would allow. "Get back in the

woods! It's the middle of the afternoon, the humans'll see you!"
And he spread his wings, as if to try to block, however futilely,
any potential view of the enormous creature from any possible
human spectator.

Comprehension dawned on Sudie Mae, and she squawked
aloud. "Dang! I'm so damn dumb!" She leaped up with a flap of
her wings and prodded the bear in the torso with her beak.
"Turn around!" she screamed. "Steven's right! Go back!"

Brian the bear, whose discomfort had only been exacerbated
by the tramp through the woods and then the emergence into
bright sunshine, was for a moment paralyzed by disorientation.
He only barely restrained the impulse to smack away the
suddenly intrusive buzzard's prodding. He growled, he loosened
his jaws to bellow and roar. Perceiving this, Sudie Mae covered
his mouth with her right wing. "Don't holler!" she squawked. Be
quiet! Get back! Get back! Before they see us!"

As vague as the pronoun 'they' was, Brian comprehended
none too soon that it referred to the humans. He was on their
turf, he could see. Just before him, many yards away but for all
of that far too close, was one of their more sizable and magnificent dwellings. And here he was right out in the open, in
broad daylight, like an absolute fool, an easy target for whatever human might be out looking for trouble. He backed away
from Sudie Mae and glowered at her. Why had she brought
him out of the woods just to expose him to danger? Once
again it was all he could do to suppress a roar. He'd been
tricked. But there was no time to lose. He fell to all four paws
and lumbered as fast as he could back into the shelter of the
forest.

Sudie Mae and Stephen lost no time following the bear.
Sudie Mae was on foot and Stephen, being smaller and thus
better equipped to navigate through the trees, by wing. They
trailed the bear until he came to rest crouched in a little thicket
of very young pines, not much taller than himself, panting as if
he was on his last breath. When he could manage to vocalize,

he barked at them between gasps. "You tried to get me killed!" he cried. "You're evil! You *do* want to eat me!"

"No!" screeched Sudie Mae. She could not look at the bear; she was so overcome by distress at her own thoughtlessness. He could have been killed, her good intentions notwithstanding. "There's enough dead critters all over this town, I wouldn't get no one killed to save my life. I was just stupid, that's all. Stupid, stupid, stupid. If I was trying to get you killed, why'd I poke you till you turned around?"

The bear just glowered and panted. Sudie Mae couldn't stand it. She took off.

Steven followed her. Smaller and swifter, he was beside her in midair before she could get too far. "Come on back," Steven said.

But Sudie Mae was too anguished to cease from flight, to respond to her friend Steven at all. The idea! That any creature would believe for a moment that she would lead them into danger just to satisfy her own appetite was so humiliating to her! It was made all the more horrible on account of the fact that her foolhardiness made it seem plausible. She just wanted to fly off the edge of the world.

Steven continued to tail her at a respectful distance. Higher and higher they soared, until they could see the vast Atlantic Ocean in the distance below. The sight of that endlessness seemed to have a slight calming effect on Sudie Mae. She stopped ascending and began to coast. Soon Steven was right beside her.

"He knows you didn't want to get him killed," said the pigeon. "He was just saying that."

Sudie Mae gritted her beak and picked up speed.

"He's in bad shape," said Steven. "He needs help. You were right to bring him. Just not in the middle of the day. But he was just as much in a hurry as you."

Sudie Mae's beak softened. She glanced at Steven. "I'm tired of everyone thinking bad about us."

Steven was silent.

Sudie Mae looked down at the dark yet twinkling waters of the ocean as she soared. She thought she could see her own shadow, vaguely cruciform, on the waters, with that of Steven, only smaller, alongside it. She felt a strange sense of release, as if she'd been holding her breath without necessity, and had finally allowed herself to breathe. "I guess if I was him, I wouldn't know what to think."

Steven remained silent.

Sudie Mae began to curve slightly to the east. Steven followed alongside. "You reckon the Reverend'll know what to do?"

"Worth a try," said Steven.

Sudie Mae's eastward turn sharpened, so that the two birds in tandem executed a neat U-turn in midair. As they descended to the grove of young pines in which the bear still crouched, grizzling, Sudie Mae declared, loud enough for the bear to look up, that she would not put up with any more ugly talk about buzzards, that Steven was going to fetch help and if he wanted help he could just stay put, and if not, well, good luck to him.

STEVEN FLEW OFF and returned shortly with Ottoline, for the Reverend was still behind the bookcase in the rector's office.

"Hey Ottoline!" said Sudie Mae. "I guess Steven told you what's going on. I wanted to bring this bear here to talk to the reverend, because he's sick. The bear, I mean, not the reverend. I forgot it was right in the middle of the day. You don't think any of the humans saw us, do you?"

"That I can't say," said Ottoline. "But I do think that if they had, we would have seen some sort of reaction by this point. I think it's safe to say they weren't paying attention."

"Whew!" said Sudie Mae. "You're right, Ottoline. Dang you're smart. Brian, this is Ottoline. She works with the

Reverend and helps run the church. She knows a lot about helping. Why don't you tell her what's wrong?"

Ottoline was at once touched and flustered by Sudie Mae's presumptuous admiration, and she greeted the great big bear warmly. "Sudie Mae is too kind, but of course I'm happy to help in any way I can. If you're comfortable sharing...?"

The great bear peered down through increasingly bleary eyes at the slim grey pigeon perched on the dusty ground before him. Again, disorientation overcame him. These little creatures... they were so different! The other birds he'd come across in his lifetime had been, like his own species and all others as far as he knew, clannish, keeping to themselves for the most part. What was it about these three, who lived in such proximity to the humans, that they all seemed to get along and to be relatively unafraid of him? It was a novelty so absorbing that it took him a moment to even remember he was suffering.

"It's too hot," he said. I'm supposed to be resting, but I can't. If I don't get some rest soon, though, I'll go crazy!"

"Oh, dear," said Ottoline. "It *is* unseasonably warm, that's for sure. It seems to get more and more unseasonably warm each and every season every year! And there's no end in sight. It's certainly unpleasant for most of us who are warm-blooded, but I can imagine, that for you larger furred creatures it's well-nigh unendurable. To be very honest, though, Brian, I'm not sure what in the world we can offer to help you... Control of the weather is beyond even the brightest creature. But I'm glad Sudie Mae brought you to our attention. And I'm just an old biddy, and there may be solutions I can't fathom. I think what we ought to do... when the time is right, of course, is call a meeting of the entire congregation, so that everyone can weigh in on how we might best be of assistance. What do you think, Sudie Mae?"

Sudie Mae wasn't sure what a parish meeting would entail or accomplish, but her friend Ottoline seemed sincerely apprecia-tive that she'd brought Brian to the church, and if Ottoline was pleased with her, surely the reverend would be too! So it was turning out that her instinct was to be trusted after all!

"I think that's a real good idea," said Sudie Mae, blushingly.

"Steven?" said Ottoline.

Steven nodded.

"I'll go back to the church, then, and let the reverend know as soon as he comes out for his evening airing. Steven, why don't you spread the word that there's going to be a meeting at that time. It will probably be best to meet here, too, away from prying eyes. Sudie Mae, you'll stay here with...?"

"Brian," grunted Brian.

"Thank you. I'm a senior bird, and don't retain new information as readily as you youngsters. You'll be all right, then, waiting here with Sudie Mae? We'll get the meeting underway as soon as we can after sundown."

Brian grunted again in an affirmative tone.

"Excellent. We'll see you soon. I'm sure that if we put all our heads together, we'll figure something out. "

Brian, for whom anything working out was a vague memory, if not a dream, closed his eyes. But Sudie Mae was as happy as a clam. The reverend was going to be so proud of her. She was a true apostle.

❧

"PROUD" was not precisely the word for what Clancy felt about Sudie Mae's missionary effort upon learning, from Ottoline and Steven, the particulars of the situation. "A bear!" he exclaimed. "Oh, Lord! What are we going to do with a bear!"

"I'm not quite sure myself..." said Ottoline. "But he appeared to be fairly well-disposed towards creatures of various species, even though, like we said, he's in a very great amount of discomfort on account of this unseasonable spell of hot weather. Apparently, it's been disruptive to his circadian rhythm."

Clancy, who hadn't seen the bear yet, could not quite get over what he imagined to be its size, and began to wring his tail. "Oh, that Sudie Mae!" he said. "I know she means well, but..."

Ottoline was well accustomed to the reverend rat's anxious hesitations. "I think in this case Sudie Mae has done absolutely the right thing. This fellow is really in a desperate strait. If anything at all can be done to help him, then I think that as a church, as a community dedicated to following the example of that admirable human being Jesus, we really are obligated."

Clancy was duly chastened and agreed vigorously. But not without pointing out a very obvious fact. "We can't do anything about the temperature, though."

Ottoline nodded in unhappy agreement, but Steven, having returned from his mission to alert the members of the congregation that a meeting was to take place in the forest and that everyone should meet at the composter after sundown, was less pessimistic. "Why not?" he said. "The humans do it."

✿

As the congregation made its way towards the young pine grove, lively and chattering with the novelty of being gathered for an impromptu emergency meeting, Brian the sick bear struggled to reconcile his preconceived notions of interspecies incompatibility with the clear indications of cooperation and camaraderie before his eyes. It was a sight so extraordinary that he found it difficult to absorb. "What do they want?!" he said to Sudie Mae.

"To help you," said Sudie Mae.

Brian shook his massive head from side to side as if, as before, to cast off some invisible yet tormenting cloud. And then, at the forefront of the procession approaching him, a very small if stout little mammal approached.

"Hey there!" it squeaked with a cheery tone only slightly strained by visceral nervousness. "I'm Clancy! I'm the pastor of

St. Aloysius Jr. Church for Urban Wildlife and All God's Creatures Big and Small, and I just want to let you know that we'd
dearly love to do anything we can to help you. Ottoline tells me
you are really not feeling good on account of all this terrible
awful muggy heat we've been having around here this late in the
year, and I'm so sorry about that. I guess I should just come
right out and tell you we aren't sure what we can do, but if
there's anything you can think of, just let us know."

Brian could hardly follow the rat's heartfelt sentiments, still
so overcome was he by the strangeness of it all. And once
again, through the obliging, sunny manner of the rat, he was
reminded of his own mother. He emitted a low, involuntary
moan, indicative not so much of heat prostration as of home-
sickness.

"I wonder," Ottoline ventured, when the bear did not
vocalize comprehensibly, "If we might be able to find some
human dwelling that is uninhabited but accessible? According
to Steven, they know how to control the temperature in their
buildings."

Brian could not believe his ears. Control the temperature?!
He stared at Ottoline. How in the world could any creature,
even one as admittedly resourceful as the humans, control a
function of nature? She must be mistaken.

But apparently, she wasn't, for the rat agreed. "They sure
can. Why, just this morning, it was so chilly up in the reverend's
office that I thought I would shiver my tail off!"

"Where!?" Brian exclaimed. "Take me! Please!"

Clancy regarded Brian, who was now on all fours and nearly
snout to snout with him, with infinite, yet helpless compassion.
"In the church... the human church, where I live. Lord knows, I
wish we could get you in there... but there's just no way..."
Clancy trailed off, because the bear's equilibrium seemed to fail
him, and he began to sway from side to side like a tempest-
tossed boat. Clancy told himself that he should have known
better than to speak of his own good fortune in being small

enough to share human spaces without being detected by them. "I'm so sorry..." he said.

Here Steven piped up. "Why not?" he said.

All eyes turned to the taciturn male pigeon. "Do what, Steven?" asked Clancy.

"You live in there... down in the cellar... Why can't he?"

Clancy twisted his tail. "Well—" He darted a glance at the bear, whose dizzy swaying had ceased with Steven's question. "Well, I don't mean to be ugly, but—he's so *big*!"

Steven spread his wings for a moment, his species' equivalent of a shrug. "There's plenty of room for him in that cellar, though. And you said they never come down there..."

Clancy felt a very uncomfortable irritation rise within him. Oh, why was Steven doing this? Didn't he realize it was mean to get the bear's hopes up? Clancy lowered his voice. "Steven... he's a bear! If those ladies ever found out that there was a bear in the cellar... I don't know what they would do!"

"What *could* they do?" said Steven reasonably. "Kill him?"

Clancy blinked. With lightning speed and clarity, the scenario played out in his mind's eye and ear of the most likely effect that finding a bear in the cellar would have upon Grace and the new lady rector. They would undoubtedly become hysterical, they would scream, they would run, they would eventually seek assistance from some other set of humans in the vicinity, likely males, likely with guns. That was the typical human response to any encounter with the wild, and that would be very bad and upsetting. But would it be necessarily fatal, and was it even likely? That, Clancy perceived, was the point of the pigeon's rhetorical question. If Brian was discovered in the cellar of the church, he would certainly be in danger. But it would be a danger easily escaped, for no one closely associated with the church was known to possess a firearm. Before anyone with lethal force arrived on the scene, Brian would have ample time to get away with his life. And the chances of discovery were minimal at best. Never in Clancy's lifetime had any human descended into his cellar. It was not comfortable for them, so fusty, so damp, the ceiling so low.

"No..." Clancy admitted. "Not those ladies. They would probably just scream a lot and run to find someone who would. But I guess he'd have plenty of time to get away..." Clancy still felt very uneasy. "I guess it would be all right. But how's he going to get in?"

"Same way you do," said Steven. "Through that little door."

"But he's too big!" Clancy said, forgetting his manners. "Even I have to squeeze!"

"Not if we can get that door open," said Steven. "And I bet we can."

Clancy just twisted his tail, fully expecting that his anxious mind would offer up another potential hazard or obstacle to the solution, but rather to his chagrin, nothing else occurred to him. And yet the very idea seemed to him to be so foolhardy as to be surreal. A bear in the cellar of the church! There had to be some limit to Christian charity! He didn't mind sharing, he hastened to believe, but so much could go wrong!

*Like what?* he heard a still, small and rather stern inner voice inquire.

And again, Clancy had no good answer. "Well," he said, "I guess it can't hurt to try."

"Praise the lord!" said Sudie Mae. "Welcome to St. Aloysius, Jr., Brian!"

⚜

AND SO, when the darkness of the late autumn evening was as deep as it could be expected to get, the congregation led the bear to the grounds of what was to be, for some time over the winter at least, so long as all went well, his lair. On the way, Ottoline and Sudie Mae discussed logistics. "I'm so glad this seems to be working out, Sudie Mae," said Ottoline to her young friend. "But we'll have to be very observant over the next few weeks, and keep a close watch on how things are going. I'm afraid I know very little about bears and how best to provide for their basic needs."

"Amen, Miss Ottoline," said Sudie Mae. "You're right. The Reverend has enough to worry about, I'm real happy to do whatever Brian needs us to do for him to get by. I wonder what he'll want to eat?"

Brian, for whom the prospect of proximity to the humans, of actually being enclosed within one of their strange monumental dwellings, was so overwhelmed that it took him a moment to realize that he was, in an indirect manner, being addressed.

"Nothing," he said. "All I want to do is rest. I may not be as fat as I ought to be this time of year, but I've got enough meat on me to make it through the winter as long as I can just sleep. Are we there yet?" he moaned.

"Just about," Ottoline said. "Look... there's the composter... and just behind that... just to the left... that's the door to the cellar. Do you think you can get it open without damaging it?"

Though his bleary eyesight couldn't be trusted to make out with any specificity the dimensions of the crawlspace door, the bear made an affirmative grunt. Oh! To be out of this heat! He loped forward as fast as he could, and with one stubby but sharp claw he flicked the hook out of the eye that held the crawlspace door shut, and with that same claw pulled the paint-flaked plywood door open. In he poked his snout, and the damp coolness was like a gift from heaven.

"Oh, so cool..." he was heard to moan. A delicious wave of drowsiness was already coursing through him, thickening his blood, his voice, his very consciousness. He felt a curious, inexorable momentum, as if the force of gravity had strengthened and was pulling him into the land of nod.

"Watch your step, now!" Clancy's bright high voice penetrated the bear's dwindling consciousness like a sunbeam through thick foliage. "There's a little drop once you get through the door."

But what was a considerable step down to Clancy was imperceptible to the bear, and he managed to thrust himself through the crawlspace door with very little resistance, as a good deal of his girth was mere soft pelt. The sudden deliverance from the soggy heat of the night was utterly transformative to his demeanor. He splayed flat against the cool, damp dirt floor of the cellar as if to gather it up into an embrace. He moaned again, with pleasure, and even thought there were no humans in the church to overhear, Clancy wrung his paws.

"Hush, now..." he heard himself say, echoing almost uncannily his dear departed aunt November whenever he, as a young rat, had become over enthused. Indeed, he sensed, as sometimes happened, her presence in this home that they once shared. He knew that she would never have allowed a bear into the cellar, and he was still not at all sure that he should have. The bear was just so big!

After a moment Ottoline, Steven, and Sudie Mae all hopped into the cellar behind Brian, and took in the shadowy, somehow hellishly homey pilot-light-lit scene. None of them had ever before been inside the lair of the rat, and each was impressed with the dimensions of the place. What a lot of room! Though it wasn't very high, and darkness obscured much of the space, there was a quality at once of vastness and enclosure that seemed uniquely humanoid. And of course, the difference in air temperature was notable.

"It's like another world!" breathed Sudie Mae.

Brian, though his mind was almost thoroughly swaddled by sleepiness, nevertheless was dimly aware of the presence of the birds and the rat now, and of being the object of attention, and thus having the obligation to express his relief and gratitude. "So good..." he growled from deep within himself. The vocalization, though not loud, seemed to cause the very air to vibrate. Clancy found himself praying that the great beast would not snore. The bear raised himself to its four feet and trundled to the far, low wall of the cellar where the darkness was deepest, and sank into a slowly pulsing heap of dark fur. The rat and the birds gazed at him in solemn wonder. "Lord!" Clancy heard himself exclaim. "He must be real worn out."

"I think so," said Ottoline in as low a voice as she could manage and still be understood. "It's been a very long day for him. Are you all right, Reverend, with how this has worked out? I know you aren't very used to sharing your space."

"Oh, I won't even know he's here," Clancy lied. "All he wants to do is sleep. And when he wakes up... well, maybe he'll want to learn about Jesus!" Clancy turned to Sudie Mae. "Sudie Mae," he said. "You may not only have saved a life—but a soul!"

Sudie Mae was grateful for the low light in the cellar, for she was certain from the heat she felt coursing along her featherless neck and scalp that she must be blushing a deep purple. "Just trying to help," she managed to gargle.

"Don't sell yourself short," said Steven.

"Amen," said Clancy.

And at the far end of the cellar, Brian dreamed of a crisp winter scene back home.

◌⁕◌

AFTER THE BIRDS DEPARTED, it was time for Clancy to say his prayers. He settled himself within the heap of discarded and slightly moldy choir robes that served as his bedding, and closed his eyes. But the soft sound of deep and rhythmic breathing from the edge of the basement now seemed rather loud in the silence of the night. And it lent the basement a sort of chthonic quality, as if this was not a man-made dwelling at all, but the depths of a primordial cave. Clancy himself felt as if preserving the great beast in slumber for as long as necessary was a natural facet of his role and responsibility as pastor, and yet somehow distinct from it. That great big body, inert yet throbbing with a vitality restoring itself, fascinated the rat reverend. Normally preoccupied with matters of the spirit, Clancy pondered the weakness of the flesh. Such a powerful creature, and yet helpless against certain conditions. *Lord,* thought Clancy, *isn't this something else? There's not a creature in this world, no matter how big and strong, who doesn't need God's love.*

## ❧ 4 ❧
## INDUSTRIA

THE REVEREND JEAN GREY did not often completely shut the door between her office and the rest of the administrative suite, and so when she did, the rat reverend hidden behind the bookshelf took notice, crept to the edge and carefully poked his snout out, the better to peer and overhear. She looked very much the same as any other weekday—dressed in a clerical blouse, the suitably sober effect of which she irreverently offset with wildly patterned skirts and shawls and statement necklaces and bracelets. Her limp chlorine-tinged grey hair clung like seaweed to her scalp, forehead and the nape of her neck, and heavy pyramidal baubles dangled from her earlobes. But something about her was decidedly different this morning. Something unusual was going on inside her. Clancy could feel it in his bones.

With the office door shut tight, Jean Grey seated herself at her desk, settling her broad bottom gingerly, as if into a hot seat, into the plush cushion of the leatherette swivel desk chair that had, like Clancy, been left behind by the Reverend DeBassompierre. She lifted her finger and pressed a key on the keyboard of her desktop computer monitor and after a moment her countenance became artificially illuminated, reflecting the bluish glare of her seascape screen saver. She typed, and then emitted a moan, and grumbled something to the effect that she had downloaded the ZOOM app Goddess knows how many times already. "Any day now..." she then muttered, and in what seemed to Clancy like a very short time, the computer began to speak. "Good morning, Jean!" it said pleasantly. "Good to see you."

"Good to see you, too, Sister Jerome," said the Reverend Jean Grey. "And just in the nick of time. I can't tell you how grateful I am, that you could work me in. I really am in something of a quandary. I tell you, if ever a woman needed Spiritual Direction, it would be me at this juncture."

"My word!" said the voice from the computer. "That certainly sounds important."

"It is," said Jean Grey. "At least, it is to me. And maybe, just maybe, to others. You see, I've just been offered a golden opportunity. And I think... I think I would be crazy not to accept it. And yet—" She put the fingertips of her left hand to her lips, hesitating. "And yet... for some reason, I hesitate. And as everyone know, she who hesitates is lost. But before I make a decision, I think I need to talk to someone who knows me and knows my history, and may be able to offer another perspective."

"I will do my best," said the pleasant female voice of the computer affably. "Why don't you start by telling me about this golden opportunity."

Jean Grey took a deep, deep breath, and exhaled with such dramatic force that her cheeks distended like those of an anthropomorphized storm cloud on an ancient seafarers' map, and her thin lips clabbered like those of a knackered horse. "It may not sound like much...but it means the world to me. My former mentor, when I was serving my internship at Metropolitan Urban Ministries, has recommended me for the position of coordinator of LGBTQ+ outreach. As a white, heterosexual, cis woman, it is quite, quite an honor, all the more so in that I would be stepping into her position, and she is a very well-known and well-respected member of that very community. And at a time such as this, when the stakes are so high for such a deeply targeted and marginalized community... well, it's the chance of a lifetime, to really make a difference. And as you know, within the next month my discernment period here at St. A's will come to an end. It all seems so providential as to be heaven-sent. So, Sister, why do I feel so—" she shook her head so that she could feel the motion of her jowls. When her sentence ended it was with a note or real bewilderment. "— so *reluctant*? Sister, I could hardly get a wink of sleep last night. I tossed and turned, and then, after finally drifting into a half-doze towards daylight, I woke up crying! What in heaven's name is going on here?!"

Behind the bookcase the rat reverend was so astonished by this admission and development that for the first time since he began eavesdropping on the human clergy, he forgot he was supposed to remain silent. It was only by the grace of God that the human reverend did not hear his squeal. And what to him was all the more astonishing was the content of the squeal, for what he heard, even if the human did not, was a very clear protest. "No!" he heard himself exclaim. "Don't go!"

*Oh, Lord!* Clancy inquired of himself. *What am I saying?!?*

The human Reverend was now pressing her hand against her clerical collar, as if to hold it in place. "Not since I made the decision to leave my marriage... and before that, when I made the decision to marry in the first place... have I felt this torn. Sister, no one knows better than you how frustrating my experience with this parish has been... almost from *before* the beginning. Even my interactions with the search committee before they offered me the rectorship were fraught with willful misunderstandings and poorly concealed discomfort with my progressive ideals and my unconventional third career path to ordination. And remember how I was almost involved in a collision on the way to my second interview, and ended up soiling myself? You'd think that would have ended the whole matter—and yet something about this church drew me in, and I guess it's not letting go so easy."

The silence from the computer was loud and clear, and even Clancy perceived it as intentionally provoking. Jean Grey's cheeks once again filled with and emptied themselves of another gusty sigh.

"It isn't as if I've made any progress here to speak of. There's really no reason why I shouldn't cut my losses and move on to the type of environment where I know I'll be appreciated by those whom I'm hoping to serve, where I can be sure to make a positive impact. Here I'm just spinning my wheels, it seems. The attendance numbers were up a tiny bit when I first arrived, but now they're steadily dwindling. The vestry is passive-aggressively uncooperative whenever I try something new and different. The roof of the sanctuary is deteriorating. I think there may even be a mold issue in the basement... something smells off in here, especially when it rains... and in this backwoods county, there's no real coalition of progressive clergy to provide support and fellowship. And yet—" She spread her arms like someone being frisked. "I'm not sure I've ever been so..." She closed her eyes and gritted her teeth as if the next word was a bitter pill to swallow. "...happy. Sister, it just doesn't make any sense!"

"Interesting," said the computer with all the maddening reasonableness of a machine. "Can you say more about that?"

"I just knew you were going to say that," said Jean Grey wearily. "But I don't know what else to *say*. All I know is that—in spite of it all, I wake up just about every morning looking forward to the day. I look forward to coming to this office, I even..." She shrugged and in so doing cracked one of her curious pursed but mirthful upside-down smiles. "I even look forward to the hassles, the absurdities. The backhanded compliments about my homilies. The hopeless but necessary grind of nudging these complacent old white people to acknowledge their own unconscious as well as systemic biases. The cussedness of it all. I guess I take a perverse pleasure in the fact that I'm hardly preaching to the choir. And maybe most of all, I look forward to the end of the day, and the suppers at Grace's house with Tommy when Grace and I always have some fresh lunacy to laugh and cry about."

The human reverend's upside-down smile returned as she reflected. "I wouldn't have lasted a day without Grace. I think it's her live-and-let-live attitude that perhaps is rubbing off on me. She has no illusions about this church, but she loves it. She cares for it and she nurtures it while maintaining iron-clad boundaries. It really is remarkable. It's almost as if we've become the parents—or perhaps, foster parents—of an incredibly willful and contentious child. We delight in its spirit even as we deplore its recalcitrance..." Jean Grey's voice trailed off, and she shook her head.

"Impossible," said the voice from the computer, "but worthwhile."

"Yes!" said Jean Grey, now nodding. "Exactly. I suppose—I guess—there's a part of me that doesn't want to leave my..." She pressed her fingers to her lips, and even from a distance Clancy could see that the human reverend's face had blanched.

"Dear God..." she said through her fingertips. "I almost said home."

"Interesting," said the voice from the computer.

❧

AFTER THE SESSION with her spiritual director concluded, Jean Grey powered down her computer, swiveled in her plush leatherette desk chair to face the window overlooking the rear of the church, and stood and gazed for what seemed like a very long time, so long that Clancy couldn't help but feel a tiny bit nervous. He was afraid that in spite of the human race's general ignorance of the lives being lived right under their extremely underfunctioning noses, the woman might catch a glimpse of some aspect of the existence of St. Aloysius Jr. Church of Urban Wildlife and All God's Creatures Great and Small. Of course, he realized, that even if the entire congregation of pigeons, possums, squirrels, deer, worms and buzzards—not to mention Veronica and even Brian—congregated around Hertz's composter as they might for a Sunday service, there was no real possibility that any human would imagine for a moment that they were gathering for worship. But there was something in the rector's monumental stance and countenance—had Clancy ever seen an ancient sailing vessel or a representation thereof, he would have been reminded of a figurehead—that suggested that her gaze was at once farseeing and inward, and superhumanly capable of perceiving that there is much more to all God's creatures, including herself, than meets the eye.

And so he felt not a little spooked when, from where she stood gazing out of the window at his parish, the Reverend Jean Grey said aloud, as if she knew someone was listening, "Well... I guess you're stuck with me."

## ❧ 5 ❧
## CASTITAS

**B**ERTRAM TOOK TO THE SKIES and flew haphazardly, hither and thither with no real destination in mind in the manner of a butterfly freshly emerged from its chrysalis, for his sweetest dream had just come true—the beautiful vulture Donna had finally, after a long period of hesitation and misgiving on her part and mistakes and misunderstandings on his, and overcome by the passage of time and his eventually undemanding devotion, expressed her own desire for the two of them to become one flesh in the sacrament of Holy Matrimony. She loved him! She'd said so! She said she wanted to marry him, even though some time before she'd accepted and then rejected his proposal, mainly because her feelings for him at that time had been those of a friend rather than a mate.

"But that was then, dear," she explained. "It was too soon after my fledglings were taken away from me by their father and his kin. I was so hurt, and so sad, and your friendship was such a comfort to me, but I knew that I was too numb to feel for you the way a fiancée should. I didn't think I would ever be happy enough to bring you happiness. But now…"

The two carrion birds were perched together, resting on the

balustrade of the access platform of the water tower where, ever since her exile from her own family, Donna had been forced to reside after she had been unjustly accused by her controlling and vengeful former mate of harlotry. Donna gazed northeastward towards the marshland where her offspring were being brought up without her and felt the old familiar pain and grief. "But now, Bertram... well, so much time has passed, and life seems so..." She rested her beautifully ruddy, wattled, featherless head against his torso and Bertram thought his heart would burst right out of it... he just wanted to eat her up, she was so elegant and fine. "Life now seems so much...richer. I still have days when I feel like I can't stand another minute away from my babies...sometimes I feel like a childless mother... but somehow in spite of that the future seems... open. I can't change the past, but I have hope now. My children might very well need me one day, even though they must hate me today. I can see that now. And in the meantime, I know that I can have the kind of life that's worth welcoming them into if the time ever comes. A life of happiness, and fellowship, and service, and love... I love you, dear Bertram, I don't know what I'd do without you. You are so kind, and brave, and decent, and strong, a true Christian buzzard..."

Ack! It was all Bertram could do to hold in his croak of elation. She loved him! She thought he was brave! Kind! Strong! Decent! True! Christian! She wanted to be his bride! *Oh Lord!* he cried in his heart. *I'm not worthy!*

As if somehow Donna herself had perceived that silent *cri d'exultation*, she nuzzled his feathered breast all the more tantalizingly. "You don't know how charming you can be, dear Bertie," she murmured. "How your attractions sneak up upon a female. You make a vulture feel so... special and unique."

"Oh! Donna!" the buzzard managed to croak. "I love you to death! You really mean you love me back? You really want to get married?!"

"I do," said Donna simply and meaningfully. "If you'll still have me."

"IF I'LL STILL HAVE YOU?!" Bertram exclaimed. "Lord, I don't want nothing else in this world!"

"I'm so glad," said Donna. "Oh, Bertram. You truly are a godsend."

The mere mention of the Almighty naturally aroused in Bertram the desire to glorify Him. "Praise the Lord!" he cried, echoing consciously his dear reverend. "It's a miracle. Donna, we have to tell the reverend!"

"Yes," said Donna. "Of course. Why don't you go ahead, and let him know, and ask him if he's still willing to perform the ceremony. I should stay here, because Ottoline is coming by soon to have a chat. And of course you'll want to let Sudie Mae know as soon as possible. I'll see you later, dear. And darling... thank you for being... gentle with me. You don't know what it means to me, that you... still care."

At a loss for words, Bertram gave his beloved a tender stroke down the length of her neck with the sharp and gore-crusted tip of his beak, then launched himself into the skies. He felt as if he could fly to the furthest star in the heavens, gobble it up, and fly back to regurgitate it before Donna so that she could share in the warmth and light he felt. *If I died right now*, he said to himself as he flew, *I'd die happy. It don't get no better than this. Does it?*

❦

CLANCY WAS, of course, delighted for Bertram, if a bit apprehensive, for he had an awareness of the ups and downs of the relationship between Bertram and Donna, and knew well how volatile particularly *Bertram's* emotions and behavior could become when it came to matters of the heart. But it was hard to imagine either one of them with anyone else, so Clancy's congratulations were sincere.

"Well, of course! I'll be so honored to do the ceremony for

you two lovebirds!" he declared. "How could you even think you have to ask?! Now, have you thought about what sort of venue you'd like? We could have a little wedding right here at the composter, or if you want something fancy, we could do it over at the birdbath. If we do that maybe we could even have a reception after, especially if we have the wedding on a Saturday, when Rev. DeBa—I mean, Reverend Grey and Grace aren't around, and..." Thus Clancy readily allowed himself to be swept up into the excitement of a long awaited consummation of a steady, if somewhat tumultuous love. Bertram was more than happy that the reverend was eager to make a real event of the occasion, and told the rat to arrange the ceremony exactly as he saw fit. "I trust you to do us proud, Reverend, and I know Donna does too. She loves you to death, and she wouldn't have anyone else marry us for the world. Matter of fact, she told me I ought to come tell you first thing! That's how high she holds you in her heart, Reverend, she thinks you're a real gentlerat."

Clancy could not help but feel gratified to hear that he was held in esteem by a creature as regal and worldly as Donna the vulture, and he flushed from the tips of his ears to the end of his tail. "Oh, stop it!" was all he managed to say, so flustered he suddenly felt. Bertram's exuberant admiration for his bride-to-be was infectious.

"I guess I better," said Bertram. "Now that you know, it's time to tell Sudie Mae. Reverend... do you think she'll be happy for us?" And, having conceived the question, Bertram suddenly felt as if a slight cloud had formed in the bright and sunny blue sky of his bliss. For the first time it really dawned on him that his own happiness did not exist in a vacuum. What if his sister did not—or could not—share it? *I'm all Sudie Mae has...* he thought. *I can't just up and leave her all by herself.*

Clancy, knowing of Sudie Mae's reliance upon her brother, shared the buzzard's misgivings, but decided that there could be no obstacle that love could not overcome. "Oh, don't worry about Sudie Mae," he said breezily, though with a real awareness that he could possibly be playing with fire. "You just remind her that she's got Jesus."

"WELL, IT'S ABOUT TIME," said Sudie Mae placidly, to her big brother's utter astonishment. "Praise the Lord, as the reverend says. Now I can have the roost to myself for once!" And she rested her own ruddy, featherless head briefly against her brother's wing, in a curt demonstration of affection.

Of course, deep down inside, Sudie Mae acknowledged some mixed feelings. On the whole she was genuinely happy for her brother, but at the prospect of being on her own she was not a little anxious. What would a future without her brother by her side hold? In any event, she had known that this day would come. She'd come to live with Bertram after the sudden death of their tyrannical father, because neither Bertram nor she wished to migrate with their ineffectual sisters, passive mother, and querulous granny back to the distant and rural mountain range from which their father had brought them all so long ago. Even then she'd known that Bertram would eventually find a mate and cleave to her. And for all of the vulture's rather unfamiliar and regal manners, Sudie Mae was glad it was Donna. Donna had class, you had to give her that. And Sudie Mae's estimation of her rose even higher when Bertram let her know that Donna wanted her to be a bridesmaid.

"That's real sweet of her," said Sudie Mae. "But what's a bridesmaid?"

"Well, according to the reverend," explained Bertram, "the humans always have a few other folks in their wedding, to help them get ready for it and then stand with them at the altar. Sometimes it's their friends, and sometimes it's their family, and since you and Donna are gonna be family and are already friends, she wants you to stand up with her. Ain't she something else, Sudie Mae?"

As Bertram gushed, Sudie Mae blinked, for in receiving Donna's invitation, it really hit home that the aloof, gracious female was going to be... family. And that meant... she would have a sister again!

"I'll be happy to," she said.

❦

WORD of the forthcoming nuptials wafted through the little community of St. Aloysius Jr. like a spray of dandelion seed on a summer breeze and filled just about every creature with a congratulatory and celebratory spirit. Weddings and baptisms and other occasional church events were always great fun, normally consisting not only of the celebration of the sacrament at hand, but of a big party afterward. And Bertram was universally liked among the members, despite the stigma of his species and his sometimes off-putting hygiene, for he was terribly nice. And there was a sense among them all, that with this marriage, a new chapter in the saga of St. Aloysius Jr. Church of Urban Wildlife and All God's Creatures Great and Small was beginning. A page was being turned. It was as if Bertram and Donna finally tying the knot was a harbinger of a new generation.

"You can't tell me..." said Hertz with gleeful sliminess, "that they aren't already doing it."

❦

DONNA WAS ENJOYING a rare leisurely afternoon just perched upon the access platform of what she had come to regard as her water tower. It was pleasant not to be obliged to provide for her own supper this evening, for it was Bertram's turn to treat her. Feeling wonderfully relaxed and at peace with her future prospects, her thoughts thus pleasantly and haphazardly fluttered, rather like a butterfly in a field of flowers, over the various details regarding preparations for their wedding ceremony. She felt no particular alarm, therefore, when she happened to glance up to spy a large, winged creature coming towards her at a good clip by air from the northeast. It was far too large to be Ottoline stopping by for an impromptu visit, and while the general proportions suggested that it was one of her own species, the speed and directness of its approach possessed a confident quality alien to Bertram's humble affability or Sudie Mae's shy brusqueness. It was still airborne, some distance from her perch when recognition dawned and her blood froze. Dear God! It couldn't be...

But diminishing distance revealed that it was, in fact, the last creature on earth she wished to have near her: Lawrence, the father of her fledglings, and the direct cause of the most unbearable suffering she had ever imagined, much less experienced. Donna's talons clenched around the railing upon which she perched.

"Hey babe!" The incoming vulture landed with a brisk, odiferous flap of his immense wings right beside her on the railing, far too close for comfort and invasive of her personal space, but she was too thunderstruck to move. He was facing the opposite direction, toward the tank, but his neck was craned so that she could practically feel his proprietary gaze raking her countenance as he tried to meet her eye. He spoke with such nonchalance that it was as if they had seen one another just that morning, and that nothing had changed.

"Lawrence," she managed to croak.

"In the flesh," he said saucily. "Nice to see you, babe. You're looking good."

Such a remark, so typical of this male, gave her a terrible jolt, as if her life since his banishment of her from their fledglings' lives—so rich at first with grief and then eventually with comfort and that lovely recent sense of renewal—had been but a dream. She couldn't bring herself to utter a word.

"Looks like you've been looking after yourself," he went on.

"I figured you would. Well, listen, babe——" He drew even nearer, and she cringed. "I've been thinking. And maybe it's too soft of me, but I've decided to give you another chance. I think you've learned your lesson. I'm willing to forgive and forget, because the kids need their mamma, even if their mamma doesn't need them. They're growing up, and you know what that means." Here Lawrence's breezy tone of address became rather steely, betraying an exasperated determination. "They need a lot of attention. And you know how it is, Donna, I've got enough to worry about." He again tried to catch her eye. "And I miss you, babe."

At this last, Donna could not suppress a moan of pure revulsion, but Lawrence did not seem to notice, and from this Donna gathered that he was really desperate, and that this did not bode well for her babies. She knew that she needed to handle this carefully. Lawrence, even under the fierce direction of his own horrible mother, was finding single fatherhood suddenly harder to handle than he'd imagined. She looked at her former mate and loathed him. Never before, not even when he'd managed to turn her own parents and siblings against her by accusing her of infidelity to him, had she felt such hatred. But to express even a hint of what she felt would, she well knew, do her fledglings no favors. Lawrence could be very spiteful when his pride was wounded.

"Lawrence. You know I would give anything to have my babies back with me," she said.

The male vulture, having recovered a bit of his poise, looked down his beak at her. He'd come, of course, fully expecting instant gratification, and was not a little put off by her standoffishness. It seemed to him to lack the excitement and deference appropriate to his having the upper wing in the situation; *she* ought to be the one asking to be reconciled. He reminded himself that she was, after all, a slut.

"Mother is getting old," he said. "The kids respect her. But she's getting hard to deal with, Donna, and she's tired, and I want her to enjoy her old age as much as she can before she croaks. It hasn't been easy for me to get over what you've done to us, but I know you love the kids, so... I think you can help keep them on the straight and narrow...if you want to."

Donna knew full well what was being insinuated. She was to put no conditions upon her life going forward if she wanted to be reunited with and have some impact upon the development of her fledglings' futures. She would be more than ever subject to their father's judgments and those of her former family. And so would her offspring. As it was now, she sensed, there were already signs of defiance. Lawrence needed her back, and he needed her penitent, as an example to them of what happens when you go against daddy and grandmother.

Still irked by Donna's mask of calm, he went for her jugular.

"But maybe you're happy way out here cooped up with that hick buzzard. Maybe I'm wrong to think you still care about the kids. We *have* been keeping an eye on you, Donna, so don't think you can fool me. Maybe I'm just giving you too much credit. But I thought maybe you have some place in your heart for your own babies..."

"You know I do, Lawrence," she said.

"Then why are we sitting here?" he said.

Donna knew there was no choice. *Oh, Bertram,* she said to herself, *I'm so sorry.* And she spread her wings, leaped from the access platform of the water tower into the air, and winged her way towards the swamp. For her children's sake she would go back to hell, but she would not follow Lawrence there. He would have to bring up the rear.

❦

"I COULD JUST KNOCK her bald head off!" Sudie Mae was vehemently outraged. "Snooty old thing! Just like the rest of them vultures! Never should have trusted her. Leaving my brother without so much as a kiss-my-tailfeathers! After all he's done for her! She better never show her beak around her again or else!"

"Sudie Mae," Clancy remonstrated. "I know you hate that Bertram's hurting. But it won't do him any good if we just give up on Donna! We don't know if she's gone away for good, and we don't know why she left, either. Something might have happened to her! I've been thinking a lot about it, real hard, and I really believe that Donna would not have done such a thing of her own free will. She just wouldn't! It's not like her. You know, when Donna and Bertram first started seeing each other, and Bertram was ready to get married, and she wanted to do it just to please him, but she wasn't sure she was ready so soon after losing her little fledglings, she was honest about it, even though Bertram sure got upset with her —and with me!" Clancy shuddered at the recollection of Bertram, possessed by jealousy, leaping to the outlandish conclusion that Clancy and Donna were conducting a secret love affair. "No, it doesn't make any sense that she wouldn't be honest now if she changed her mind. It just doesn't!" he insisted.

"The reverend is right," said Ottoline. "To just vanish— without any explanation—is not like Donna whatsoever. Sudie Mae, dear, take a moment to think about it... Do you really believe that Donna doesn't care deeply about your brother? About all of us?" And here Ottoline's low, pleasant and resonant voice broke under the weight of her own sadness, for the vulture and the pigeon had become close female friends.

Sudie Mae, though hardly mollified, had to admit that the rat and the pigeon were making sense. "I don't know..." she muttered, sounding very much like Bertram. "Daddy always said that them vultures and us buzzards shouldn't mix, that the vultures would always feel like they're better than us."

"Forgive me, but your father was mistaken about a good many things, wasn't he?" Ottoline said gently. "I think we have to give Donna the benefit of the doubt. For Bertram's sake, as much as for hers. It won't help Bertram for us to assume the worst."

"Well, I don't know..." grumbled Sudie Mae, unconvinced but unwilling to baldly contradict the kindhearted pigeon.

The creatures, gathered around the composter at dusk as was their habit, fell into a melancholy silence accentuated with seeming empathy by the moonlight. This was broken by the padding approach and the jaunty, rasping, hissing salutation of Ometa the opossum. "Hey, y'all!" she called. "What's new and different?"

Those gathered at the composter were slow to respond, for although Ometa couldn't have known that anything was the matter, the jollity of her greeting felt jarring to them and kindled unease. Naturally quick to tune into the atmosphere of her surroundings, Ometa was instantly on guard. "Well, y'all sure are quiet! What's the matter?"

"Good evening, Ometa. We didn't mean to be rude... I guess you can tell, we're all a bit upset. It's Bertram... It seems that Donna has—" The pigeon paused. What had Donna done? What was the truest way to put it? Had she absconded, disappeared, was she gone, or lost, or missing, or God forbid, dead? She was absent, that was all that could be said, but whether of her own free will or not... who could say? "We don't know where Donna is. She hasn't been seen since this morning, and Bertram was expecting to see her this evening, but she's... she's not where he expected her to be. And since it's just before the wedding... well, you can imagine, he's very hurt."

Ometa, her own young clinging to her pelt, bristled. "Do what, now? Donna took off? And didn't say anything to Bert? That don't sound like Donna to me."

"Nor us," agreed the pigeon. "But there's no sign of her, and no indication, pardon the expression, of foul play. And according to Bertram, she seemed perfectly content and at ease when he left her earlier in the day to scavenge something for their supper."

"Has he gone to look for her?" Ometa said.

"He don't have to look for her!" snapped Sudie Mae. The thought of Bertram bringing home a meal to a missing fiancée causing her to revert to her outrage. "He knows where she's at. If she's anywhere, she's back with her snotty old family and flock. Back to them vultures who feel like they're better than everyone else because they've been here a long time. Well, good riddance, they can have her if she don't appreciate my brother!" And with that, Sudie Mae leaped off the ground and into the sky, nearly knocking over Clancy as she outstretched her wings before takeoff.

"Oh, this is so awful," said Clancy, steadying himself. "I don't know what to do."

Ometa was already on her way. But before she was out of earshot, she came to a pause, and as if the gravity of Donna's disappearance had only just struck her, she blinked, turned and addressed the little gathering. "I never have spent too much time with that Donna... gotta admit, I've had my run-ins with vultures before, and so maybe I kept my distance. But I know how to size folks up pretty good, and one thing I can say, she's got class. If she's gone somewhere without a word, I believe it's because she didn't have no choice. Don't y'all?"

"I do," said Ottoline. "But I'm afraid that doesn't help Bertram."

RETURNING to her current home in a particularly picturesque old oak stump that had been hollowed out to form a den capacious enough for herself and her eight youngest ones, Ometa gently but vigorously shook herself loose from their sleepy but firm clutches, and waited for them all to blink awake. It wasn't often that Ometa took time for herself away from the mostly enjoyable but occasionally aggravating burden of her own very young, who were, like her, fairly irrepressible and could be a pawful, but tonight was one of those nights. The sudden and unexpected disappearance of Donna shook her for some reason that she couldn't quite put her claw on, and she felt like she needed some time to herself to think. "Babies," she said, "look here. Mama's gonna go shopping by herself tonight, 'cause I want to go way across town and I don't wanna be carrying a lot of weight. I'm gonna ask your lazy Daddy to come over and watch y'all, so be good, and I'll bring everyone back something real good to eat. Hear me?"

"How come, Mama?" said Lessie, the most outspoken and the smallest of this latest brood. "Why're you going way across town? There's plenty to eat at the shopping center right down the street! And why're you having Daddy watch us? You know all he's going to do is sleep."

Ometa gave this little one a gentle but firm poke with her snout. "None of your business, nosy. You just behave while your Daddy's here whether he's asleep or awake."

Little Lessie was not a bit cowed. "You got you another male friend, don't you, Mama?" she said. "You're getting ready to start a new litter."

Ometa bared her teeth. "I told you to mind your business," she said. "I ought to beat your tail, talking back like that." But her reprimand was half-hearted, for she liked it when her young showed spunk. And after all, little Lessie wasn't half wrong. This brood was growing up fast, and she wasn't one to stay single for long. "Last thing I need right now is another bunch of mouths to feed," she said. "I work hard enough as it is." And so saying, she nudged Lessie over to the far side of the stump, where her seven siblings, Lenny, Lorna, Lester, Lurlene, Lulu, Ladbrooke and Luther wriggled with glee, for it amused them to see Lessie, who had a tendency to try to boss them around, get put in her place.

"Whup her, Mama!" cried Lester.

"Shut up, Lester, or I'll whup *you*!" hissed Lessie.

"You both shut up or I'll whup you both," threatened

Ometa hollowly, for she knew, as all naturally gifted mothers know, that corporal punishment only instills cowardice. But consequences were another matter. "Now, y'all settle down, or I won't bring you back nothing for breakfast."

And although this too was an empty threat, it was delivered with sufficient sternness so that the entire brood, even Lessie, expressed compliance through a collective silence. Ometa waddled out of the hollow stump over to a nearby hole in the ground to nag her most recent ex to haul his tail over to the stump and pay some attention to his children.

⚮

THE FOUR VULTURE fledglings were prepared for the return of their prodigal mother, and greeted her with a formality that made her strong stomach sink. "Welcome home, Mother," said Terrance, the largest and first hatched. "We're so happy that you decided to come back to us, and we forgive you." In an unmistakably practiced manner, he sank back down to a resting roosting position in the large nest in the boughs of the ancient cypress which was home to Lawrence, the fledglings, and their formidable grandmother.

"Welcome home, Mother," Tiffany stood next, and regarded Donna briefly, then kept her gaze demurely upon the floor of the nest. "Now that you're back with us, I may stop having the terrible nightmares that began when you left. I hope so, because I have suffered every single night. I've missed you very much, and hope that from now on you will do all that you can to set a good example for me as a female and a mother." And like her brother, she sat back down before Donna could begin to respond.

"You're so pretty, Mother!" piped up little Todd, hopping to his feet with such swiftness that he actually lost contact with the floor of the nest for a split second before Tiffany poked him with her beak.

"That's not what you're supposed to say, Todd!" she hissed. "You're supposed to say you hope she'll teach you how to pay attention to your elders who only want what's best for you!"

"Oh, yeah!" said Todd. He stood up. "Welcome home, Mother," he recited. "Now that you have learned your lesson, you can help me to remember that I must always obey my..." Here the effect of his conditioning seemed to falter, and he poked Tiffany with his little beak. "What comes next?" he said.

"Never mind, Todd." Lawrence, who stood behind Donna, so close that she could feel his familiar and foul breath against her cowl. "Just sit down. See how fucked up he is, Donna?"

Though Donna's flesh felt clammy with horror, her vocalization was warm. "Oh, darlings!" She said. "I've missed you more than you will ever imagine. And I'm so glad we're all together again." And she spread her wings, and her three fledglings, with little Todd leading the way, rushed forward and into her waiting wings. And for an all too brief moment, as they nuzzled her breast with all of the natural affection of young for their first provider, Donna felt sure she'd done the right thing to come back.

"That's enough," said Lawrence, bringing the all too brief moment of warmth to an end. "You three go back to Grandmama's. Your mother and I have some things to talk about."

One by one, the fledglings rose and exited the nest to file down the branch to an opposing bough where Lawrence's hawkeyed mother made her home.

"See, Donna," Lawrence moved forward to confront her. "The way you took off really screwed the kids up. You can tell they aren't well developed mentally. They're retarded. But maybe, just maybe, now that you've come to your senses, you can help them grow up. We'll see. There's a lot of damage to be undone."

"I can see that," said Donna.

THOUGH SHE DIDN'T SCORN the quotidian and the mundane, Rev. Jean Grey really, really hated the chore of grocery shopping. It had nothing to recommend it whatsoever. She went about it out of necessity, nonetheless, every Tuesday upon leaving the church in the evening, stopping at the supermarket located on the boulevard just before the turn onto the old beach drawbridge.

It was always so discouraging. In many of the other cities she'd inhabited before coming to this still rather unreconstructed and unsophisticated southern beach town, there had been, if not a co-op, at least one or more of the more socially responsible grocery chains represented. But here there was only the run-of-the-mill corporate supermarket with its mass-produced packaged poison and its largely genetically modified produce. One nearby historic hamlet just across the river was beginning to attract a moneyed and potentially progressive retiree population from which she hoped to court at least a handful of new parishioners who might be willing to bankroll a local co-op, but in the meantime she was stuck with what edibles she could scavenge from what was for the most part capitalist trash. Summoning what forbearance she could, she maneuvered her Volvo into a parking space under a four-part stadium light and far enough from the entrance of the store to get a few hundred steps in, and summoned, as an exercise of her active imagination, a force field of lavender light surrounding and protecting her person from negative energy.

But her concentration and thus her protection shattered in the effort of wresting a cart out of the stubborn logjam at the front of the store, and so the babble of voices and the unnatural glare of the light made her obliged to suppress a moan as she maneuvered her way into the produce section, which was blessedly and also unfortunately the least crowded and the least harshly lit. Here she took her time, selecting what appeared to be the least tainted fruits and vegetables that her IBS could tolerate, before steeling herself for the gauntlet of the dry goods and frozen aisles. She wanted to make it quick, as it was usually in the context of these narrow lanes of plenty that she tended to attract the most unwanted attention.

It was of course, primarily her clerical collar that elicited the most hostility. But it wasn't just the collar. It was her general and overall demeanor—that of a woman, a professional woman, and an outsider to what was basically an insular and deeply reactionary community outside of the lucrative tourist season. On top of that, she was a woman who would stand out with or without a collar, on account of her height and the post-menopausal bulk that had widened her hips so that she was no longer the slim lady she had once been, but instead, as her friends of Ashkenazic heritage might have said, zaftig. She preferred to wear long loose skirts and flowing tops and colorful shawls to offset the austerity of the clerical collar and comple-ment her collection of statement necklaces and ornate earrings. It didn't help that her almost daily morning series of laps at the YWCA swimming pool lent her pale grey hair a greenish tinge from the chlorine. It took precious little imagination to discern the perception in their narrow minds: *This old lady isn't from around here.*

*I'm an alien,* she could not stop herself from thinking as pale eyes in weathered faces looked her up and down with the complacent contempt of an overfed and thereby pacified peas-antry. *Yes!* She wanted to declare. *I am a woman. I am a priest. And I am not of your narrow, bitter complacent world. I am something you will never understand.*

*Divine Feminine, strengthen me!* was her mantra, empowering her to withstand the blunt but nonetheless piercing and de-energizing glances of her fellow shoppers as she filled her cart. And so by the time she reached the checkout aisle, which was staffed by a young person of, at first glance, indeterminate gender with a mass of brightly and artificially colored dread-locks and a hoop through their septum and a tattoo consisting of illegible gothic script down their forearm. At the sight of a youngster so visibly in rebellion against the corporate and provincial miasma that surrounded them both, Jean Grey smiled broadly at the cashier as she swiped her credit card. "How is your evening going?" she said.

"I'm blessed," said the cashier, and reached for her first item to swipe it across the scanner before meeting Jean Grey's eyes. The smile tightened and the brow lowered as her clerical collar registered with the cashier. Jean felt her heart sink even lower into the depths of her exhausted spirit. Once again, as so often happened in this culture of commodification, appearances had proven deceptive. This young person, whose stubbled chin and thin wrists hashed by coarse dark hairs upon closer inspection suggested the male gender, was, for all of his own "alternative" self-presentation, clearly an example of one of those young conservative evangelicals whose recruitment tactic was to appear "edgy." A second look at his forearm revealed that the gothic script spelled out, of all things, a verse from Scripture, complete with reference. "Seek ye first His Kingdom and His Righteousness... Matthew 6:33 NIV"

Jean Grey's response, which was silence, was drowned out by the beeping of the scanner and the general tumult of the store. The young crusader did not appear to notice at all that his proclamation of his blessing had gone unheeded. As he rang up her total while she placed her items into her recyclable reusable totes, his eyes once again lingered on her collar before meeting her gaze. "Have a blessed evening, ma'am," he said. "You need your receipt?"

"No." Assuming the burden of her purchases, she steered her cart out of the store, into the parking lot, and toward her distant Volvo, waiting for her like a faithful friend, alone under the stadium light. It was only when she reached the car and opened the hatchback with a beep of her key fob remote that she spied—in the shadow cast by the low brick retainer wall separating the supermarket lot from that of the discount furniture retailer next door—a sight to freeze the blood. There, just a few yards from where she stood, a lone vulture was pecking at the fresh remains of a dead opossum that had doubtlessly been mortally struck by some careless vehicle earlier in the evening.

As unpleasant as the sight certainly was, Jean Grey couldn't take her eyes off it. In the shadowy parking lot the two figures, one inert, the other probing that inertness with a savagely hooked beak, muttering faint, gurgling sounds that were presumably expressive of delectation, presented a phantas-magoric, ghastly, yet somehow eerily magnificent tableau. All her life, the sight of a vulture, especially in the act of feeding, had struck her as being inauspicious. But as a *sequela* to the distressing and disappointing human encounter she had just experienced, to come upon this most pure representation of the endless cycle of life was a kind of inexplicable affirmation. Here, before her very eyes, as the nadir of the day, was a literal manifestation of the paradoxical concept of death sustaining life, a prefiguring of the ultimate Resurrection. Nature was nurture, and transformation as inevitable as it was eternal. The vulture, as if it had become aware of and yet untroubled by the fact that it was being observed by a nearby human, paused in its investigation of the freshly killed corpse, and seemed to look right at her.

The tips of the fingers of her free left hand rose to Jean Grey's lips in a swift, unconscious gesture. The vulture did not seem alarmed in the least by this sudden movement; rather, it was as if for a moment time was without measure as human and vulture regarded one another, each in the act of gathering provision. Even though there was no way for Jean Grey, not being well- versed in ornithology, to discern the gender of the creature before her, she felt strongly that she was beholding what was essentially a mystery evocative of the Divine Femi-nine. Here she was impressed with the sense that the vulture shared with her the predicament of a female creature obliged to provide for herself without the support of a male. She felt that she was in the presence of a familiar spirit indeed.

"Holy Mother of God," she murmured, a Roman Catholic oath alien to her upbringing that nonetheless felt appropriate to this visitation. She subsequently felt a peacefulness rising within herself, like a wellspring of something pure that had the power to purge from her heart the lingering despair and bitterness engendered by the ordeal of grocery shopping. She genuflected. This vulture, for all the morbid associations it stirred up within the human, or at least the modern Western consciousness, was on the side of life, and was in fact rooted in what was even deeper than life itself... a feminine glory in transformation that was unmerited grace.

The vulture returned its attention to its meal. Jean Grey understood this to be an acknowledgement of their shared essence and received it humbly. Jean Grey's mouth pursed into the upside-down smile of noble mirth that came most naturally to her, turned away, loaded her bags into the hatchback of the Volvo, and folded herself into the driver's seat. She backed out of the parking space and steered towards the exit onto the boulevard. As she reached that turning point, she gave one last glance in the rearview mirror toward the beautiful vulture as it leaped up, having had her fill, and winged its way towards the marshland.

"Godspeed," was the Rev. Jean Grey's benediction as she made her way home to her own humble lodging to prepare her supper.

☙❦❧

As she loped within the stormwater culvert that ran along the boulevard, feeling so light she thought she could go on forever, it occurred to Ometa that she had not had a whole entire night to herself since her latest litter was born.

Since that first litter she'd had—let's see... six more, each by a different male, for Ometa liked novelty and change, and felt it was best for everyone concerned if she handled the upbringing of the offspring, since her experience was that on the whole, male opossums were ill-equipped to handle a lot of responsibility. That was just the way things were, and there was no point in pretending otherwise. And in any event, single motherhood was rewarding. She was the boss, and she liked it that way. And she considered herself to be a well-rounded parent, with just the right balance of toughness and good humor. And with every litter, the job got just that much less exhausting. Except maybe for this last one.... They sure could be feisty. She supposed that was no less a sign of success. A possum had to have gumption to survive in the wild, Lord knew.

She stopped for a moment to investigate a KFC bucket some human had apparently tossed out of their automobile, but apart from a few delectable crumbs of special seasoning, the bucket was empty, so she moved right along. Sometimes it was hard to believe she'd raised six whole litters, but it was true, and she had offspring all over the county, and she loved each and every one of them, live or dead. (Because there were a few that had not made it.) That, like the constitutional irresponsibility of the male of the species, was the way things were. Every mother possum knew that not all of her babies would survive to maturity unless she was either extremely lucky or ruthlessly strict. And Ometa figured she was neither. There were just too many dangers and predators out there to fool yourself into thinking you could keep them all safe forever, especially for a female as fertile as Ometa. The law of averages had to apply. It hurt, of course, to lose a young'un, but you had to keep on going for the ones that survived. It didn't mean you didn't care. It meant you did.

A concentrated night glare signaled that she was approaching her destination, the expansive asphalt parking lot of the supercenter shopping complex across from the drawbridge leading from the mainland to the barrier island beaches. She picked up her pace once she crept onto the lot, for she knew that while it was a rare human that would molest her, these supercenter parking lots did attract the sort of humans that liked to carry a firearm and wouldn't hesitate to use it just for kicks on a harmless lady possum. Once she approached the far edge of the lot, shadowed by the chain link fence that separated it from the lot of the discount furniture showroom next door she felt less conspicuous, and began to contentedly explore the plentiful little piles of litter that the sea breeze regularly deposited along the base of that fence. As she investigated the contents of a family-sized and not quite empty bag of cool ranch Doritos the stale but still mouthwatering aroma brought back memories of Sidney, the runt of her third—or was it fourth?—litter, as cool ranch Doritos had been his special comfort food. Sidney had been a sweet and winsome little fellow, but from the beginning Ometa had feared for him, for, apart from being a runt, his eyesight was terribly weak. And, there being nothing she could do to remedy his disability, she could only try to keep him close, and look out for him herself. And that had kept him safe for a good while, well past the time that his siblings went off on their own. He'd been a help to her with her next litter, but of course, eventually, like every male, he began to feel the need to extend himself, and she knew it would be worse than death and destructive of his spirit to discourage him. And it wasn't long before one of those sneaky red-tail hawks got him as he was running up on an old broken fan belt some human had tossed under some shrubbery, thinking it was a dead garden snake. His brother Simeon, who'd witnessed the attack, had shared with her all the gory details, and that poor Sidney had the idea that the snake would impress a female that he'd had his weak eyes on. It was a real sad time. But there had been good times, as well...

As if the memory had summoned the shadow of his death, Ometa sensed a circling presence high overhead, and she swiftly withdrew her snout from the Doritos bag and glanced above. At first her heart skipped a beat, for the sight of a spiraling descending cruciform shadow in the sky always—or almost always—meant the sort of trouble that had taken poor Sidney. It meant a bird of prey, and her fur spiked as she prepared to dash for cover underneath the nearest vehicle, a Volvo parked luckily or providentially nearby, far away from the entrance of the store and the majority of the other vehicles. And yet, just as she was about to flee, something in the aspect of the distant, circling figure struck her as being vaguely familiar—the wingspan was far too broad to be that of a hawk, and the fan of the tailfeathers extended at the apex, like those of a buzzard or—why, a vulture! Of course! Ometa recognized that it was a vulture spiraling down to get her, and it was gonna be in for a surprise, because she was far from dead!

For safety's sake, she kept an eye on the descending figure, for although in general living breathing possums have nothing to fear from vultures, it was never a good idea to let your guard down when approached by strangers. But the closer the vulture came to the asphalt surface of the parking lot, the less apprehensive Ometa became, because it was, of all creatures, Donna! Ometa emitted a hearty hiss of salutation, but even as she did so she could hear Donna hissing back to her with a sibilant urgency.

"Play dead!" Donna was pleading. "Quick!"

Do what? Ometa was, fortunately, too puzzled to do anything but remain still, and when Donna landed, practically on top of her, she'd had enough time to see the point in Donna's command. She relaxed every muscle, her snaggle-toothed jaws slackened, and her beady black eyes assumed a vacant glaze.

"Ometa!" Donna gargled *sotto voce*. "Oh, I was praying it was really you! Thank heavens. I can't stay long... I know they're watching me when I'm looking for provision... but if you play dead, they won't have any idea that I'm doing anything but nibbling. Oh, Ometa! It's so good to see you. How is everyone? How is Bertram?"

Ometa knew better than to mince words. "Tore up," she

said. "Real tore up, honey. I ain't gonna lie. He don't understand how come you just up and left without saying a word. Me, I figure whenever someone does something out of the blue and quick like that, it's always for a good reason. Anyone with any sense knows that. Not that Bert ain't got no sense, you know what I'm saying... he's just real tore up."

"Yes." Donna felt such heartache that it was for a moment difficult to keep up the pantomime of consuming Ometa's flesh. She lifted her heavy head, looked up to the heavens to somewhat reassure herself that there were none of Lawrence's clan within earshot, and emitted a low moan before aiming a soft peck at the ground near Ometa's lolling tongue. "Ometa, I feel so terrible. But you're exactly right. I had absolutely no choice. As you probably realize... I'm under duress. Lawrence, my children's father, you know, Lawrence came to my tower, and he— well, he's got me in a terrible bind. He's allowing me to see my children again... but only if we are reconciled, he and I, and under his terms. And Ometa, I have to do what he wants... he's got the entire flock... even my own dear parents and siblings turned against me, and as for my fledglings... the poor things don't know what to think. He's really a very clever bird"

Ometa held her lolling tongue.

Donna continued to pretend to feed. "I know it must be difficult for you to understand. You're so independent. But Ometa, as much as I wish I was back with Bertram and the rest of you, I can't leave my fledglings—not as long there's any way that I can be a mother to them. Ometa, I really believe they need me, that my presence back there, as stifling as it is for me, is doing them good. It's a terrible choice to have to make, but I've made it. I just hope Bertram can forgive me..."

"Oh, he'll forgive you," said Ometa. "Especially if he knows you didn't just leave him high and dry on purpose. I know Bert. He's a hothead, but he's got heart. He'll forgive you, but he ain't gonna be happy."

"But I want him to be!" lamented Donna. "Oh, Ometa, I

really do love him." And the sorrowful vulture made a few half-hearted stabs at the opossum's abdomen. "Ometa, tell him he must move on. He'll make such a fine mate and father one of these days. Tell him I wish it could be different, but—" She stiffened, and Ometa sensed that another vulture was approaching.

"I'll tell him," said the opossum. "You hang in there, lady."

"I will," said Donna, and in a flash, she was gone.

<br>

THE FOLLOWING EVENING, as dusk settled upon the churchyard and Clancy emerged for his habitual informal conference around the composter, Ometa with her babies clinging to her back once more was the very first to arrive, and with an air of urgency. "Where's Bertram at?" she demanded. "I got to talk to him pronto."

"Bertram?" Clancy was a bit jarred. "Well, I don't know, Ometa. You know, Bertram's been keeping to himself lately. You know how upset he's been since Donna left and the wedding is off. What do you need to talk to him about?"

Ometa hesitated, for she felt Bertram ought to hear about her conversation with his lost love directly from her—but at the same time, if he was off in the treetops somewhere, how was she, an earthbound marsupial, supposed to reach him? While she pondered this dilemma, irrepressible little Lessie made the question moot by piping up, in her teakettle whistle of a vocalization, that Donna had told her mama that she was back with her old mate and their young.

"Lessie!" Ometa growled, at once incensed and relieved. "Dadgummit! I ought to swat your tail. I don't know why I open my mouth around y'all. And that's only part of the dadgum story!" Rolling her eyes, she regarded the reverend rodent. "Well, I meant to tell Bertram first since it's his busi-ness, but since this one had to run her mouth... yep, that's what's going on. But it ain't like Donna wants to be back there with her old mate and his nasty family—she can't help it! They got her by the tailfeathers, Reverend. It's a real sorry business."

"Oh, Lord!" Clancy reached for his tail with his forepaws and twisted it anxiously. "Ometa! How did you find all this out?"

"Donna told me!" Ometa declared. "I seen her last night at that big old store by the bridge. I was looking for grub and I guess Donna saw me or got wind of me somehow, 'cause she came down and told me what was going on. I had to play dead, 'cause she said she believes they're always on her tail, making sure she don't meet up with Bertram no more, but she figured they'd never guess she'd be friends with a possum, much less a dead one. Anyway, she told me that old mate of hers has the young'uns all mixed up in their heads about her, and on top of that they're scared of making him mad, and she feels like they're better off with her there. She says she wishes she could come on back, but she can't leave her babies all alone with that bunch. Says she misses everyone and misses church, but there ain't nothing she can do. It's a damn shame. Makes me so mad I could spit."

Ottoline descended from the rooftop of the church accompanied by her usual salutation, her familiar chuckling coo. She landed beside the composter and was joined just a moment later by Steven. "Oh my stars!" cried Ottoline. "Poor Donna. Ometa, how did she look... is she hurt?"

"Looked all right to me," said the possum. "At least, it don't look like he's whupping on her or starving her or nothing. She just looked tired. I guess those vultures down to the swamp are real bastards. I know I'd dearly love to get my teeth into that old mate of hers..."

Clancy, who deplored any mention of violence, even in the service of justice and liberation, swallowed his reprimand. "Oh, this is just awful. Oh, I wish there was something we could do!"

"I think we all do..." said Ottoline. "But there doesn't seem to be anything. But Ometa, I'm sure it did Donna a world of good to have the chance to talk to you and pass along her farewell, and I'm sure that it will be of real consolation to poor Bertram to learn that Donna is doing the only thing she can to make sure her dear offspring have some guidance and support in what sounds like a terribly oppressive environment. Bertram is such a dear soul; I know he'll understand. Ometa... in the midst of a tragedy, you have brought glad tidings. I wish Bertram was here to hear them. There's no telling where he is, though..."

Steven, who always knew more than he said, spread his wings. "I'll tell him," he said, and he was off.

❧

HAVING TOO much sense than to bypass the most likely place Bertram might be, Steven first stopped by the roost shared by Bertram and Sudie Mae at the top of an ancient maple not terribly deep into the woods. "He ain't home," said Sudie Mae. "I don't know exactly where he's at. He doesn't tell me much these days about what he's up to. Sometimes, I know, he goes over to Donna's old place, to see if maybe she might be there, so you might check there. And he still goes out looking for meat sometimes, but his heart isn't in it like it used to be. Matter or fact, if it wasn't for me, we'd starve. I don't know what to do about it all, Steve... I'm worried he's just gonna curl up and die. Maybe you can talk to him... he always did set great store by you. He always said, you treated him more like a son than our mean old daddy ever did."

Touched, Steven thanked Sudie Mae and took off towards the water tower. Bertram was nowhere to be seen, so Steven took a moment to consider other possible locations. He perched on the railing of the access platform beneath the massive tank and closed his eyes and thought about what Sudie Mae had said. He and Ottoline had raised several offspring, and while their brood ran high to females, Steven was father to plenty of sons, whom he cherished. He felt honored, that Bertram considered him to be something of a father figure, but it was hard for Steven, with sons of his own, to think of Bertram as a son in the same sense. And yet there *was* a sense in which he felt with the young and normally enthusiastic and cheerful buzzard a bond just as vital. It was akin to, though not identical with, the bond he felt with a number of his grandsons —paternal, yet with a dimension of fellow feeling that fathers and sons can rarely share due to the responsibilities and expectations inherent within their relations. Dissimilar in temperament as they were, Steven saw in Bertram much of his own spirit. He understood Bertram's ardent devotion to Donna, for Steven himself felt it, if in a less dramatic manner, for Ottoline. Steven knew that if Ottoline left him, he would more than likely find it difficult to enjoy life without her, but his capacity to bear her absence would be greater if he could be sure that her going was not of her choosing. Abandonment is one thing, rejection another. Particularly for the young male. Steven knew that Ometa's message would bring some measure of consolation to the poor buzzard.

A strong and acrid and familiar odor reached the nostrils of Steven's beak, and his eyes opened. Sure enough, it was Bertram, flapping the air as he descended to perch alongside Steven on the access platform railing. "Hey Steven." His croak was pitifully morose. "Thought that was you. What're you doing here?" He eyed Steven, whom he normally loved to see, with a hint of irritation. Why couldn't they all just leave him alone? All he wanted was Donna, and she was gone.

Steven was not unaware of how misery was distorting his young friend's spirit, so he did not mince words. "Bert," he said. "Donna didn't leave because she wanted to. Her old mate made her go back to the swamp if she wanted to see her fledglings. That's why she's not here anymore. If she could be here to marry you, she would. That's the truth, son."

Bertram, so wounded by recent disappointment and bewilderment that he could scarcely follow the consoling gist of Steven's words, could only respond with a bitter disbelief. "Yeah, right," he said. He glared towards the distant swamp. It wasn't that far away. If Donna really wanted to, she could have found some way to get word to him. No, Steven was just trying to make him feel better.

"If she really wanted to marry me, nothing would stop her. Nothing would stop *me* from marrying *her!* How do you know where she is anyway?" He had never before spoken with such sullen stubbornness to his friend. "Did you see her?"

"Ometa did."

Bertram grunted with surprise.

"It's a long story," Steven said. "I'll let Ometa tell it. I told you the important thing. Donna didn't have any choice but to go back to her fledglings. You know that. They need her more than you do. You've got us."

Bertram felt as if his mind was being stuffed too full of information to absorb, like a swollen corpse about to burst with hastily expanding gasses. He regarded Steven as one being shaken out of a deep slumber would regard their rude awakener. Donna was gone, Donna had left him without a word, and now it came to light that Donna was... in a very real sense, a captive. Bertram became incensed. It was an animal and invigorating sensation. His every feather pimpled, his neck stretched, and the skin of his head flushed bright burgundy. His talons gripped the railing. "I'm going to get her back!" he cried. "Nothing's gonna stop me!"

Steven saw it coming. "Don't do that, son," he said gently. "Don't go out there and make trouble for her. I know you want to see her, and help her, and bring her back to where we all care a whole lot for her... but the best thing you can do for her right now is let her be." And having delivered what was for him a lengthy speech, Steven fell silent.

Bertram slowly deflated. His still flushed head hung. Of

course, the pigeon was right, as usual. He got right to the heart of the matter, and there was no arguing with the truth. It was beyond dispute that Donna was in a bind, that nothing Bertram could do, no matter how courageous and loving, could ever loosen. But for the love of God, he couldn't just do nothing!

"Oh, Donna!" he cried, unable to contain his anguish and longing. "I love you so much!"

As buzzard vocalizations are more guttural than voluble, there was no possibility that this outburst could ever reach the ears of his erstwhile love, but just giving voice to his hopeless devotion did serve to lighten, just a little, his heaviness of heart. "Steven..." he moaned. "What am I going to do without her? We were going to start our own family... Now I'll be all alone forever..."

"Things can change," said Steven. "You just can't always *make* 'em change. Don't give up hope, son. And it looks like now there's one thing you can do... you can get word to her that you understand. Come on. Let's go find Ometa."

※

BERTRAM HUNG on Ometa's every word. "Did she look all right?" he asked, once Ometa had related the conversation. "Are they hurting my sweetie?"

"Looked pretty good to me," said Ometa, which observation did not exactly reassure Bertram as he wished it might have. "Hard to say; it ain't easy to get a good look at someone who's pretending to eat you up. But she was the same old Donna, nice and clean, not too stout but not too scrawny...but you could tell she's not real happy. And she was nervous, you know? Said they're always watching her."

"Oh, Donna!" Bertram groaned. "Why you?" And he let himself collapse onto the leafy forest floor upon which he and Steven and Ometa were talking, right outside Ometa's current residence.

"It is a shame," Ometa said. "But no point crying about it. Donna ain't crying... She's just doing what she has to do to keep her young'uns with her. That's the way it is, when you're a single mama."

"She wouldn't be single if she was with meeeee," Bertram lamented piteously. "Oh Donna! Ometa, I thought I'd feel better knowing she was all right, but right now I feel worse. She may be all right, but she's not happy! And there's nothing I can dooooo!" Bertram began to extend and collapse his wings with impotent impatience like a bird too young to fly.

"Calm down," Ometa said. "Or I'm going inside. All this whining isn't doing nothing but getting on my nerves. Matter of fact, there is something you can do. You can let her know you know what's going on, and you ain't got no hard feelings, and that you know she's doing what she has to do and she don't have to worry about your sorry tail. That'll help her more than anything. She feels bad enough without having to feel bad for you."

Bertram expanded and collapsed, taking a deep breath as Ometa's reprimand sank in. She was right, of course. The last thing Donna needed was to be on a guilt trip. "But how can I tell her?" he cried. "If I go around those vultures, they'll kick her out like they did before. And then she'll hate me!"

"Well," said Ometa, "if I see her again, I'll tell her. I was planning on going back out there tonight. If she got away with pretending to eat me once, chances are she can get away with it again. Playing dead has gotten me and mine out of more scrapes than I care to tell you. Easy, too. I don't know why it's only us that figured out how to fool the world."

And so saying, Ometa fell to her side, snaggled jaws agape, her tongue lolling and her form as still as a rock. The illusion was so convincing, that Bertram's stomach growled, signaling if nothing else, a resurgence of his appetite for life.

As for Donna, following the chance, or perhaps providential encounter with Ometa, she returned to the stifling habitat of her former mate with a renewed sense of determination, alongside a glimmer of hope. Her spirits had been sinking for some time on account of the oppressive atmosphere of the clan and their constant scrutiny of her every word and action. But now her spirits were on the rise, if only slightly and if only for a moment. Ometa, bless her heart, had served as a reminder that there was more to life than her unfortunate situation allowed her to experience. Donna, whenever she thought about it, mourned the loss of Bertram, and the idiosyncratic little crew of feisty creatures that surrounded him, and she even missed the water tower of her once lonely exile. But it was no little consolation to know that the church missed her and was praying for her. She only wished she could share it all with her fledglings for they all, but especially Todd, displayed real curiosity about the life she had led beyond the swamp. As it was, she didn't dare even speak to them of the friends she'd made in town. Lawrence would take it as an attempt to undermine him, and she couldn't be sure that Tiffany wouldn't inform on him.

"Where were you before you came back home, Mother?" said Terrance one day.

"Oh, I lived in town, near the waterfront," she said warily.

"All by yourself?" said irrepressible little Todd.

This was treacherous territory, but Donna didn't want Todd—or the others—to feel as if she were hiding anything. "I made a few friends," she said. There being no perceptible hint on the part of Tiffany that she found her mother's admission of outside friendships to any degree noteworthy, Donna went on. "There can be friendly and helpful creatures wherever you might find yourself, darlings, never forget that..."

A familiar shadow approached.

"Toddrick!" Lawrence's mother cawed warningly. "Stop

being so nosy. Your mother wants to put her past behind her. As she should."

Todd glanced at his grandmother and back at Donna with a further question in his eyes, but Donna dare not encourage him. Then Tiffany, with a wheedling quality that reminded Donna of Lawrence during their courtship, inquired, "Did you miss us?"

"More than you will ever know," said Donna.

"...and Daddy?"

Donna looked at her unreachable daughter and felt heartsick. "I missed him terribly," she said. She knew that in a very real sense she was walking on eggshells in just about every conversation she had with Tiffany, for the young female fledgling was clearly deeply attached to her father. But in a sense Donna was obliged to be circumspect with *all* her offspring, for she couldn't be certain that anything she said, no matter how benign, wouldn't be interpreted by Lawrence and his mother as some sort of subversion of their authority. They simply did not trust her.

It was painful because she could sense, at least on the part of Todd and Terrance, that their frayed bond with her was gradually mending. Their curiosity about her life beyond the swamp was just one of many indicators of this. "Father said you had another mate while you were away. Did you, Mother?" asked Terrance.

Donna proceeded with caution. She didn't want to dismiss the question, because she heard within it a certain anxiety of her son, that she might go away again. At the same time, she wanted him to hear from her that there was a life worth exploring beyond Lawrence's control, should he ever find it all too much to bear. "I had a friend," Donna said. "Darling, I was so unhappy being away from you all. But like I said, wherever you find yourself, if you try not to despair, you will find... good creatures. I met quite a few lovely individuals who helped me to bear being away from you all. But I didn't have a mate." Donna considered that technically this was the case, as her relation-ship with Bertram, though it grew beyond being simply platonic, was never consummated. "Just friends."

"Father says that only vultures can be trusted," declared Tiffany. "He says that other creatures don't like us, because we clean up after them, and that buzzards are low class and jealous of us because we're better scavengers and we have the whole swamp to ourselves and don't have to feed on what the humans run over."

Donna gritted her beak. How typical, and how calculating of Lawrence, to instill bigotry unnecessarily in the burgeoning minds of his own offspring. "There *is* some prejudice towards us among the creatures who only know of our diet, no doubt," she said. "But I believe that there are always creatures willing to... question their presuppositions. We should all take that atti-tude, don't you think, darlings? It makes life more exciting."

"I'm confused," said Tiffany, with what seemed to be sincer-ity. "Why would father tell us that other creatures don't like us if they do?"

Donna extended her left wing, a wordless invitation to her most apprehensive and enigmatic fledgling to come closer, to trust her. Tiffany didn't advance, but she didn't retreat. She looked to her mother as if for a real answer. "Your father and I have had different experiences, that's all," Donna said. "It's only natural that we would see the matter differently."

"But who's right?" pressed Tiffany.

Donna had the sensation of being backed up against a wall. She could have, in that moment, torn Lawrence's heart out with her own beak for what he'd done by making this daughter his favorite. "Your father just wants you to be careful around strangers," said Donna, "as you should be."

Tiffany was silent. Donna found herself praying for this flesh of her flesh.

FROM THE STENCH OF IT, it was as if the town itself was going bad, rotting like a corpse left out under the blazing sun, so foul was the miasma that wafted inland all the way to the far end of the boulevard upon the sea breeze from the oceanside beach. It was so noxious, in fact, that Grace and the Reverend Jean Grey had to cover their snouts and mouths with little light blue cloths held by strings that looped around their ears whenever they walked between the church building and their vehicles. Even the nonhuman members of St. Aloysius Jr. were not a little affected by the odor, and much speculation went into what could possibly be the cause.

"Smells like when the human church had that thing they called a barbeque, and put all that burned leftover meat into this here composter to go bad," said Ometa. "Only worse."

"It is really unpleasant," said Ottoline. "And so lingering. What on earth could it be?"

It was not until Sudie Mae descended to join the regular impromptu evening gathering that the curiosity of the other creatures was satisfied. "Smell that blubber?" she enthused. "Ain't it scrumptious?!" And she inhaled noisily through the gore-encrusted nostrils of her hooked bill, savoring the sweet smell of putrefaction. "One of them big old whales has done washed up on the beach. This time it's a real big one! 'Bout as big as one of them eighteen-wheeler trucks that are always going up and down the boulevard. It's so big the humans can't figure out what to do. Lot of times they get a boat and pull it back out into the water before any of us can even get a few good bites out of it, but this time none of their little boats are strong enough. Oh, it's gonna be a real feast for us buzzards!" And as if her enthusiasm and high spirits had reached a zenith, they suddenly plummeted. "Except for Bert," she moaned. "Oh, y'all, he's still so tore up over Donna—he don't even care. It's a damn shame. If he was in his right mind, he'd be off getting his fill already. He always did love fresh blubber."

The other creatures who happened to be gathered at the

composter, Clancy, Ottoline, Steven, Ometa, and Christopher P. Martin, vocalized their agreement and sympathy. Bertram still was not himself lately, and it was a shame that Sudie Mae's own brother could not share with her the pleasures of this windfall.

Hertz, poking his tip out through one of the ventilation slots of the composter casing, offered his unsolicited opinion. "Bertram needs to get a life," he remarked.

"I'm trying to let him be," Sudie Mae said. "But it ain't so easy. I know he feels like it's the end of the world. But it ain't! He's still got me, don't he? and all our good church friends." She shook her head. "I guess I just want the old Bert back."

"It's understandable, dear," said Ottoline. "It's difficult to just stand by and watch our loved ones struggle, especially where there is nothing we can do to help."

"You got that right," said Sudie Mae. "Well, I guess it won't do anyone any good for me to sit around when there's such good meat out there. Won't be the same, though..." And so saying, she was off and airborne, and in a very short time she was a mere cruciform speck in the sky, dwindling as she headed east to the banquet.

"Stupid buzzard," said Hertz, just to be unpleasant.

❧

THE SCENE at the beach was fantastic, phantasmagoric, and wild. Sudie Mae, as she flew closer, once again marveled at the size of the creature that lay prone and rotting upon the stretch of sand, its carcass seeming to pullulate with the activity of the birds that swarmed around and upon it. Seagulls predominated, but there were also plenty of buzzards and vultures drawn from the nearby towns and stretches of countryside. Sudie had never seen so many members of her own species in one place in her life, and she hesitated before landing. Her father having been highly antisocial, and she and Bertram having obviously thrown in their lot with a community made up primarily of the members of other species, Sudie Mae felt paradoxically alien and self-conscious in the midst of so many creatures who looked like her. She almost turned around. She wished more than ever that Bertram was his old self, there to accompany her and enjoy the bounty with her and to help smooth her way into a new social situation for which she felt ill equipped. But with the smell of rot so strong upon the sea breeze, delectation overcame diffidence and Sudie Mae, in spite of herself, joined the throng.

She landed upon what was relatively the most open spot on the corpse, that being located towards the tail end, where the exposed anus of the whale puckered under the bright hot sun, and seemed to be sprouting some diaphanous scrap of something that fluttered in the wind. Upon closer inspection, Sudie Mae recognized it as a bit of one of those increasingly ubiquitous thin plastic bags that the humans used to convey purchases from one place to another and which she could see often clinging to the branches of trees and in ditches and culverts along the roads. No doubt this bag, along with others like itself, had been ingested by the hapless whale and had led to its demise. Sudie Mae resisted what was in the end a fruitless urge to pull it out, realizing that it would then likely find its way inside and sicken or kill another helpless nonhuman animal. Best to leave whale enough alone...

Dismissing the unpleasantness of the plastic bag, she set about gobbling up her fair share of carcass. She was enjoying herself immensely when, having lifted her head to facilitate the swallowing of a particularly generous mouthful of warm blubber, she spied, at some distance, toward the head of the dead whale, a very familiar and elegant figure. It was Donna! Sudie Mae was about to cry out, when Donna shifted her own gaze to meet hers, and the cry froze in Sudie Mae's throat. Donna looked away with lightening quickness, and Sudie Mae instantly perceived that for the two of them to acknowledge one another in this situation would spell trouble for the poor vulture. Sudie

Mae only wished that she could somehow communicate to Donna her complete understanding. Poor Donna.

She couldn't help darting another swift and she hoped surreptitious glance in that general direction, though, and her spirit sank when she saw that one of the male vultures accompanying Donna was looking right back at her. *Dang!* Sudie Mae cursed herself. *Now I've done gone and got Donna in trouble.* She ducked her head and tried to gobble up more whale, even though she had lost her appetite. She could feel the male vulture's gaze continuing to regard her, however. And when she lifted her head to swallow, she could not help but see that the male vulture was coming toward her. *Oh, durn,* she said to herself, *I just knew I should of stayed home.*

But as the vulture drew closer it was impossible not to perceive that the steady gaze was not expressive of suspicion but of sheer unbridled carnal interest. Sudie Mae felt her own flesh and blood grow warm from the tip of her scabrous scalp to the claws of her feet. This vulture was looking at her as if, like the unfortunate creature they both stood upon, she was a particularly delectable piece of flesh. And, God help her, she found herself ducking her head back down again in a manner that could only be described as coy. What was happening to her?

She forced her attention away from the male vulture, and plunged her strong beak into the softening flesh of the dead whale as if with a vengeance. Only when she had occasion to lift her head in order to facilitate swallowing did she note that Donna no longer seemed to be in the area, and that the male vulture was still regarding Sudie Mae intently. After a quick glance, she blushed, and bent down again to her feast.

In what seemed like a flash, the male vulture was right in front of her. Never before had a stranger so boldly entered her personal space, and Sudie Mae was taken aback. She found herself ducking backwards, compelled to create some distance before she could collect herself. She regarded him. He was a large and healthy-looking vulture, about Bertram's size, but far more polished in appearance, without Bertram's rugged, disheveled quality. "Hey, babe." The vulture addressed her with total confidence. "I'm Lawrence. What's your name?"

Sudie Mae, still somewhat taken aback, hesitated before responding. Instinct led her to avoid the truth. "Prudie," she said, with downcast eyes. This had been the name of her grandmother, her father's mother—a complicated figure in her early life.

"Prudie." He repeated this not once, but twice, as if to mentally incorporate it. "Pretty Prudie. I don't think I've seen you before, Prudie. If I had, I know I'd have remembered. Are you just here for the meat?"

"Yes, sir," she said, affecting a deference that felt as foreign and unnatural and yet potentially useful to her as a set of teeth. She wasn't sure why she was behaving so unlike herself, but there was, she found, something deliciously exciting about it. Being someone else reminded her of the thrill of learning to fly. She was getting the hang of something.

"Glad to hear it," he said. "We need more pretty, young females like you around here, in my opinion. But why are you here all alone? Don't you have friends with you? Family?"

There was no question in Sudie Mae's mind what this vulture was after. Curiosity and vanity and a glimmer of possibility that she may somehow be able to help Donna by engaging with this nasty mate of hers nudged Sudie Mae mentally into the idea of Prudie as into a concealing shadow. "Not around these parts," she said. "I came here by myself. I'm all I've got."

"That's a shame, Prudie," said the debonair, slick vulture. "Pretty young thing like you. Don't you know it can be dangerous around these parts for a female without someone looking after her?"

"Dangerous?" "Prudie" affected astonishment. "But I've always heard folks were friendly at the beach. Not like way back in the hills, where I'm from. When you fall on hard times back there, they turn their back on you..." And her tone became forlorn. "I guess there just ain't nowhere safe for a gal on her own..."

"Oh, that's the truth," said Lawrence. "Take it from me. I've seen many a good female go bad by taking up with the wrong type. No, don't let all the bright lights and the fancy humans fool you. Where there's too many humans, it just draws lazy types who don't want to take care of themselves, as my mother always says. And especially in those woods along the boulevard. Those nasty buzzards around there are nothing but lowlifes. Trust me, I know."

Sudie Mae allowed her beak to fall open, affecting alarm. "Oh, no! That's where I thought I'd stay until all this meat is gone! I heard they were real kind in the woods! That's what a little purple martin told me!"

The vulture named Lawrence leaned in. "Oh, Prudie. Don't you know any better than to listen to just any bird? No, Prudie, take it from me. You'd be much better off staying out in the swamp, just north of here, than anywhere near the humans. In fact, why don't you come on back with me? I'll introduce you to my mother and—" He paused. "—the rest of my family. You can stay with us as long as you want."

Though Sudie Mae had no intention of going anywhere with this slick vulture, "Prudie" could not resist a coy riposte. "Do you think your mate I saw you with when I first got here would appreciate that?"

The vulture named Lawrence sidled closer. "So you had your eye on me, too," he said. "You vixen! Well, Prudie, Don't you worry about my mate...my ex-mate. She's my fledglings' mother, but there's nothing between us anymore. I'm just too nice to run her off, and besides, the fledglings' need someone to look after them when I'm busy." He regarded Sudie Mae with a thoughtful air. "Do you like fledglings, Prudie? You seem like the motherly type."

"Oh!" "Prudie" said. "I just love little hatchlings. I'm the oldest, and I helped my mama with all my brothers and sisters after my daddy died." She ducked her head, as if to hide an overwhelming sorrow. When she looked back into the vulture's red-rimmed eyes, her own were shining. "I sure miss them."

"What happened to them?"

Sudie Mae shook her head and managed to convey a tragic air.

"You poor thing," said Lawrence. "All alone. Prudie, let me help you. Come along with me."

Sudie Mae thought fast. Suddenly, in spite of the pleasure she found herself taking in this strange pretense, she experienced an almost physical aversion to this smooth operator, and she had no real desire to involve herself with him any longer. And yet it was dawning on her that he was practically inviting her to provide Donna with some measure of aid and comfort. But of course, he didn't know that and mustn't ever figure it out, lest Donna be subjected to some consequence or other. And of course, Sudie Mae knew that she couldn't just go with him just because he was inviting her. For one thing, that would be stupid. And for another, she couldn't just up and leave the church, and especially not her grieving brother, without any explanation.

"Prudie" ducked her head in a gesture at once demure and saucy. "Oh, I couldn't," she said. "I don't even know you."

The vulture spread his wings. He too knew that playing hard to get was an effective tactic. "You have to start somewhere," he said. "But suit yourself. I'll be back tomorrow. The offer stands... I could help you out a lot, babe. My family has been in these parts for generations. But don't take it from me... ask around."

"I just might do that, Mr. Lawrence," said "Prudie."

"Good girl."

FEELING AS LIGHT AS A FEATHER, for all that she was full of dense and succulent whale meat as well as the admiration of a male, Sudie Mae dashed away, back towards the woods. Not since encountering Brian on the tracks and leading him to the church had she felt so significant. She, Sudie Mae, had been noticed, and not by just any old vulture, but by the one that had stolen Donna away from Sudie Mae's own beloved brother. And Sudie Mae, as she flew across the sound and along the boulevard back to St. Aloysius Jr. Church of All Creatures Great and Small, had no doubt that it was all happening for a reason.

The question now was what she should do?! Here the Lord had led her to, or had led to her, the potential to help Donna, and maybe even Bertram. Playing the role of "Prudie," a role she'd adopted without conscious intent, had opened something up inside her, and revealed a hidden capacity—with which she might make a real difference. She could cover up the truth, and apparently she could do so convincingly. She had pretended to be other than she was. It was like being hatched again. She wanted... needed... felt called, perhaps... to see just how far she could take this charade.

But how? How could she be Prudie and Sudie Mae, how could she be two critters at once? How, for that matter could she be in two places at once, for if she did not join Lawrence and Donna in the swamp like Lawrence had asked her, then the whole thing would go nowhere. But how could she leave St. Aloysius? How could she leave her brother in the state that he was in? She could never tell him the truth. He would take off like a lightning bolt to the swamp and ruin everything. It was a real problem.

Shoot. Sudie Mae came to the conclusion that she'd better slow down and figure some things out before she did something stupid. She came to a perch atop an old telephone pole along the boulevard and gazed down at the vehicles whizzing past underneath her beak. But then, as if to illustrate that she had not just her brother, but an entire community to consider, who should come along to perch on the power line right beside her but that stuck-up little Christopher P. Martin—the last creature on earth she felt like dealing with.

"Why the long beak?" chirped the pert little bird, hoping, as always, to get a rise out of her.

Sudie Mae had recently resolved to ignore his cheap shots as much as she could, so she made no response. But then Christopher, with a perspicacity uncommon to him, sensed, perhaps from the absence of a furious comeback, that something really was troubling her, and that it likely had to do with her brother's troubles. "Oh, I guess you're still upset about your brother and that Donna, aren't you? Ometa told me all about what happened. It's a real shame. She's not the prettiest thing I've ever seen, but I thought she and Bert *were* kinda cute together, and she did always have a lot of class. She carried herself well. That's rare, with big birds like you lot..."

Sudie Mae's feathers ruffled, but Christopher chirped blithely on, oblivious to his own renewed insensitivity. "Anyway, it's too bad. Nothing any of us can do. I guess it's just one of those things..." And so saying, Christopher, who was finding empathy to be as uncomfortable as it was unfamiliar, spread his wings for takeoff.

But the little songbird's expression of sympathy for her suffering brother, for all that it was plainly shallow, struck Sudie Mae as being nonetheless sincere. She wondered if maybe—just maybe—he might actually come in handy. "Wait a minute," she croaked. "Look here... If I told you you could help Donna... would you?"

Christopher drew in his wings. Certainly, he felt sincerely bad for Donna and Bertram, but that didn't mean he wanted to commit himself to any course of action. After all, a bird has to look out for himself first and foremost, especially when he has a gift. But of course, he wasn't about to say that to Sudie Mae. "Certainly!" he chirped. "I'm very well known for my altruism. I'm not just a pretty voice."

"You sure aren't," said Sudie Mae, not a little pleased by her own subtle dig. "Listen. I think I can get Donna and her kids away from that vulture... but I need your help."

Christopher felt as if he'd flown into a sudden fog. "I didn't say I'd do just anything," he fudged. "I said I'd do anything I could. But I have responsibilities. I'm not going to do anything that might get me hurt, or in trouble, or compromise my deeply held values."

"What if all you have to do is lie?" said Sudie Mae.

"Oh, *that's* no problem," said Christopher P. Martin.

☙❧

THE NEXT DAY, after an almost totally sleepless night filled with second guessing, Sudie Mae returned to the rotting carcass of the beached whale, which by that time had decomposed sufficiently to draw carrion birds from across three coastal counties. The scene was even more chaotic than before, with fights breaking out among vultures and gulls, and Sudie Mae, her prudence guiding her to take her place upon the nearly inedible tailfin of the dead creature, was tempted to take this unexpected crowd to be a sign that she should abandon her mission. But soon after she arrived she saw him coming, insouciantly winging his way through the crowd, as if drawn to Sudie Mae by an irresistible force. "Hey babe," he croaked as he landed just in front of her. "Couldn't resist, could ya?"

"Prudie" responded without missing a beat. "No, sir," she said demurely. "I came back for seconds."

Lawrence shot out a wing to knock aside a seagull that was diving too close and leered approvingly at his sassy new interest. "And *I* came back for dessert."

"Prudie" affected a becoming blush and turned her head. "Where is your mate today? I was hoping I could meet her too."

"Ex-mate, Prudie." Lawrence craned his long, thin, featherless neck forward. "And if you want to meet her, all you have to do is follow me."

"Are you sure it's no trouble?" said Prudie. "I don't want to be any trouble."

"No trouble," said Lawrence. "Trust me."

⚜

THE ST. Aloysius Jr. Church of All Creatures Great and Small had weathered countless ups and downs in official membership as well as attendance over the period since its inception, but never, ever before, lamented Clancy, had so many upheavals shaken the foundations of the community. It was as if Donna's disappearance and the cancellation of the wedding had opened a chasm into which the spirit of fellowship was seeping. Bertram was behaving like a veritable recluse, and now Sudie Mae had taken off on what seemed to him to be a potentially foolish mission. Clancy had been left thoroughly puzzled by her sudden departure, and even more so by the manner in which she'd announced that she was going. She had arrived at the composter, just as Clancy was emerging from the cellar of the church after a busy day of observing the new female human reverend, and Sudie Mae was accompanied by, of all creatures, Christopher P. Martin. What's more, the two birds, so perpetually adversarial in their interactions with one another, were behaving with none too convincing bonhomie.

"Reverend," Sudie Mae had said. "I need to ask your blessing. Chris here has been telling me about this place that he used to go to with his folks every winter, and he says that down there there are a whole lot of buzzards, and none of them have ever heard of Jesus. He says that the way they live is just terrible, and that they're always fighting with each other, and he thinks that all they need is to hear the Gospel from someone like them. Reverend, I really feel like the Lord has put it on my heart to go minister to these poor critters and share the Gospel with them. But it's a long way away, and I might be gone a long time, and I know that with Donna gone and Bertram in such a bad way, that means that the choir would be missing another singer. But Reverend, everyone knows I don't sing too good anyway, and Chris here is the real star of the choir... Anyway, I think the Lord is calling me into the mission field. I think it may be my anointing. Look at how I brought big old Brian into the church..."

Christopher P. Martin, who hated it when anyone abbreviated his name, submerged his irritation about that and seconded Sudie Mae's appeal. "I think she's right, Reverend," he said. "I know you must be extremely surprised, but let me tell you, when I was telling Sudie Mae about conditions down in Brazil, well, it was just like she was struck by lightning. I could see that God was touching her. And to be honest, Reverend... I think Sudie Mae needs to get away for awhile. All this business with Donna and Bertram is really getting her down. I know she wants to be here for her brother, but the way he's moping around all the time, I'm worried that it might start to rub off on her. She needs a change of scene; she needs to find some purpose for her life beyond just looking after her family. You know me, Reverend; you know I want everyone to be happy. And I think Brazil is where Sudie Mae can find happiness... but she needs your blessing. She's going to need all the help she can get, making such a long journey on her own. I'd go with her, of course, but..." Christopher, who as a matter of fact had joined St. Aloysius Jr. following a conflict with the leadership of his flock *en route* to Brazil, in which he'd been chased from the formation to find sanctuary on the rim of the baptismal birdbath, knew that Brazil was the last place he'd ever journey now. "...but I'd hate to leave the choir without strong leadership."

"Thanks, Chris," said Sudie Mae. "But I believe I'll be just fine without you, as long as the Lord is with me. Reverend, I'm leaving today. Reverend, tell Bertram I love him, and not to worry. Tell him..." Sudie Mae had to swallow a lump in her long, narrow throat. "Tell him if he needs me, Chris can always come find me. He knows the way. And Reverend..." Sudie Mae bowed her head. "Reverend, *can* I have your blessing? It sure would make me feel good..."

Clancy was deeply unsettled by this strange behavior on the part of Sudie Mae, and not a little disapproving of Christopher P. Martin for encouraging her to go on what sounded like a harrowing journey, but he certainly was not going to deny her a blessing. The rat reverend made the sign of the cross against the pale fur of his chest, closed his eyes, and raised his paws, palms out, slightly above the crepey, featherless scalp of the female buzzard.

"Dear Lord," he petitioned, "Bless and keep our Sudie Mae as she leaves us to carry the Good News of your sacred love to the lost buzzards of Brazil. Guide her, dear Lord, in Your Hands, and protect her against all predators and dangers that she might have to face..." Clancy then paused, as one who has awakened themselves by talking in their sleep. He opened his eyes and saw that Sudie Mae, still humbly bowed, was trembling. *Oh, Lord!* he thought. *She's scared to death!*

He kept his eyes open as he resumed his prayer, and with a far greater awareness that something beyond his understanding was at work in Sudie Mae. This awareness sparked a sincere concern and ambivalence which he could not keep out of his direct address to the Almighty. "Lord, I don't understand what You are up to with Sudie Mae, asking her to leave us so suddenly and for some place so far away, and right when we're all kind of upset about Donna leaving, but Lord, I do know that Sudie Mae is a good Christian buzzard, and that she wouldn't be doing this if she wasn't real sure that it was Your anointing upon her life. Lord, I pray that You will give her peace and strengthen her with Your Spirit as she journeys among creatures who don't know you and your Precious Love and your Holy Ghost. Keep her real close to You, Lord, because I just feel it in my own spirit that she's going to need You where she's going, where there's not anyone close by to remind her how precious she is in your sight. Stay near her, Lord, and remind her of Your Presence, especially when she might be sore afraid. Speak to her in the sounds she hears, in the thoughts she thinks, in the dreams she dreams and in the souls she's there to save. Show her Your beauty in the light and in the dark and the near and the far and in the faces and forms of your creation. Never leave her alone, Lord. We want her back home safe when her mission is accomplished, to share with us, who love her as she is now, what she has become and what she will be. All this I pray, in Jesus' Name, Amen..." And as if he'd suddenly surfaced following a dive into some fathomless ocean, Clancy took a deep breath, and fell to all fours. Sudie Mae lifted her head, and her red-rimmed eyes were glistening.

"That was real nice, Reverend," she managed to say.

"Gosh!" was all that Christopher Martin could manage to speak.

"Bye, y'all," Sudie Mae said, and off she flew to the dismal swampland that lay due north.

&#10086;

"DONNA. This is Prudie. She's new around here, and she's gonna help us with the kids."

Donna's blank silence, her unflappable manner borne out of necessity, could not thoroughly mask her astonishment, which Lawrence accepted as being natural to a scorned mate being introduced to her presumed replacement. But of course, it was the fact that this was Sudie Mae, perched beside Lawrence and wearing a look of sly demure self-satisfaction, which was causing Donna to doubt, for a moment, her own red-rimmed eyes.

Sudie Mae could, of course, imagine Donna's surprise, and hazarded a quick glance, directly into the eyes of her once potential sister-in-law, hoping to communicate, with a look alone, that she, Sudie Mae, was there to help, but that she could only do so if Donna kept her beak shut and her recognition hidden.

"Hello, Prudie," said Donna, with shaky dignity. "Very nice to meet you, and welcome to our home. Lawrence, may I speak to you in private...?"

"Later, Donna," said Lawrence. "We'll talk later, but right now I don't want to hear any of your beak. The kids are a wing-full and you know it, and that's why I wanted to bring in some help. I know you *think* you can handle them, but the fact is, they're still all screwed up by being left without a mother during an important time in their development, and it's going to take a lot of time before they ever trust you again. In the meantime, they need consistent discipline, Donna. And Tiffany especially needs a nice young female role model, one who hasn't disgraced herself by taking off after some lowlife buzzard."

Sudie Mae gritted her beak.

"...Prudie here is on her own... her father just died, you know... and I think it would be a shame if she got mixed up with all the trash over in the city. Now, I want you to be a good sport about this, and not get in the way of Prudie bonding with the kids. You understand?"

Donna felt stupefied. Lawrence...and Sudie Mae?!? And what was this "Prudie" business? Donna glanced at Sudie Mae, but Sudie Mae avoided Donna's gaze, hoping to give the impression to Lawrence that she was just being bashful, as befit a sweet young thing meeting her admirer's significant other.

"Pleased to make your acquaintance, Miss Donna," she said mincingly. "I really appreciate Mr. Lawrence's kindness to me, to let me stay here and help look after your young'uns for y'all. I want you to know, I'm going to everything I can to help you, and make sure those kids know how lucky they are to have a daddy who cares." And, just to ensure that Lawrence did not detect the slightest hint of insincerity, she turned to gaze at him with an exaggerated adoration that he was all too willing to accept.

The utter disingenuousness of Sudie Mae/Prudie's speech and behavior was not lost on Donna now. She wasn't sure what Sudie Mae was up to, but it was clear that she had somehow managed to convince Lawrence that she was thoroughly fascinated by him. Donna was touched to the heart, to think that Sudie Mae would disguise her identity in order to somehow help her, but she knew it was a lost cause. If Sudie Mae thought she could keep Lawrence in check when he thought he was entitled to something, she was going to learn the hard way. *Oh, Sudie Mae!* she thought, and had to force herself not to say, *It's not worth the risk. Get out while you can.*

"Welcome, Prudie," she said instead. "Glad to meet you as well. I think, though, that you'll find the fledglings are very well behaved. I'm sure they'll enjoy getting to know you."

"They've been through a lot," said Lawrence. "I know you'll be good for them. Help them see what a mother's supposed to act like." He turned to Donna. "Go get them," he said. "Tell them it's time for supper, and Daddy's got a surprise for them."

⁂

THE EVENING MEAL, for these rather stiff-necked vultures, was always a formal affair, and the fledglings were expected to be on their best behavior as the family gathered to consume the regurgitated remains of whatever creature had been scavenged that day. On this occasion, of course, whale meat was the main course for the third evening in a row and unfortunately Todd couldn't bring himself to finish his portion.

"Toddrick," his grandmother reprimanded. "Don't play with your food. Eat it. Your father works hard to provide for you, and you ought to be more appreciative."

Todd took a token bite and then appealed to his father. "It's great, Father," he said. "But tomorrow, do you think we could have possum?"

Donna cringed. She was learning quickly that of her three fledglings, little Todd was at once the most eager and least likely to please his father and grandmother, given his youth and high spirits. Donna ached to defend him from the wrath to come, but she knew well by now that any attempt on her part to interfere would be futile and might meet with another exile. She closed her eyes.

It was not, however, Lawrence's mother who responded to Todd's innocent, if unwise appeal to his father—it was Sudie Mae. Donna opened her eyes in astonishment as Sudie Mae reprimanded the youngest vulture, in a manner so saccharinely pedantic that Donna was forcefully reminded that Sudie Mae, at least for the time being, must be more properly thought of as "Prudie," someone she did not know at all.

"When I was a little one, back in the hills where I grew up, I would have eaten whale meat every single night if that's what my daddy brought us. Back in the hills, we were lucky if we even got a whole squirrel between the twelve of us... But we were always grateful. Our daddy worked hard to keep us fed, but he just wasn't the scavenger that your daddy is. I guess you all can afford to be particular when you have a daddy who'll go all the way out to the human beach if it means he can bring home a real treat, and not just one time, but two, three times in a row..."

Todd hung his featherless little head.

"Prudie is right," said Lawrence's mother approvingly. "You youngsters have it far too easy these days. It's high time we had someone around here who can recognize all the advantages we provide for you fledglings and your mother, in spite of her disgraceful behavior. We don't do you any favors by mollycoddling you. Todd, since you can't be bothered to finish your supper, you may go to your roost. Immediately."

Todd, stricken, looked towards his mother, but Donna

could only hope that he understood on some level that she was as helpless as he. "Do as Grandmother says, darling," she said.

With a baleful little scowl at Sudie Mae, Todd left the bough upon which the family gathered for meals and made his way along a branch and down the trunk to the bough below where he shared sleeping quarters with his brother and sister. Donna glanced at Terrance and Tiffany, and was chilled by the look of sheer loathing that Tiffany was directing towards Sudie Mae... or, rather, Prudie, who for her own part was gazing with adoration at Lawrence.

"Donna!" Lawrence's' mother addressed her sharply. "I hope you realize that you, too, could learn a great deal from our... guest."

"Yes, Mother Lawrence," said Donna. "I do realize that."

⚬⚭⚬

"MOTHER..." said Terrance in his careful manner to Donna when she made her way down to the bough upon which the children slept. "Why has Father brought Prudie to our bough?"

Before Donna could think of a sufficiently anodyne response, Tiffany spoke, and without a hint of her older brother's emotional reserve. "I don't like her," she said. "I want her gone."

Donna, of course, proceeded with caution. "I think your father wants to be a good neighbor," she said, and instantly felt a lump in her long throat, for she had very nearly said "good Samaritan," the reference to which would have been lost on her unchurched fledglings. "Prudie apparently doesn't have any family of her own, and that makes her vulnerable to... predators. It's good of your father to offer her some protection, and something to do to be useful. We should all try to make her feel welcome."

"I don't want to," said Tiffany quite heatedly. "She's ugly, and it's not like we need anyone else around to tell us what do to.

*She's* not our mother. *You* are. Mother, you should tell Father not to let her stay."

"Oh, Tiffany..." Donna was disturbed by her daughter's ruthless condemnation of a creature she scarcely knew, but understood that the child felt threatened. She was and always had been, after all, the apple of her father's eye. "Dear heart, it's ugly to judge by appearances. And darling, there's always room for someone new. That's what it means to be a family."

"Not our family," said Tiffany, not without justification.

"Prudie's mean," added little Todd. "She made Grandmama send me to bed without any supper."

Donna found Todd's denunciation harder to counter, in that Prudie had in fact behaved rather uncharitably toward him. "I'm sure she didn't mean to," she said. "Remember, she doesn't know us, and she couldn't have known that grandmother feels very strongly about finishing our meals. I think S... Prudie was just trying to be helpful." This, at least, Donna knew to be true. But she also knew that Sudie Mae had no idea what she was getting herself into with Lawrence and his mother.

"Don't worry, darlings," she said, as much to reassure herself as her fledglings. "And sweet dreams, and don't be too hard on Prudie. She's just like the rest of us, she wants to fit in. So it's our job to welcome her in to our family. It'll all work out, you'll see."

"No it won't!" said Tiffany, with terrible conviction.

⚘

"THEY'RE CRAZY ABOUT YOU ALREADY," Lawrence reassured "Prudie," who held back none of her complaints about how the meal had gone, how the young vultures seemed to prefer their mother.

"Are you real sure?" she said. "Oh, I wish I could believe that. Ugly as they are to me, I think they're all precious. Even that pretty little Tiffany. Isn't she something! Smart as a whip.

Says just what she thinks. You don't see that a lot in most females."

Lawrence heard the veiled disapproval of his daughter's outspokenness loud and clear.

"She *can* be a little sassy," he admitted. "She gets that from her mother. But deep down, she's a good girl, she just needs to be reminded sometimes that good girls keep their opinions to themselves. Don't worry, Prudie. She loved you to death, I can tell."

"Well, I guess you would know," "Prudie" said. "I can tell she's Daddy's girl."

Lawrence craned forward his neck in an attempt to caress "Prudie's" but Prudie took a demure step back on the branch upon which they perched and did not stifle her yawn. "Mercy!" she said. "I'm worn out! I reckon all that good blubber has made me sleepy."

Lawrence withdrew, but Sudie Mae noted that his pate was flushed deep red with frustrated desire, and Sudie Mae determined that indeed he and Donna were no longer mates in any technical sense of the word. Bertram'll be happy about that, she knew.

"Night night," she said. "See you tomorrow."

"You sure will," said Lawrence adamantly.

৩১৩

IT WAS, Clancy felt, the most lackluster and discouraging Sunday service in the history of St. Aloysius Jr. Church of All God's Creatures Great and Small. Attendance was noticeably poor, and even though Sudie Mae's voice had always been more voluble than melodic, its absence from the choir really did evacuate from it some necessary grit.

It was too bad, because Clancy had worked very hard on his sermon, as he'd been stirred and inspired by what the Reverend Jean Grey, in what she called her zoom meeting with her women in ministry group upon which he'd eavesdropped, had discussed around the Hebrew Scripture for the week. It was a story with which he had only been vaguely familiar, preferring as he did to preach upon the more Christocentric and generally more ethically straightforward parables and pericopes of the Gospels, but in light of the inexplicable departure of Sudie Mae in spite of her own brother's troubles, he felt it spoke to perhaps some hidden dynamics among members of the church's inner circle.

"Friends!" he exhorted. "In this world, where everything is so mixed up, and it's hard to know what to say or do sometimes, especially when we're scared or we don't think we're going to be treated fair, it can be real, real tempting to tell a story. Things aren't always the way we want them to be, and we aren't always the creatures we wish we were, and that's why it can seem okay to pretend things are different from what they are, or that we are somebody we aren't, like Jacob in the Scripture that Ottoline just recited so beautifully. But friends, when we act like Jacob did, when we aren't honest about who we are and what we're doing and what we want, then we are really asking for trouble! Look at Jesus! Jesus always told the truth! Now, I know that sometimes—just sometimes—you have to pretend just to survive. Like when Ometa pretends she's dead so that she won't get eaten up... but when it comes to our friends and family that we trust, we should always be honest. Because when we aren't honest with our nearest and dearest, then how can we ask them to trust us? And that's no way for a church family to be. All we have to do is listen to what happened to Jacob. Jacob wasn't honest with his daddy, and don't you know that it caused all kinds of problems for him in the long run, didn't it? And on top of that, he did it all because his mama wanted him to! And that just goes to show you, that when we aren't honest with everyone we care about, and we tell lies and secrets behind each other's backs and try to trick one another, and team up against one another, it usually isn't just one person's fault, it means that something isn't right among us somewhere and we need to get together and find out what it is and fix it! And we need to do that as a family and as a church, and do it out in the open. Maybe Jacob didn't feel like his daddy loved him as much as he loved his brother Esau, and that's why he tried to be more like Esau by making himself seem furrier. But he was taking advantage of his daddy's bad eyes, and he was not being himself, and if he'd stood up to his mama Rebecca and said, no, Mama, I'm going to be honest with Daddy, and just tell him that even though I wasn't born first, I'm still your son, and I need your blessing just as much as big old hairy Esau does! Now, don't you think Isaac his daddy would have blessed him? I sure do! And friends, let me tell you, I'm not Isaac, and Lord knows, I'm not the Lord, but I am your pastor, and I love you in the Lord, and let me tell you there's no reason why you can't be honest with me. There's not a thing in the world that any of you could say or do that would make me want to withhold my blessing from you. I want every one of you to feel blessed, and to be the best that you can be, and that means you can be yourself. You *have* to be! You have to let the ones who love you see you as you are to bless you... Not as you want to be or wish you were. Because that way you can be sure that who you are is God's gift to you. That's what Jacob learned in the end, but he sure learned the hard way, didn't he! He had to leave his house and his whole family and live with strangers for years and years and marry two sisters and two other ladies on top of that, and he had to wrestle with an angel who left him with a bad leg, and you know all that time he must have been wondering, what would Esau do to him if they ever saw each other again? Lucky for Jacob, his brother Esau was a good Christian and forgave him. And that's what I believe we should learn from Jacob and his mistakes. Not that we can just go around lying and cheating and running away from our problems and fight with God and our brothers, but that even if we do all that, we can still be forgiven. But before we can be forgiven, we have to tell the truth. Amen?"

"Amen," dutifully recited the congregation, in their usual babel of grunts, whistles, chirps, growls, hisses and croaks.

Christopher P. Martin wondered for a moment if the rodent, with all this talk of deception and forgiveness, might be hip to the ruse that he had concocted with Sudie Mae. But how could he? The confident songbird dismissed the discomfiting possibility at once. Still, the question remained... Under what circumstances, exactly, would it be permissible to, as the rat reverend so saccharinely expressed it, "tell a story?" Never before having considered the ethical ramifications of any of his actions or desires, Christopher felt somewhat unsure. But not for long. There were lies, and there were necessary disguises for the truth, and to his mind the distinction seemed as clear as his own mellifluous and pitch-perfect voice. And yet the sense, awakened by the story of Jacob, that Sudie Mae had perhaps put herself in a precarious situation was not so easy to dismiss. If anything bad happened to her, would Christopher P. Martin bear any responsibility? But he'd promised not to tell, and promises were made to be kept.

Well, he knew one thing. He wasn't going to make any more promises. It made things too complicated. He just wanted to sing and mind his own business. "Amen!" he said, a beat behind the others.

⊘⧓⊘

THE ATMOSPHERE of the swamp was, as far as Sudie Mae was concerned, something else indeed; at once rich and lushly beautiful and overpoweringly treacherous. Death was everywhere, with animal and vegetable in various stages of decomposition omnipresent alongside abundant life—these diametrically opposed phases of existence keeping apace in the swampy terrain and blending into one another in a manner unimaginable elsewhere. Just as there was no clear delineation between earth and water here there seemed to be no clear distinctions whatsoever. Having been brought to the family ostensibly with the object of providing care to the fledglings, in actuality Sudie Mae/Prudie interacted very little with them, and that primarily at meals. It was soon obvious that their grandmother considered herself to be their primary caretaker and disciplinarian, and that she was not about to relinquish this role to "Prudie" any more readily than she had relinquished full parental authority to Donna or even her beloved son. The old vulture kept them under her figurative and sometimes even literal wing night and day, managing their every breath, it would seem. She was always close by. It did not take long for Sudie Mae to determine that it was the old lady who really ran the show, for all that Lawrence claimed and fact believed in his own agency. He was who he was, self-indulgent, immature, and volatile because it suited his mother's need for control for him to be so, and it kept him complacent and thus complicit. Donna's submissiveness for the sake of the fledglings served the same purpose, and the old lady was determined to snuff out all vestiges of recalcitrance from the fledglings, particularly headstrong Tiffany and guileless Terrance. From "Prudie," the old female required a mere fawning distraction for her son and so that was what she got. But it was deeply wearing upon Sudie Mae, who, as if in the swampy spirit of ambiguity and dissolution, sometimes felt as if she were losing all sense of the distinction between her own self and the mask of "Prudie." She knew that she'd better work fast. This place, and these creatures, were more insidiously dangerous than she had foreseen.

Opportunities for the subtle emotional sabotage she knew was necessary were, thankfully, not infrequent, and indeed proliferated, as if her very sense of urgency called them into being. Lawrence, ever ardent, approached her following another contentious suppertime with his usual forwardness, and

"Prudie," rather than responding with her usual coy evasiveness, froze solid.

"Hey, what's the matter, babe?" he said with not a little indignation.

"Prudie" did not reply.

"Come on, Prudie," Lawrence pressed. "I don't have time for this kind of crap. Spit it out. What's up your craw tonight?"

"Prudie" knew better than to press her luck, and so melted with a simpering sulkiness. "Tiffany hates me," she said. "I just know it. I think all those kids hate me, but especially her. Did you see how she was looking at me at supper tonight?"

Lawrence had only noticed that Tiffany had been a little touchy when the family gathered for the swamp rat he'd regurgitated, and that she'd barely touched her portion. "Oh, Tiffany's just touchy," he said. "She's at that age. She loves you to death, babe, trust me."

"No, she doesn't!" "Prudie" insisted. "Oh, she's too smart to really say anything, but I can tell she thinks she's better than me. Just because I come from up in the hills..."

"Babe, no one gives a damn where you're from! You're being stupid. You've just got low self-esteem. Well, I got something that can help you feel real good about yourself..." And Lawrence craned his neck around hers suggestively.

"Prudie" stiffened, but did not, as Sudie Mae would have done, strike out. "Oh, I don't know," she whined. "Maybe I am too touchy. It's just that I see Donna with them, and she's so high and mighty and never says a word to me and they act just like her. I just wish I had some fledglings of my own that would love me like that..."And she allowed herself to ever so slightly relax under the pressure of Lawrence's embrace, which tightened not insignificantly.

"That's not a bad idea," he said, and he began to mount.

The resistance he met was swift and pointed, and in less than a moment the two were flushed face to flushed face. "No babies of mine are going to take second place to a bunch of snooty spoiled brats and their hoity-toity mama!" "Prudie" vocalized warningly through a tightly closed beak. "I may be poor, but I've got my pride." "Prudie" stretched her neck and looked down her beak at Lawrence in a parody of Donna's elegant manner. "Those three need to learn how to show respect. Especially that Tiffany," she added.

Sudie Mae knew she was taking a real gamble, but it was all or nothing at this point. She regarded Lawrence with a wariness that she prayed was effectively masked by "Prudie's" wrath.

Lawrence, who only took ultimatums from his mother, was not a little put off. Who did this little hillbilly buzzard think she was, badbeaking his kids? And yet, he could, now that she mentioned it, see where she was coming from. Since he'd introduced "Prudie" to the mix, the fledglings did seem to be drawing a little too close to their mother. This was not to be tolerated. Like it or not, "Prudie" was a barometer for the degree of influence Lawrence and his mother maintained over his brood. "Don't worry, babe," he said. "Tiffany'll come around. I promise."

Several evenings later, the tension in the swamp was as thick as it could be as the "family" gathered to their repast of regurgitated feral pig, which was nobody's favorite meal on account of the toughness of the flesh of this indomitable creature, for feral pigs almost always die of old age. It was the best that Lawrence could come up with, so preoccupied was he with Prudie and her moods. There seemed to be no consistency to her responses, not only to his advances, but also to the family life he was so generously inviting her to share. He thought that once he made sure that his fledglings knew that they were supposed to love her as their mother whether they liked it or not, she would return his affections to the full. But "Prudie," for all of her feminine wiles, was so far living up to her name. How could he be expected to take care of everyone else when no one was taking care of him?! A little old feral pig never hurt anybody.

Of course, no one complained about the menu. But even Lawrence's mother merely picked at her portion, and little Todd found the meal so distasteful that he couldn't even swallow one bite. His grandmother had to scold him for allowing his helping to grow cold, even though she left half of her own unfinished. Sudie Mae saw her chance, and forced "Prudie" to gobble down every bite and then remark, with an adoring look at Lawrence, that the meat was "just yummy."

At this, Tiffany merely closed her eyes, but "Prudie" saw her chance. In a tone suggestive of deeply wounded feelings, she spoke, addressing no one in particular, but glowering right at Tiffany. "I see that someone here thinks I'm making a pig of myself. Well, I'm sorry I'm not always as high class..." Here she turned her craftily aggrieved expression toward Donna, "...as some of y'all, but where I came from, I never got a chance to be picky about what I eat. I'm grateful for whatever anyone puts in front of me... and if that makes me just another trashy country buzzard, well, then I guess that's what I am. Maybe I ought to just go on *back* where I came from!" And she stood, as if to spread her wings, and glanced balefully down at Tiffany, who glared right back.

"Sit down, Prudie," said Lawrence with real heat, and "Prudie" sat.

"Now Tiffy—" Lawrence's tone was at once stern and wheedling. "—I want you to apologize to our guest."

"For what?! Daddy, I didn't do anything. Prudie just hates me and you know it, and you just let her be mean to me!"

"Prudie" gritted her beak.

"Don't talk back to me, Tiffany!" Lawrence warned. "You know better than that. Now, you can apologize to our guest, or you can go to your roost. It's up to you."

"Father... " Terrance spoke tentatively. "Tiffany didn't—" But the young male faltered as his father hissed at him.

Sudie Mae broke "Prudie's" glare at Tiffany to glance at Donna, who looked at once terribly controlled and terribly troubled. But she could sense Sudie Mae in that brief glance, and felt a swift stab of relief, for "Prudie" had established in Donna's mind her own reality, so distinct did this unpleasant character seem from her dear friend and erstwhile sister-in-law Sudie Mae.

Then "Prudie" turned her petulant attention to Terrance, whose timid appeal to Lawrence for clemency for his sister had not escaped her. The fear and courage that the minor confrontation with his formidable father required had left him flushed. Sudie Mae could not help but feel some remorse for what "Prudie" was about to do.

"Prudie" began to screech with indignation. "And now Terrance is over here just looking at me like I'm nothing but a piece of dung. These young'uns hate me, Lawrence, they don't have any respect for me! I've tried and tried to help y'all raise them, but their mama just won't let me, and she's turned them all against me. Oh, I never should have come here. I ought to just go on back to the hills where I belong."

Terrance, nearly fully grown though not yet quite as large as his father, shrunk into himself at this accusation, for all that it was so baldly unwarranted. Beside him his sister Tiffany stood and spat at "Prudie." "You shut up and leave my brother out of this, you bitch. I wish you *would* go back to the hills, you hick!"

"Prudie" screeched as if her tailfeathers had been plucked out.

"Tiffany!" Lawrence's croak was as crepuscular and cold as an ancient grave. "Go to your roost. And stay there. I don't want to see your face until you apologize."

Tiffany rose on her crusted claws and spread her wings. "I'm leaving," she said. "I'm going to my roost, and I'm going to stay there until SHE leaves. I don't care if I starve to death. It's HER or me, daddy."

"Oh, this is all my fault," said "Prudie" disingenuously. "I'll just go. Don't worry about me, Lawrence, you tried your best. I'll get by..."

But, as Sudie Mae had intended and scarcely dared to hope, "Prudie's' presence, as she'd intended, had become for him a matter of pride. "You stay put," he commanded. "And you!" He shouted at his daughter, "Get out of this tree."

"Father!" Terrance cried.

"Oh! Father!" Lawrence mocked his son with affected breathlessness. "You stay out of this, mama's boy. You can get out of my tree, too, before you turn my other son into a pansy."

At this attack upon the very heart of her eldest son's gentle strength, Donna's resignation gave way to fury, and she leaped across the bough at her former mate with beating wings and a gaping beak, out of which, like lava, a gout of steaming bile disgorged onto Lawrence's face, coating his astonished eyes and temporarily blinding him. Beside her bespattered and gasping son, Lawrence's mother flew at Donna and the two female vultures stood beak to beak and the sultry air of the swamp fairly crackled with tension.

"Terrance. Tiffany. Toddrick." As Donna faced her mother-in-law she spoke to her fledglings, her vocalization calm, yet unyielding. "I will not allow your father, nor anyone else, to disrespect you, or me, any longer. We are leaving."

But the fledglings were paralyzed.

Sudie Mae wondered afterwards how on earth "Prudie" had known just what to say to break the spell. She certainly wouldn't have come up with it on her own.

"Oh, Lawrence," Prudie simpered. "Don't be mad at these babies. It ain't their fault. I know I ought to have more patience with them. They can't help it if their mama puts all kinds of ideas in their heads about me. It ain't their fault she's jealous. Don't send your own babies away, honey. I promise, when their mama's gone, and they get used to us being together, then they'll be just fine. I love them just like they were my own." And she nuzzled her crepey, featherless neck against Lawrence's wing, and began to lick away the filth from his face with her black tongue. And with a quick, sharp glance at Tiffany, she added, "...and I bet I'll have some of my own real soon."

It was, for Tiffany, the last straw. "You're disgusting!" she said. "I hate you. I'm leaving, too. I'll go with my mother. My real mother."

"Oh, no you won't," her grandmother ordered. "You're going to stay right here, and remember that you can't just have your way all the time."

"Oh, shut up, you old hag!" seethed Tiffany, sounding remarkably like her father.

"Tiffany!" Terrance was terrified, and could not contain himself. "Father! Grandmother! Why are we fighting? We're family! We're supposed to be nice to each other!"

"Aww, ain't he precious," "Prudie" said, her tone dripping with the blistering contempt of the insecure female for any perceived femininity in a male.

"Like I said, he's always been a mama's boy," said Lawrence, glaring at his shamefaced son with eyes now licked clean of Donna's bile. "Well, all that's about to change, believe me."

Tiffany spread her wings. "Come on. Let's go."

"Where are we going?" said Todd

"Away from HER," said Tiffany, meaning "Prudie."

*Not for long*, thought Sudie Mae.

"Lawrence!" Lawrence's mother commanded. "Stop this nonsense! These are your offspring. You have a responsibility to see that they are brought up decently."

But with a sure thing beside him Lawrence couldn't be bothered. "It's no use, Mother," he said. "They're hopeless. And I'm not so sure they're mine in the first place."

"Would God they weren't!" said Donna, and with her three heartbroken, disowned fledglings, off she took.

❧

"Believe it or not," said Christopher P. Martin, with surprising but not totally uncharacteristic aesthetic objectivity, "I don't think I should be the one to sing the solo verses on this one. They're too... I don't know... too wordy, I think, they don't suit my phrasing. I'm not saying we shouldn't do it. It's an interesting arrangement... but I think someone else should sing the verses. Someone who likes to belt a song out. It's too bad Sudie Mae's not around."

The choir of St Aloysius Jr. was gathered at its usual space for practice, at the foot of the churchyard birdbath that served as the baptismal pool. Consisting now merely of Christopher Martin, Ottoline, Steven and the often-dispirited Bertram, the choir was not what it once was, in spite of Christopher's talents as a singer and leader. He had to admit, her poor range and sometimes recalcitrant attitude notwithstanding, Sudie Mae really brought something to their performances, something he couldn't put his wing on, and for which he couldn't compensate. The show, however, must go on.

"Bertram, why don't you try it? You've never done a solo, at least, not as long as I've been around. Have a crack."

"No..." Bertram said, with that note of forlornness that was becoming a rather unpleasantly predictable aspect of his formerly ebullient nature. "I don't really feel like it, Chris."

Christopher was not one to take no for an answer. At least not without a struggle. "Now, what kind of an attitude is that? I thought you were a Christian. Don't you want to make a joyful noise unto the Lord?"

"Not lately," said Bertram.

"Bertram, dear..." Ottoline was careful not to betray her own exasperation with Bertram's entrenched disconsolation. "I think Christopher is right. We have to keep our spirits up, even in the worst of times, and our music and worship is what brings us together to support one another. And I also think Christopher is right to suggest that you have just the voice for this type of number, which calls for a sort of... vocal heft... that birds of our size can't really deliver. Do give it a try, Bertram. I think you'll feel a lot better."

Bertram remained reluctant, but it was so much harder to resist the encouragement of the pigeon than that of the songbird, that he had to give in. "All right," he said. He took a deep breath, and began to wail the words to the hymn that the choir had memorized. And, oddly enough, he did begin to feel a sort of release, so fitting were the lyrics to his general sense of abandonment.

*"Will the circle be unbroken/by and by/by and by/Is a better home a'waiting, in the sky, in the sky..."*

Such was the impact of Bertram's heartfelt delivery, that the chorus was not immediately taken up by the other members of the choir, and when Bertram came to himself sufficiently to look at each of them inquiringly, he was taken aback by the clear appreciation that their silence expressed.

"That was quite good!" said Ottoline.

"Well!" said Christopher P. Martin. "There you go! I didn't even know you had it in you, to be honest. Bravissimo! One more time, and this time, we'll pick up the chorus on the one..."

Obliging and gratified, Bertram launched once more into the first verse of the hymn, and this time with all the more spirit and a taste of his old spunk. He was beginning to feel the burgeoning sense that he was being heard by someone or something apart from the small gathering at the birdbath, and this gave him the sense that in spite of how life seemed at the moment, nothing on earth ever stays the same, forever, and that there was never reason not to hope for better days ahead. He lifted his beak to the heavens and took a deep breath through his nostrils, to fill his lungs for the chorus, and in so doing he caught wind of an unmistakable and deeply familiar and pungent odor from a dwindling distance. His red-rimmed eyes widened. "She's home!" he crowed.

All heads turned to follow Bertram's gaze, to a distant but approaching cruciform darkness in the dusky sky, from the general direction of the vast swampland that formed much of the northern portion of the county. As it approached it became clear that it was a bird, a large bird at that, followed by three smaller but similarly shaped figures, and the closer it drew the more evident it was, from the length of the neck to the span of the wings to the fanlike shape of the tail feathers, that it was in fact a buzzard.

Or something like that. "It's Sudie Mae!" sang Christopher. "She's come back home from Brazil!"

"No!" said Bertram, who knew the difference. "It's Donna!" And off he took, like an arrow from Cupid's bow, to reclaim his beloved.

❦

AS WOULD BE EXPECTED, news of Donna's return from the swamp and the presence of her three lost fledglings spread through the inner and outer circles of the St. Aloysius Jr. Community like the Holy Ghost at Pentecost, and all who heard gathered around the composter that evening intending to welcome Donna back and her three young ones in. They were disappointed, however, as Donna, in keeping with her concern for her fledglings' traumatized state, had accompanied Bertram with her offspring to his roost and had not budged from there. It was going to be difficult enough managing the fledglings' understandable mistrust of Bertram and their reticence around him, of whom they had only heard terrible things from their father. Donna was not about to immediately subject them to the certainly overwhelming and intrusive, if well-meaning scrutiny of the congregation.

"I'm real happy to have y'all!" an ebullient Bertram assured Terrance and Tiffany and Todd as soon as the five of them reached his roost and were settled. "And I want y'all to make yourselves right at home here. My roost is your roost. Your mama and I have been real good friends for a long time now, and I'd do anything in the world for her and for you. She'll tell you! So you just let me know, anything you need, and I'll take care of it. Your mama and me, we've got a lot of good friends here in the woods, and I know that they're ready to help you any way they can, too. So don't worry about anything, hear? I know all this must be real strange to you, but it's all gonna work out. You'll see."

Terrance and Todd, subdued with traumatized bewilderment, murmured vague acknowledgements of Bertram's friendly overture, but Tiffany eyed the buzzard with deep hostility. "He talks like Prudie," she growled towards her mother after Bertram left to rustle up a late supper.

Donna's heart sank, but she managed a tone meant to be at once tolerant and firm. "I suppose you're right, darling," she said to her daughter. "They share similar turns of phrase... That's because creatures from the same general area or environment do tend to adopt similar patterns of speech. I imagine that anyone listening to the two of us might say that you and I sound alike."

"I sound like my father," said Tiffany challengingly.

"Yes, you do," said Donna. "In many ways. The important thing to keep in mind is that no one manner of expression is necessarily better than any other. It's a matter of what's best for you. Variety, as they say, is the spice of life."

But Tiffany didn't seem to be listening.

"Darlings," Donna said. "It's been a long, hard day for all of us. I think you should try to rest now. Bertram and I will be right down the branch. He and I have a lot to discuss, but don't hesitate to call if you need anything. I'm your mother, and you are my first priority. Don't ever doubt that. Ever again."

"We won't need anything," said Tiffany.

❧

LATER THAT NIGHT, Bertram's croak of astonishment woke all three fledglings from their troubled slumbers.

"Do what now?!" he cried. "You mean Sudie Mae...!"

"Hush, darling..." Donna's murmur was as urgent as it was placatory. "You'll scare them. Yes, Bertram. Sudie Mae saved us. I don't know why or how she ever imagined that she could pull it off, but she did. It was as if, from the moment she saw him, she recognized what it took me a long, long time to see: he's weak. He puts on a good show of strength, but he's as weak as they come. There's something very special about Sudie Mae..."

"My sister!" he cried, and Donna was obliged to stifle his beak with her own. "I've got to go get her!" she said, much more softly, when she withdrew.

"Let her be," Donna said. "There's more to Sudie Mae than even she ever knew."

❧

"AH, baby! Free at last! Finally! It's just you and me. Just you and me! You see how crazy I am about you? I'd do anything for you, you can see that. Now—don't you think it's about time you did a little something for me...?"

It was the dead of night in the depths of the swamp on the edge of town, and now that Lawrence's mother, after performatively bewailing the defection of each and every one of her three grandchildren and cursing and upbraiding Lawrence for having taken up with Donna against her advice in the first place, had retired to her bough in the topmost branches of the cypress in a snit. Sudie Mae was well aware that she was on her own now, with nothing to stand between herself and Lawrence's sense of entitlement to her affections, and she knew that her virtue was at stake. Her mission to liberate Donna had ended in what looked like success, but at what cost? If she didn't allow this vulture the liberties he wished, there might be hell to pay. He was, after all, bigger and stronger than she was, and in his own territory at that. And if she did let him have what he wanted... did it really matter? Certainly no one else wanted what he was after. And it would be so nice to have fledglings of her own, even if they were his. She'd rescued Donna and her fledglings, certainly she'd find a way to rescue herself and her own, if it came down to that. And really, was he all that bad? Selfish, for sure, but isn't everyone, deep down? She felt Prudie welling up within her like a belch. She also felt weary. It was so heavy, the atmosphere of the swamp... It would feel so good just to close her eyes, let "Prudie" simply take over...

"Your mama doesn't like me, Lawrie," "Prudie" complained, relishing her power. "You see the way she looks at me? I'm not doing anything unless your mama shows me some respect. I've got my pride!"

"Quit playing games," grunted Lawrence, and he attacked. And that was what it took to strengthen Sudie Mae and deliver her from evil. Like a bat out of hell she flew, guided by sheer determination and the indomitable instinct for home and the familiar. Over the marshes, over the town, across the boulevard and with Lawrence in hot pursuit, she made her way back to the churchyard, and descended like lightning from heaven to the lid of the composter and there tried with all her might, by thrusting her sharp beak and beating her powerful wings, to fend off Lawrence and his foul advances. But even from that platform she was no match for Lawrence's aggression, fueled as it was by his sense of entitlement. When he couldn't shove her off of the composter he began to shove against the composter itself, and Sudie Mae imagined in a flash the catastrophe that would befall Hertz and his colony if their tower fell. With a flying leap she took off to the treetops, but Lawrence was able to gain on her and force her to the ground beside the garden.

"Get off me, you nasty thing!" She cried, in the dead of night having no real hope of being heard by any creature that might be able to help her. But she underestimated the power of her voice to reach and rally, even from the depths of slumber, her fellow Christian creatures. Clancy poked his snout through the gnawed out corner of the crawlspace door to see what all the ruckus was about, and Percy clambered up to the edge of the opening of his dumpster. Ottoline and Steven emerged from within their decorative belfry and were immediately joined by Veronica who, her sharp compound eyes perceiving instantly that Sudie Mae was under attack, made a beeline to the most tender and exposed portion of Lawrence's anatomy, and fixed him with her stinger. With a shrieking vocalization that could have raised the dead, Lawrence took off into the night and Sudie Mae was free. Percy and Clancy and Ottoline and Steven all rushed to her side, where Veronica lay spent in the dust. The feeble waving of the bee's forelegs was the only sign that she lived, until, in that faint burring voice that was so signaturely hers, she said, looking straight at each one of them by virtue of her multifaceted eyes, "I'm all right." And so saying, she became perfectly still, the thorn in her flesh having been sacrificed.

"Naw!" wailed Sudie Mae.

IN THE IMMEDIATE aftermath of Veronica's death Sudie Mae could not be convinced that the little bee's blood was not on her talons. "It's all my fault." She cried. "I should have just let him get what he was after. I never should have gone out to that dadgummed swamp in the first place. Donna would have got away one of these days, and Veronica wouldn't have got killed. Oh, Reverend I've sinned big. I lied to you and told you I was going to Brazil and I got Christopher to lie for me, and I played the harlot to make that nasty vulture get all hot and bothered and then when I couldn't handle him I hightailed it back here like a dadgummed coward. I shoulda known someone was bound to get hurt, and I just didn't want it to be me! Oh, Reverend, I swear, I was trying to do something good...I even prayed about it, and now Veronica ends up dead. Why, Reverend? Why didn't Jesus stop me?"

Clancy, even if he'd had the words, did not have the where-withal in the moment to tackle the thorny theological questions of Divine Omnipotence and creaturely free will. And he sensed that none of that would matter in the moment anyway. Sudie Mae was bearing the weight of the Cross, that no mere explanation could lift. He could only stand beside her, looking at the tiny, lifeless little black and yellow striped figure on the ground.

It was Ottoline, with the perspective of an elder, who though feeling keenly the horror of the moment, felt called to offer some consolation. "She was tired, Sudie Mae." She said, as she looked down at the little corpse, remembering. "Even though we all did our best to look after her-- Steven and myself sharing our roost, Ometa and Percy foraging packets of honey from the dumpsters-- it just wasn't enough. She was out of her element...there was just something missing. But she never complained, and she just kept saying that she wouldn't go back to the colony to save her life. "I'm free." She always said, and when you feel free, you can do anything. And that's what she did, dear. I'm sure she was happy to do what she could to help you." And, overcome with maternal affection, the little pigeon leaned against the shuddering buzzard to convey her love, which after a long moment began to penetrate Sudie Mae's anguish, for she trusted the wise little grey bird.

"I hope Lawrence's pecker falls off," said Sudie Mae through her gritted beak after some time. "This is all *his* damn fault, too."

"Amen," said Ottoline.

⚜

CLANCY ASSUMED his place atop the lid of the composter and lifted his forepaws for silence, to signal that the eulogy was about to begin. He looked out among the impressive gathering of mourners with a markedly unClancylike and somber mien. The circumstances surrounding Veronica's death had shaken him deeply. He hated violence of any kind, he couldn't bear to accept that it could ever be a Christian response to conflict, and he had been very disturbed by Sudie Mae's confession that she'd lied to him about taking a mission trip to Brazil to undertake such a treacherous campaign to rescue Donna. The whole affair struck him as being terrifically sordid, and made him wonder what else might be going on right under his snout. To think that sweet, innocent Sudie Mae could come up with such a scheme!

And so it hadn't been easy to come up with the right words. In the end, he gave up on crafting a prepared eulogy, and made the risky decision to speak from his heart and trust the Spirit that it would not lead him into error.

"Dearly beloved…" He addressed his congregation, without knowing why he chose that particular opening. "I just want to thank you all for being here on this sad occasion, to mourn the loss of one of our newest but most treasured members, sweet little Veronica. Poor Veronica wasn't with us all here at St. Aloysius Jr. for a real long time, but I believe God brought her to us for a reason. I think you all can remember when we first met Veronica…she just happened to drop in on one of our services, and to be real honest, I don't think we were too welcoming at first…we were all scared, because we all know that nothing hurts like a bee sting. But Veronica wasn't just any old bee, she was a unique individual, and God led her to us so that she could come to know Him, and in coming to know Him, she could come to know herself. Veronica didn't have a whole lot of encouragement, where she came from, to try new things and to get to know new critters and to make her own way. Veronica didn't even have her own name before God brought her to us, that's how different life was for her. But in the end, Veronica didn't let what she knew before to stop her from following Jesus. No, Veronica showed us all that she wasn't afraid to do what Jesus asks all of us to do in some way...to give up everything we know and that makes us feel safe, and start a new journey. To be born again, Amen?! And once she started to follow Jesus, when the time came she followed him all the way...she laid down her life for her friend."

At this a low moan escaped the lowered beak of Sudie Mae, who was at the front of the gathering flanked by Ottoline and Steven, with Bertram and Donna and Donna's three offspring close behind her. Clancy's heart hurt, for he knew this was hard on Sudie Mae. But there was no avoiding what happened.

"Yes...I know it feels like Veronica's gone too soon. She gave her life, it doesn't seem fair, when she was so good, and had so much to offer. But we just have to remember, that Veronica has followed Jesus further than any of us has ever seen, and that her soul is with Him in Heaven, looking down on us remembering her, and I know that she's happy. The closer we are to Jesus, the happier we are, and no one is closer to Jesus than someone who has followed him all the way. Veronica isn't the first to follow Jesus unto death, and she won't be the last, but she'll always have a special place with Him, and a special place with us. You know, there's a whole lot of human beings who have given up their lives just like Jesus, and we call them saints and martyrs, and it just could be that Veronica is the very first bee to be among them. Isn't that something! Why, she's right up there with St. John and St. Mark and all the others who wrote about Jesus, and Jesus' mother Mary, and his daddy Joseph, and St. Aloysius whoever he was, and a whole bunch of other humans who gave up a lot for Jesus. And when you're a saint like that, you're so close to Jesus in heaven that folks down here on earth can even come to you in prayer, so you see, St. Veronica really isn't gone after all. Just because we can't see her, doesn't mean she isn't with us. And you know what? We can all tell her right now how much we love her, and appreciate her, and that we are proud of her for doing what she did." And, caught up in the logic and spirit of his eschatology, Clancy clasped his forepaws together, closed his eyes and began to pray to one of his very own parishioners. "St. Veronica, we're all gathered here and we're so happy that you are safe in heaven with Jesus. We miss you being here with us, but we know you're in a better place, and we know that we can always call on you to help us be as brave and true as you've been. St. Veronica, we'll never forget you, and just like the humans' name churches after their saints, we are gonna honor you like that. Of course, our church already has a name, and I don't think we ought to change it, because that can be confusing...but we can name something else for you, that will remind us that you're with us, and so I declare that this very altar, where I preach and bless the sacraments, ought to from now on be dedicated to you, because you deserve our respect. I proclaim, with the power vested in me as a minster of the Gospel, that this here composter is named St. Veronica's Shrine, and all are welcome, to visit it whenever they feel like it, to remember you and come to you in prayer. Amen! And now, let's all sing along, as Christopher leads us in a hymn that was real special to Veronica..."

And with that Clancy opened his eyes, and his mouth and began to accompany Christopher P. Martin's stirring rendition of, "There is a Balm in Gilead," and every single member of the church joined in, even Hertz, who was not exactly thrilled about his colony becoming even further appropriated by Clancy's zeal, but who had become too fond of the little bee to object...at least not right in the middle of her funeral.

# HUMILITAS

"WHERE'S PERCY?" SUDIE MAE was curious. It had all of a sudden occurred to her, after Veronica's funeral and the gradual softening of her guilt and sorrow, that she had not seen that enigmatic companion of the Reverend's whom she found at once so objectionable and intriguing.

"Why, come to think of it, I'm not sure!" answered Ottoline. "I haven't seen him in a few days, at least. I hope nothing's wrong..."

The two female birds each glanced over towards Clancy, who, as was his usual custom following the service gleefully greeting parishioners just at the base at the composter. The nature of the relationship between the rat reverend and his fellow and far from reverend rodent was a favorite question for those members of St. Aloysius Jr. who troubled themselves to speculate about their pastor's private life. Certainly the two rats were close friends, but what was the nature of that closeness? Was it friendship, fellow feeling between two male members of the same species, or was it something more? And, if it *was* that 'something more,' why did they not proclaim themselves, and sacralize their bond? The natural variation of same sex coupling being, for the most part, an uncontroversial reality accepted among most of the species who attended St. Aloysius, it was doubtful than anyone in the congregation would have been the least bit scandalized or disapproving. At the same time, there was something about the reverend that seemed perpetually virginal.

"If there was something wrong, the reverend would let us know," said Sudie Mae with somewhat wistful wisdom. "Hard to tell for sure, though. Sometimes things get past him."

Ottoline had to agree.

☙❧

PERCY LIKED to think of himself as being bi-locational... an inhabitant of two very different worlds, both of which were essential to his complex and expansive nature. He loved the church, for all of its naïve drama, and he liked his church friends, *and* he loved the haunts of his youth, the waterfront alleys and gutters and dark delights, and his old cronies there. As time went on, he found that if he went too long without partaking of one or the other he would begin to feel somewhat pleasantly restless and discontented. On account of this fluidity of sensibility, he felt uncommonly lucky, if not to say blessed. And he was also lucky (if not to say blessed) that his pious little pal Clancy understood and seemed to appreciate, that he, Percy, was just not one to settle down completely. He wasn't sure he ever would be. He was pretty sure, too, that Clancy felt the same sort of ambivalence in his own way.

Hence Percy always felt a rush of pure vigor when he approached the bustling waterfront district of the town, the sights, the sounds, the smells of rowdy nightlife. Here in the alleys and the dumpsters and the sewers of the waterfront was where he'd been born and raised and learned to survive on this own as an orphan. Possessing a bold charm and an abundance of physical advantages, Percy's struggles and triumphs over early misfortunes had had the rare and salutary effect of disposing him kindly towards those less capable than himself, and so in the end he'd become something of a celebrated figure among the rodentine denizens of the wharf, and while this was gratifying, it could also be draining. In fact, it had been the demands upon his attentions—among other things—that had led him initially to seek occasional refuge and solitude in the dumpster of the convenience store next door to St. Aloysius, and which had attracted him to the relative stability of the little community of creatures, and to Clancy, whose guileless, indomitable innocence at once challenged and complimented his own experience. It was hard to believe that in fact Clancy, too, had been born on the wharf, though he'd been raised in the church, far away from his squalid beginnings.

"Well, look who's here..." came a familiar voice, interrupting Percy's ruminations as he crawled out of the sewer grate in front of the waterfront flower shop. "Hey handsome! What brings you back to the old neighborhood?"

"Call of the wild, baby," said Percy. "How's it going, Smokey?"

The pale grey rat swished his tail sassily. "Oh, there's always something," he said. "You know me. What about you? Here to see Rowena?"

"Not if I can help it," said Percy, Rowena being the most difficult and demanding of his former paramours.

"My lips are sealed," said Smokey. "I mean, if you *want* them to be..." He executed another saucy snap of his supple, scaly, hairless tail. "By the way, how is that friend of yours that you brought around to meet everybody not too long ago? We hear he's been keeping you out of trouble. He must be a real angel! What was his name again...?"

"Clancy," said Percy. "He's a good influence, I guess. But I'm still me."

"Like they say, you can take the rat out of the wharf..." Smokey tittered, then grew thoughtful. "Clancy..." he murmured. "You know, it's funny. I thought that sounded familiar. Just earlier today, someone asked me about someone named Clancy... How about that!"

"What, now?" Percy was understandably surprised by this tidbit of information. "Someone was asking about Clancy— around *here*?"

Smokey, always pleased to get a rise out of Percy, tittered again. "I guess so! You don't run across too many Clancy's... not in these parts."

"Who was it?" Percy suddenly had a terrible thought. "It wasn't Rowena, was it...?"

"Oh, nooo..." Smokey trilled. "Definitely not *that* tacky thing. It was actually three females, but I doubt they were any that you have to be worried about... a little too long in the tooth, even for you, I think. No, in fact I don't think I've ever seen any of those three old dears around here before. And they as much as said that they're just looking for their sister, who they haven't seen in ages, and that the last they knew she was living around here with a grandson or something named Clancy..."

Percy's heart leaped like a flea. It couldn't be—could it? He affected a disinterested tone. "Did they say what the sister's name was?"

"November, I believe," said Smokey. "Isn't that cute?"

Percy was so stunned his pelt bristled. What luck! What synchronicity! What were the chances, that on one of the very days he, Percy, decided to visit the waterfront, that some long lost connection of Clancy's would come around in search of his dead great aunt! It was almost as if there really was some sort of divine plan. "Smoke," he said. "Where did they go? Did they say?"

"Well, it was first thing this morning, around eleven, and last night I had one of those nights, if you know what I mean, so the whole thing's a little fuzzy, but I believe they said they were going to try and ask around some more before they went back home to who knows where. I wish I could tell you more."

"That's all right, Smoke," said Percy. "You didn't know."

"Know what, if I may inquire?" said Smokey with concern as sincere as his curiosity. "You aren't in any trouble, are you, hon?"

"No trouble," said Percy. "Don't worry."

"I didn't think so," said Smokey. "But with a cutie like you, one never knows!"

✺

AMIDST THE TEEMING throng of humans, rats, gulls, alley cats, insects and mollusks that made up the populace of the waterfront shopping and dining district of the town, Percy had precious little hope of encountering three elderly female rodents who were more likely than not well on their way out of town, but he had to try. The prospect of surprising his little buddy Clancy with not just one, but three long-lost relatives, was just too captivating to give up on so soon. He knew that Clancy would be thrilled.

After a long afternoon and evening of fruitless searching, ending with a night on the town, Percy finally had to give up the search, and skittered in the dawn's early light down to the flower shop to bid farewell to good old Smokey.

"Hey, handsome!" The little grey rat hailed him and rushed out from underneath the porch of the flower shop. "Do I have a surprise for you!"

THE THREE SENIOR female rats peered through the whitewashed wooden latticework below the florist's porch as Percy and Smokey approached. "My land, he's all grown up, isn't he!" He heard one of the females exclaim.

"And big and strong looking, too!" said another.

"Who would have thought..." mused the third.

"Hi ladies!" Smokey called as he slipped through the lattice-work into the cool darkness beneath the porch. "Back as promised! And here's the fellow I was telling you about—Percy! Percy, this is September..." He indicated the stoutest of the three elderly females, who raised a paw. "October..." The piebald, placid-looking middle rat bared her teeth in a friendly manner; " ...and last but not least, December." The slimmest rat narrowed her eyes at Percy, as if she might be shortsighted, and nodded her salutation.

"It's a pleasure," said Percy, gazing from one elderly yet energetic countenance to another. "I don't know if Smokey told you, but I've been hoping to catch up with you. See, I think I can help you find who you're looking for."

"It's true, then!" the stout old female said. "They're still together! Bless your heart! Is she treating you all right!"

"Do *what*, now!?" asked Percy.

"No, dear heart," Smokey interjected, addressing the stout lady rat. "I think you're confused. This isn't Clancy. This is Clancy's dear, dear friend. *Percy*. Not Clancy... *Percy*."

"Oh!" exclaimed the piebald rat. "Where's Clancy?"

"Just up the boulevard," said Percy. "I'll take you. Boy, he's gonna plotz!"

"So will November!" said the squinting, skinny female rat, December, with what sounded like rather gleeful foreboding.

◌▓◌

KEEPING to the shadowy places along the boulevard as the sun rose higher and higher in the east, Percy and the three elderly females arrived at the gathering behind the church building just as the Sunday Service was beginning. Percy led them past the gravel driveway of the human church to the asphalt parking lot of the convenience store beside it, and then to the dumpster behind, which he considered his primary residence. He clambered up to perch upon the plastic lid of this dumpster, and beckoned the three elder rodents to join him. " Hop up," he said. "You can see him in action from here."

The three females, each still spry enough to make the necessary climb, perched beside Percy to look over the chain link fence that separated the two lots into the back churchyard, where, perched upon a green plastic vermicomposter bin, surrounded by creatures of various species, a young and rather stout and bright-eyed male rat was holding forth with great animation. "There he is!" Percy said with pride and joy. "That's your Clancy!"

"Well!" September exclaimed.

"Just as cute as can be!" said October.

"Looks just like his father," December remarked.

Then all four of them watched in silent absorption as the service progressed, from the sermon in progress to the Eucharist and then the announcements and then the processional hymn.

"Well, isn't that something," said September. "It's like one of the services in the church where we grew up."

"It *is* a church service!" said Percy. "He's the Rat Reverend Clancy now."

"Well, my stars!" said September.

"Isn't that precious!" enthused October.

"*Rat* Reverend!" December exclaimed. "How did *that* happen?"

"You'll have to ask him," said Percy. "Come on!"

❧

"PERCY!" Clancy squealed when he saw his dear, dear friend approaching through the gaping gap at the base of the chain link fence. "There you are! Praise the Lord! Sudie Mae and I were just wondering if you were going to be back in time for fellowship hour! How was everything down at the waterfront?"

"Wet and wild," said Percy. "As always. Listen... I got a surprise for you." He gripped Clancy's right ear and led him forward with irrepressible excitement. "Rev, these three ladies right here are September, October, and December. And, Ladies, this here is the Rat Reverend Clancy of St. Aloysius Jr. Church of All God's Creatures Great and Small. Ladies, this is your great-nephew, and Rev, these are your great-aunts... Now, how about that!" And Percy skittered back and behind the three beaming females, as if to present no obstacle to a joyous family reunion.

Clancy was utterly speechless. He gazed from one rat to the next, over and over, as if to determine which one was the more likely to leap forth and attack him. "You ...y'all... are my great-aunts?!" he breathed.

"Yes, indeed," said September.

"You look just like your pa!" exclaimed October.

"Where's November?" demanded December.

And Clancy gasped, stared, gasped again, and then fell forward, overcome with vertigo.

❧

WHEN THE OVERCOME reverend rodent revived, he was not a little disoriented, surrounded as he was flat on his back and with the countenances of a menagerie of creatures peering down at him. For a split second he thought he might have died and was waking up in Glory. But as the familiarity of the various snouts and beaks looking at him registered, he realized he'd lost consciousness and he immediately wriggled himself up onto all four paws. "Oh, Lord!" he cried. "Was I just slain in the spirit?!" He directed this inquiry to Ottoline, the one to whom he most often tended to turn when in distress, due to her placid and maternal nature.

"I don't believe so, Reverend," she said. "I believe you

hyperventilated. Try to be still and measure your breaths, and I'm sure you'll feel better in a moment."

"But why on earth would I..." Clancy began to say, but then he remembered the three old females and felt his head swim again. He looked through his circle of friends and parishioners to where four rats stood at a distance. Closing his eyes, he waited for his head to steady, and then made his way tentatively through the circle to where Percy and the three elderly females crouched. "Y'all... y'all are looking for my Great Aunt November?"

The three sisters murmured in the affirmative.

"Y'all are my Great Aunt November's sisters?"

"We certainly are!" said September.

"No doubt about it!" said October.

"In the flesh!" said December.

Clancy gazed from one to the other, again and again, as if he thought that if he took his eyes off of one of them for too long, they might disappear.

"You certainly look like your father," the slim, squint-eyed rat named December declared. "Like he spit you out of his lying mouth. Hasn't November told you that? I suppose not. Where is she? I bet she'll die when she sees us!"

Clancy felt his respirations dangerously accelerate again. He closed his eyes and ground his teeth and thought of Reverend DeBassompierre at the altar, an image that never failed to soothe him. "After a moment he felt able to respond. "I'm real sorry..." he said, "but Aunt November passed away some time back. I'm sure she would love to see you... and you know, I believe that in the spirit, she can. I believe she's looking down on us from heaven right now, and that she is truly rejoicing."

"Passed away!" cried September.

"She's dead?" demanded October.

December turned and squinted at Percy.

"I wasn't sure if I should tell you or not," he said. "I figured not. I'm not good with giving bad news."

September, October and December drew closer together physically, as if with the news of November's death their sisterly bond had tightened. "Well, I'll be," said September after a while. "November is dead."

"I was afraid of that," said October. "It's been so long."

"Just like her," muttered December. "Hardheaded to the end."

Clancy, sensing genuine if complicated grief, and disinclined to revisit his own ambivalent feelings about the loss of his beloved aunt, slipped intentionally and with no little relief into pastoral gear. "I know it must be a shock. She was in her prime. But I want you to know, she didn't suffer, she died in her sleep. I believe the Lord just decided it was time to bring her home, and He wanted to do it without any fuss. I know she would be so happy to see y'all if she was here..."

"I bet you anything she never even mentioned us," said December. "Did she?"

Clancy wasn't sure he cared for the tone that this slim, squinting aunt was using. He reminded himself that she was blood family as well as a child of God. "Aunt November didn't talk much about the past," he said, and immediately glanced upwards, as if fearing some contradiction from the heavens. Because of course Aunt November had talked about her idyllic childhood in the cellar of a little church way out in the country, where life was simple and orderly and her mother and father were strong and good. But she had never mentioned any sisters. "But she always said that there was nothing that meant more to her than family..." That, at least, was true enough. She had said that. Frequently.

"I'll just bet," said December.

"Hush..." said September.

"It doesn't matter now," October murmured.

Clancy felt as if he had stumbled into a cloud of locusts. His impulse, then, was to seek cover. "Would you ladies like to see the church?" he appealed.

AFTER FELLOWSHIP TIME, it was customary and indeed necessary for the congregation of St. Aloysius Jr. to disperse somewhat quickly, as at that time the human service concluded, and, as not many of the human congregants tended to stay for their own fellowship time, the animals were mindful of not presenting a spectacle. Clancy watched his flock dissipate with more than his usual wistfulness, for something deep within him was reluctant, even though he had suggested it, to welcome his Great Aunt's estranged sisters to the basement where she had lived her last days and eventually and unexpectedly perished. It was, in a sense, uncovering her nakedness. But what was he supposed to do? He was very relieved that Percy seemed to show no intention of leaving him alone with his new family.

"Follow me," Clancy said stoutly, and he led the old females around the cornerstone of the foundation to the crawlspace door, the corner of which had been gnawed by Aunt November herself to provide access. Percy loyally brought up the rear. Through the roughly triangular gap in the corner Clancy wriggled with some effort, for he was increasingly thick around the middle these days, and the three long-lost great aunts followed. He made the little leap from the threshold to the cool damp earthen floor. "Watch your step," he said. "It's not too high, but there is a drop." And he waited in the familiar cool dimness of his lair for his eyes to adjust and the four other rats to join him.

"My land," said September. "All this room!"

"So nice and cool," agreed October.

"Help!" cried December. "What is *that*!"

Such was the unexpected volume of December's squeal that all five rats were drawn together by alarm and faced the north-side wall of the basement with stiffened whiskers and pelts. Clancy was the first to recover. "Oh! I should have told you. That's just Brian. He's so quiet, I just forget all about him sometimes. He's my guest, for a while, while the weather's still warm. It's hard on his constitution. Sudie Mae—she's a member of the church—brought him here, and I've enjoyed having him. He's certainly a big ole bear, but like you see, there's lots of room, and he's no trouble at all..."

The three elderly female rats exchanged murmurs of astonishment. Percy felt a rush of pride in his little pal, who, for all of his occasional fretfulness, was essentially courageous, when push came to shove.

"Can I get you ladies anything?" Clancy was saying. "There's plenty. I always make sure I have some Triscuits or Little Debbie snack cakes from the dumpster next door—Percy here is real good about sharing—and there's always some water to drink in the little pan around the bottom of the humans' water heater over in the corner. After a while, when the new human reverend leaves, we can go upstairs and I'll show y'all around the church... It's so beautiful, especially the sanctuary, y'all just won't know what to do, will they, Percy?"

"Aren't you sweet," said September. "But we don't want to be any trouble to you, dear. We really were just hoping to see Sister November. I'm just sorry we waited so long. Now it's too late to... catch up on all that we've missed. I'm sure you were a real comfort to her... you really do look so much like your father." She glanced nervously over to the cinderblock foundation wall, to which the sleeping and softly pulsing great furry bulk of the bear named Brian was turned. "Isn't this something," she marveled. "We grew up in a church basement out in the country, and so did our father before us, and his father before him. But I don't believe I've ever heard of a church rat ever starting a church of his own! It was just something that the humans did. How on earth did you get the idea to do such a thing?"

"Jesus," said Clancy stoutly. "Jesus called me in the night, to feel His sheep and spread His Word. And I'm so glad He did..."

"What did November have to say about that, I'd like to know," said December.

"Well, Aunt November had passed on by the time Jesus

called me to pursue the ministry," admitted Clancy. "But I know that Aunt November would have been real happy. She was a good Christian rat if there ever was one. We used to sneak upstairs before every Sunday service, and watch from under the Hammond organ. She loved all the songs, especially 'Onward Christian Soldiers,' and she loved old Reverend Bickle's sermons, though she didn't care so much for Reverend DeBassompierre's. But she never missed a service, until the day she died, and—" Clancy, even in the throes of his nostalgic reverie, could not help but notice that the three elderly females were uneasy.

"Are y'all all right?" he said.

The three females exchanged tentative glances.

"We're just sorry that we missed seeing her," September said again.

"We're glad she took good care of you," reassured October.

"I suppose it was the least she could do," said December.

The silence that fell was very, very heavy and tense, as if December's remark had spilled blood. In that silence they could hear overhead, muffled through the flooring yet discernable, the footsteps and the voices of two human women preparing to leave the church. The moment became one of decision for Clancy, in which he decided he would rather not pursue any further conversation about Aunt November with her sisters. A line from scripture occurred to him and was quickly dismissed: "Let the dead bury the dead."

"There they go!" he said brightly, changing the subject with determination. "That's Grace and the new rector, Reverend Jean, locking up and going home. Let's go on up, and I'll show you around. Oh, I just know you'll love it to death!"

The three females were elderly, but not stupid. They glanced at one another, then at Percy, and followed Clancy as he loped up the stairs and squeezed underneath the door that opened into the broad hallway of the education wing. Only

December vocalized, and that in a mere sigh that could only be heard by Percy, who was right behind her.

"Feels like she's right here with us," December said.

⸙

CLANCY CHATTERED nonstop as he led the females and Percy through the corridors and into the open spaces of the church: the administrative wing where Grace and the Reverend Jean Grey spent the workdays, the various dusty, seldom used Sunday School classrooms, the vestibule, and finally the sanctuary. "Here it is!" proclaimed Clancy, scampering ahead toward the altar and turning to face his guests. He rose up on his hind legs and held his forepaws up and out and gazed up to the crucifix that was suspended from the arched beams above the altar with thin wire. "This is where I first learned about the Lord... right here in this sanctuary. Oh, I wish you all could have been here when Reverend DeBassompierre used to preach the word and celebrate the sacrament. I like Reverend Jean all right, I guess, but there was no one like Reverend DeBassompierre when it comes to preaching. Why, you've never heard so many long words in your life! And he knew the bible like it was right inside his head. I just hope that one of these days, I'll be as fine a priest as he was." And Clancy dropped to all fours and closed his eyes, as if praying.

"It's unreal," December whispered. "He sounds just like her when she'd..."

"Hush, December," September said.

"Let him be," October agreed.

⸙

"IT CERTAINLY IS A BEAUTIFUL CHAPEL," said September when they returned to the cellar with the sleeping bear. "And I know we all enjoyed seeing it. But I suppose it's time we headed back to the country..."

"Oh, can't you stay the night?" said Clancy with admirably masked relief. "I'd love to hear more about you all, growing up with Aunt November, and your own families, and all that." And he held his breath, determined not to betray his hope that they would not change their minds.

"Some other time," said September. "Now that we know where to find you. But for now, I think we'd better get back. As you get older, dear, you'll find that you don't rest well away from home... and we have a lot to digest. I still can't believe November is gone."

"It's such a shame," agreed October.

"We should have known," said December.

"Well, you're welcome back anytime," said Clancy bountifully. "And I hope you'll come back soon. And join us in worship. I know that Aunt November would be real pleased. I believe she's rejoicing in heaven right now, now that we're all together."

"That's a nice thought," said September.

"So sweet," said October.

"Anything's possible," said December.

WITH A LONG, questioning look at Clancy, which was met with a performative yawn, not at all subtly signaling that the rat reverend was not in the mood for company, Percy followed the three elderly females to and through the gap in the crawlspace door. Once outdoors, he poked his snout back in and said, "See you tomorrow."

"See you tomorrow, Percy," Clancy said.

The night had indeed fallen, and the three females were already near the front of the church, facing the boulevard, when Percy caught up to them. "Hey!" he said. "Listen... I guess that didn't go too good. I guess I should have warned you—not just that she was dead, but that he's really touchy about some things, and that Aunt of his is one of them. As far as he's concerned, she's the next best thing to Jesus."

"As far as *she* was concerned, too," murmured December.

"It's all right," September reassured Percy. "No harm done. Everything happens for a reason, our father used to say."

Percy felt a curious sense of keen failure, as if a burrow he had dug had suddenly and inexplicably filled itself in. He'd hoped, with this family reunion, to spark joy, but it had instead ended in this strange discomfiture. He should have known better, he told himself, than to bring up the past.

But how could he have known that she had never mentioned her sisters? he demanded of himself. You don't know anything unless you ask. And then, the more you know, the less you fuck up...

"Listen," he said. "It's too late for you gals to be traveling by yourselves. The owls are out and about, and they're hungry this time of year. I'm coming with you."

"It's a long way out in the country..." warned September.

"I got no plans," said Percy.

෨෨෨

IT WAS A LONG TREK, through parts of the surrounding landscape that Percy had never had any cause to explore, and he was intrigued by its flat regularity and the sameness of the brick structures that were human dwellings along both sides of the two lane road that led far into the northwesternmost section of the county which was bordered by a wide river just before it broadened all the more into the sound. It was near the river— he could tell by the faint brackish tang of the air so reminiscent of the brine of the waterfront—that they reached a curving dirt driveway that led some distance across a great expanse of meadow to a small and somewhat dilapidated steepled building.

"Hepzibah Free Will Baptist," said September, somewhat breathless from exertion. "Home Sweet Home."

Percy wasn't sure what he had expected... Something a bit more grand, like the old stone churches downtown, or the sprawling megachurches along the interstate, and he was pleasantly struck by the rustic and humble presence of this particular building. He followed the three females up the gravel path and around the back to where, just as with the crawlspace door at St. Aloysius, a small chunk had been gnawed out of the corner of the ancient wooden slab that had been jammed into the sill of a window whose glass was no more now than a dust-caked jagged remnant in the top left corner. Through this tiny aperture the four rats squeezed, and found themselves in a dark space much like the cellar of St. Aloysius, only much smaller and with a higher ceiling—and with no sleeping bear. Streaks of dim light overhead drew Percy's gaze.

"Wooden floor," said September. "Not much between us and them. And in the old days, when the church was full every Sunday and Wednesday, why, we were never sure that floor wouldn't come right down on top of us. But it never did. And these days, of course, there's only a few that show up. And they're as old as we are..."

"They still get pretty loud," remarked October.

"Only the preacher," said December. "And that's because half of them can't hear. Won't be long before they're all gone, and we won't hear any more preaching. Of course, we might be dead by then ourselves."

"Poor November," said October. "I still can't believe it. Oh, I wish we'd gone looking for her sooner."

"Maybe it's for the best, sister," said September. "It sounds like she was still..." She hesitated, regarding Percy. "Oh, I'll just be quiet."

Percy ducked his snout, to signal that he knew he should be leaving. "I'll head on back," he said. "You ladies take care."

The three sisters exchanged glances. "Don't rush off," said

September. "It's all right. There's no reason you shouldn't know the whole story. After all, you're one of us."

Percy felt strangely warmed, though he wasn't sure what September meant by "one of us." Was she referring to their shared species? Or was it something else, something more... familiar? He settled down upon his abdomen, much as if he were back in Clancy's cellar, resting alongside his friend at the end of a full day and/or night.

"She was still...?" he prompted.

"Proud," said December bluntly. "Too pleased with herself for her own good."

❧

"NOVEMBER ALWAYS DID SET HERSELF APART," September said, "even as a little, bitty thing. She was always kind of..."

"Spoiled," interjected December. "Father never put her in her place."

"Father never put *you* in *your* place either..." Normally easygoing September sounded almost stern in her rebuke. "He was *always* more permissive with you younger ones. I suppose he assumed that with me and October to look after you, you wouldn't need as much... discipline."

"You could be a pawful yourself, December," agreed October. "Oh, how you and November used to bicker!"

"Squabbling fit to raise the dead!" agreed September. "It's a wonder you didn't get us all found out by the humans, with all your squealing. But it is true that November *could* be bossy, especially with you, since you were younger. She didn't take comfortably to you having your own mind. Strange, because she certainly had hers."

"She hated me," December declared.

"Now that's not true!" remonstrated October. "She just wanted you to be her pet."

"Yes," September said. "She had to have her way. I'll never

understand why she was so bossy. It isn't as if she got it from Mother and Father. Of course they were strict... they had to be... but they were never unreasonable..."

"Oh, we're making November sound just awful." October turned to Percy. "And she really wasn't. She had her ways, and her moods, and her airs, but oh, she could be so much fun! Why, she loved to watch the humans up in the church, and imitate their strange ways, the singing and the dancing and the preaching and the praying. She thought it was all so strange and funny—we all did—and she was so good at making believe..."

"Of course, we never took any of it seriously. It was just like all of the rest of what humans get up to, trying to make themselves feel superior and safe. As if anyone could really believe that the world was made by some great big human in the sky... and in less than a week. And the ribs, and the floods, and people walking on water... so fantastic!"

"We did like the snake story, though," said December. "Such a troublemaker. Just *like* a snake. To a T."

"Yes," said September. "Those stories could be amusing. But of course, we knew they were just stories, and November would be the first to tell you they were preposterous. Really, it wasn't until Andreas came along that she seemed to change..."

"He gave her attention," said October.

"He gave more than that," December said.

Percy's ears pricked up. This sounded juicy! But the females fell silent. "Who's Andreas?!" he cried.

Once again, the three elderly sisters exchanged glances.

"Let's let her rest in peace..." said September. "What's done is done. It doesn't really matter, after all this time."

"It all works out in the long run," October added, rather inexplicably.

Percy felt wild with frustration. But he knew he had no right to pry.

"I won't say nothing to Clancy," he promised. "Unless... you want me to."

"He *should* know the truth," said December. "But *we* don't even know the truth. We just know what Andreas told us... and he was as bad as November when it came to having airs. Who knows what really happened between those two? All I know is, when Andreas came up the river and begged our Father to take him in, November sure enough met her match..."

"Andreas didn't fool Father for a moment!" contradicted September. "Father was simply helping out a stranger, the way he always did."

"Fool him how?!" Percy was driven wild by vagueness. "What happened?"

October reached over with one paw and patted Percy's paw in a rather motherly manner. Percy could not recall ever having been touched by any female rat with such uncomplicated tenderness, and he felt a rush of warmth toward her and her sisters, and even the formidable ghost of November by extension. He felt, for a moment, infinite forgiveness for every sentient creature, including himself, and was ready to hear the whole story of November's undoing without judging her.

"Andreas was Clancy's father," said October. "At least, that's what he said."

❦

"HE WAS, in his way, kind of... dashing. We all thought he was cute, with his foreign way of vocalizing. He came up to the church one evening, looking terribly wet and bedraggled, but still with a sparkle in his eye, and he told Father that he was stranded, that he'd been found by a cat and chased off of the yacht he'd been living on, and just needed a place to stay for the night before he hitched another ride down the river to the waterfront. Now, when you think about it, none of that makes sense, because he also told us that he'd came to the waterfront on a freighter that sailed from his home, a place the humans called Amsterdam, and he never explained how he got from the waterfront to a yacht coming from upstream, but Father never was one to pry. Anyway, Father told him he could stay, and when after a while he made himself so useful helping mother keep the cellar as nice and fresh as possible, we all stopped wondering why he never made his way onto any of the boats heading down the river to the waterfront. Like I said, he was charming, and he was always willing to help out—though he wasn't much for foraging with Father—and he was very sweet to all us girls, and now, looking back, it's clear that he knew he had an admirer in November from the very start. She didn't like to let it show, but anyone paying attention—which I suppose we weren't—could see that she was fascinated by his stories about all his travels, and all the seaports all over the world that he said he'd visited, and I think he could tell that November had always felt a little... underappreciated and stifled, way out here in the country, and we were all getting past our prime. But still, we were all surprised when the two of them..." She paused.

"Eloped," supplied September.

"Ran off," said December.

October pressed Percy's paw again. "Of course, it didn't take us long to figure out what happened. Apparently, they had planned it for a while, and they just took off one night while Father was out scavenging and the rest of us were asleep. At first it was a real shock, but looking back, it all made sense... November tried not to let on, but you could tell she loved the fact that he paid her a lot of attention. Oh, he paid attention to all of us, and was always quick to flirt—it was like he just couldn't help himself—but I think November felt like he had his eye on her especially and that she was finally getting her due. When she put on her little church act, Andreas just acted like it was the most hilarious thing he'd ever seen. But I suspect *she* was the one who talked *him* into taking her away, because I don't think he would have left if it was up to him... He liked us all, even if maybe he did have a sure thing in November. Anyway, they disappeared, and Father was just frantic, and he looked all around and I guess he heard from some of the river rats that Andreas and November were down on the wharf and setting up a nest together. Well, Father went on down there... he wouldn't let Mother or any of us females go with him... he said it might be too rough... and when he came back a couple of days later he said that November was determined to stay with Andreas, and that all we could do is just hope for the best. "She's full grown now," he said. "All four of you are, and when you're full grown, you have a right to make your own decisions and your own mistakes. Andreas isn't bad; I do think he's very immature, but maybe November can teach him some sense. If there's one thing she has, it's sense enough to get her way..."

"So we waited. And we waited. And we heard...or Father heard, after a while, that Andreas had left November on her own, and then we heard, before Father could even make arrangements to go see her, that they were back together. So Father let her be... he didn't want to make her feel embarrassed... and then, after a while, lo and behold, who comes crawling into this cellar one night, all wet and bedraggled and with a hunk torn out of his ear and a kink in his tail and a few whiskers missing, but Andreas. He wouldn't say how he got so... roughed up... but he did admit that he and November had been at sixes and sevens, and that he hadn't realized that she was so... attached to him... and that he was afraid that he just couldn't handle her moods and that Father had better go get her and bring her back home. Well, Father hadn't been born yesterday, and he knew that November was too proud to ever run off with any rat who hadn't encouraged her, and he backed little Andreas right into that corner right behind you, and he made that silly rodent admit that he'd trifled with November's affections. And Andreas said he was sorry, and that he'd gotten carried away and that he'd never meant to hurt her, that he was just trying to show her a little more of the world that she always wanted to see. And then he said that Father might as well know that November probably wouldn't come back home or go anywhere without the baby..." October paused and closed her eyes as if witnessing, with her inward eye, a shameful scene. "And after Father got off of him, he swore up and down that the baby wasn't hers. 'I mean, *l'enfant* is of my loins, but not of November, you see... when we were... how you say? ...*séparés*... I'm afraid I was... how you say? ... *infidèle*. The baby was born to a... *paramour* of mine, a very enchanting but rather... irresponsible young female named Trixie. And November has... how you say?...taken charge of the child. And won't give him back to his *maman*. It is perhaps for the best. How I long to be a part of my *enfant's* upbringing, but I'm afraid... November won't allow it. She's very... *adamant*, as you perhaps can imagine."

"Well, it was just awful," said October sadly. "I felt *so* embarrassed for November."

"Heartbreaking," September said.

"Typical male," said December. "Present company excluded," she amended, rather begrudgingly.

Percy was so captivated by the narrative that he had not even registered December's tongue-in-cheek female chauvinism. "Wow!" he said "Wow! So Clancy's pop was a player!"

"*If* everything Andreas said was true..." said September. "And October has pretty much put it in a nutshell, then yes. Clancy was the offspring of Andreas and some poor tramp from the waterfront. But November, right or wrong, for better or for worse, took the baby in and brought him up. And named him after Father, which I must say, does suit him better."

"Better?" Percy said. "You mean, Clancy isn't his real name?"

"Depends upon what you mean by real. November named him Clancy. Andreas said that she refused to call him by the name his mother gave him, which was, apparently, Rocco."

"*Rocco?!?*"

"Yes, isn't that silly?" said October. "Apparently, the natural mother was fond of that name. In any event, even Andreas didn't think much of his child's mother, because he seemed perfectly content to leave 'Rocco' in November's custody, and take off to who knows where. Well, after he left, of course we made our way down to the waterfront to try to find November, and let her know that there was nothing to be ashamed of, and that she should come back home to the church, and we would all help with the youngster, but by the time we got there, of course, November was long gone. We might have known that she wouldn't stay where she might look foolish. But she'd left without a trace! We had no idea where to begin looking for her. But every once in a while we make our way down there, just on the off-chance that someone there might have heard something of her or little Clancy, and of course, this time we found you! And now..." October patted his paw. "Now we know, that the poor Clancy has grown up to be a very fine rodent, with an... interesting career and lovely friends. So it all works out in the long run."

"Yes, indeed," said September.

"And we know that November's dead," said December. "Just as well. She wouldn't have been happy to see us."

"Oh, December. You don't know that," September remonstrated.

"Rocco wasn't too happy to see us," she said.

The other two elderly females could not argue with that.

Percy felt another upsurge of all-encompassing understanding. He knew that if these elderly relatives of his pal were left with the impression that Clancy was merely a product of their sister's pride, they were missing the point of him. "Listen, he's just kind of protective of old November. She did make sure he had a nice, safe home. That's more than I ever had," he said. "Just give him time. And don't be strangers. Come back to church whenever you feel like it. I promise... he'll come around. It's not every day you find out you have long lost family."

The three females, as seemed to be their unconscious habit, exchanged glances before September responded. "Of course, you're right," she said. "It's a lot to take in. Three strangers show up out of nowhere, and don't even know their own sister is dead."

"Anyone would be on guard," agreed October.

"And he doesn't even know the half of it," added December.

"You are a very wise young rat," said October to Percy. "Clancy is lucky to have you as a friend."

"And I'm lucky to have Clancy," said Percy. "And Rocco," he added.

❦

POLITELY, without pressure, September, October, and December encouraged Percy to stay for the rest of the night, but as oddly refreshing and amusing and illuminating as he found their company, he found he could not relish the prospect of an overnight spent so far out in the middle of nowhere. On top of that, he felt very much in need of some time alone in which to collect his thoughts and impressions. With sincere appreciation and affection, he bade the three elderly female rodents farewell, and assured them that in spite of their long-lost great-nephew's unexpected diffidence they would always and forever be welcome at St. Aloysius Jr. "Trust me," said Percy. "I can always get him to loosen up, no matter how wound up he gets."

"I believe it. I don't doubt that you are just as charming as Andreas when you want to be," October fondly observed. "But far less self-serving. Good-bye, dear. And thank you for understanding."

With that, and a few frail embraces, he was off. Southbound he loped along the grassy shoulder of the two-lane state highway towards the city, under the weak and distant light of a fairly new moon. As if to keep himself company as well as to process what he'd discovered about his friend's beginnings, Percy chattered to himself along the way, enjoying, as if he'd just made a new friend, the sound of his own voice.

"Holy shit!" he carried on. "Ain't that something else! Old Aunt November wasn't so holy after all. Well, it just goes to show you, you never know about folks. Poor old bag got swooned by some hustler, he probably had a babe in every port. No wonder *she* was such a prude. I guess I would be too, if I let myself get taken for a ride like that... It's a shame, though, she didn't have enough sense to just live and learn. Those old sisters of hers are about as neat as they come, and I know they wouldn't have given her too hard a time. She should have gone back home with little baby 'Rocco' and let them help her out. It takes a village, like they say. It would've been good for Clance to have more family around, to maybe know a little something about who his dad was, and where he came from. No, she had to hide herself up in a whole 'nother church, away from everybody, and keep poor Clancy all to herself." Percy paused as he rounded a curve and the lights of the boulevard came into view from a considerable but comforting distance. "Well, I guess all's well that ends well. For better or for worse, she croaked in time for the little guy to have to figure things out for himself, and so far, he's done a pretty good job. Started a church from nothing... made a lot of friends... and who knows what else he might do, if he keeps it up. Still, I wonder what he would have been like, if she'd brought him back home, or if she'd just let him stay with his real mom." Percy, who could all too easily imagine the irresponsible type of female that Clancy's mother most likely had been, allowed himself a contemptuous defecation along the roadside. Moving forward, he resumed his reflections. "Nah. It all worked out okay. After all, if it hadn't been for his nutty Aunt November, he wouldn't even be Clancy... he'd be Rocco." Percy looked up at the distant moon, as if for confirmation. "And without Clancy... who would I be?"

Percy's mind quieted into a pleasant alertness to his surroundings as he approached more closely the edge of the city and the boulevard across which his heart lay. Once safely past the intermittent and heedless traffic, he skittered up the

gravel driveway of the church, and along the side of the building, and squeezed through the gap in the crawlspace door into
the cellar, where Clancy was wrapped up in his pallet of slightly
moldy choir robes, fast asleep. Suddenly overwhelmed with
drowsiness after his long journey, Percy wriggled in and
wrapped himself cozily around his friend. *Just wait till I tell you*,
he said silently as he fell asleep, *who you are! You'll never believe it!*

## ❧ 7 ❧

# PATENTIA

D ONNA'S ELDEST SON TERRANCE perched atop
the power line pole in front of the church, along the
boulevard, and observed the young male human
being as he maneuvered a small yet unpleasantly loud and odiferous machine on wheels up and down the uniform expanse of
grass between the church building and the road. The young
human seemed perturbed neither by the effort of pushing the
little machine, nor by the noise, nor by the petroleum stench,
nor by the violence he was wreaking upon the tender blades of
grass. Terrance, observing, felt a keen and unexpected sense of
outright envy. It would be so nice, he figured, to be like that. By
"like that," Terrance wasn't precisely sure what he meant, but
he sensed, about the young human, a general contentment that
he, Terrance, who had never before felt anywhere near as at
ease as he had since leaving the swamp to come here to live
with his mother, was not at ease with feeling at ease. Shouldn't
he miss his father and grandmother, even just a little bit? His
little brother Todd had moments of longing to see their dad,
and his sister Tiffany was very plainly pining for the way life
used to be. But he, Terrance, found himself wishing that things
had always been the way they are now. He'd missed his mother

when they were apart; he liked Bertram, and the more time he spent with the various creatures that made up the congregation of St. Aloysius Jr. Church of Urban Wildlife and All God's Creatures Great and Small, the more he found them absolutely fascinating. And he particularly was impressed by Bertram's friend, the Rat Reverend Clancy. And he couldn't help but think that the Rat Reverend Clancy took a special interest in him. He'd even asked Terrance if he would like to serve as an usher! Terrance had accepted with deep gratitude, too deep even to express. How good it was to have something to look forward to every single week, and to have a part in it! So often, back in the swamp, the days had passed with such monotonous similarity that there was no concept of time passing. The only regular event that Terrance could remember looking forward to had been the coming of the cold season, which, for a while now, had not even been that cold. And after every single Sunday service, the Rat Reverend Clancy had made a point, during the announcements, of thanking him. Terrance believed that he would do just about anything to please Reverend Clancy. And this made him wonder—why had he never felt this way about his own father?

The roar of the machine came to a drawling, sputtering end, and the young man pushing it paused and removed the billed cap from his tousled hair and wiped his brow with his sleeve. Terrence, from above, retracted his neck and brought in his wings as close as they could come to his sides and clenched his talons against the rough wood of the pole, attempting inconspicuousness in lieu of invisibility. He continued to observe the young human as it pushed the now silent machine into a small outbuilding to the left of the church building, then enter the church through the bright red double doors. And now that he was out of sight, Terrance found that he missed him. Just being in the presence of such contentment, he realized, was a real comfort.

෴

"Finished," Tommy Holbach announced to his mother in a loud voice. Grace looked up at him from her desk in the open area of the administrative suite. "That's thirty bucks," he stated, his voice even louder.

"Go see Jean," said his mother, indicating the slightly open door to the rector's office.

"What?"

"Go see Jean," Grace repeated.

"What?"

Grace sighed, stood, stomped over to her son, plucked the airpod buds out of his ears and pressed them into his clammy palm. "Go see Jean!" she shouted.

"Oh, okay," said the young man with maddening nonchalance, and he sauntered into the Rector's office.

Jean Grey, having overheard the interchange between mother and son, already had the check written out. She smiled as the young man approached her desk and handed it to him. He stuffed it into the pocket of his shorts without looking at it.

"Thanks," he said.

"You are welcome," she said. "Twenty-five dollars, as agreed."

"Wait!" The young man dug into his pocket, pulled out the crumpled check, and peered at it. "You said thirty!"

"Did you edge? I didn't hear the edger."

Tommy did not answer.

"Thirty when you edge," she said with a smile. "Would you like to edge now? I can write you another check for five…"

Tommy considered. "Nah," he said. "I'm beat."

"Very well," said the Rector. "I'll do it myself. And apply the extra five dollars to the Bishop's fund," she leaned back in her leatherette chair, so that the back of the headrest nearly touched the window looking out over the rear churchyard, and regarded Grace's son with a fondness not untouched by concern. The boy, though apparently doing well in his culinary program at the community college, and involved, with three of his friends in what he referred to as a 'post-hardcore emo experimental band' which was distastefully and provocatively called 'The Vomiters,' still lived at home with Grace and did not feel the need to contribute by obtaining steady employ-ment. That said, he was not uncooperative. Jean just worried that he lacked initiative. He seemed to be putting more energy into The Vomiters than his restauranteur ambitions. And while neither Jean nor his mother wished to discourage him, none-theless it gave them no little *agita*. Tommy had, in fact, approached first his mother, who had then approached Jean, about the possibility of his band using the chapel as a practice and potential performance space. It was an idea that was not unappealing to Jean Grey, though she felt that in this case it would not be prudent to give something for nothing. She was prepared, however, to make a deal. "While I have you here," she said, sensing that he was waiting for her to bring the matter up, "...I've given your proposal a good deal of thought." She effected a facial and vocal expression of dourness, so as to keep him on tenterhooks. "And I've decided... that it would be fine for you and your fellow musicians to make use of the sanctuary from time to time as a practice space."

"For real!" Tommy sat up from his slouching position. "Thanks, Jean!"

She held up her palm. " ...Under certain conditions. One: the only evenings that we are not hosting weekly AA meetings or other community groups are Monday and Thursday, and for the sake of flexibility I ask that you choose only one of those. That means, in general, only one evening a week. Two: You must leave the space as you find it. That means, any alterations in the arrangement of the furnishings you may make in order to accommodate your equipment must be put right before you leave the building. And, last but not least: Three: You will agree to provide a concert as a part of the Stewardship Benefit Jubilee your mother and I are planning to hold next month. And you will encourage as many of your friends and fans as you can to attend and contribute. Now. What do you say? Do you think you can agree to these not unreasonable conditions?"

"Hell yeah!" said Tommy. "I mean, Yes sir! I mean, ma'am!"

"All right, then." Jean Grey extended her slim, pale right hand over the desk, and Tommy shook it vigorously. "It's a deal. And, it being Thursday, I suppose I should probably ask if you'll be needing the space tonight? If so, I'll have your mother leave the alarm code with you. Please do not share it, not even with the members of your combo."

"Whatever you say!" he said, and he stood and dug in his pocket for his phone. "Dude!" he crowed into it after pressing a contact. "It's me. Mom's boss said we can use the church. Do you want to jam tonight?"

A brief silence, throughout which Tommy grinned like a happy skull. "'K. I'll come to your place. Mom'll drop me, and we'll get Stuart and Ellis in your van. See ya!" And he stuffed the phone back in his pocket, heedless, it seemed to Jean, as to whether or not the connection had ended.

"Luid says thanks, Jean!" Tommy said. "And I really mean it, this is a lifesaver. We'd have to pay 250 a month at least for some shitty storage space, now that we've gone electric, and Luid doesn't want us using his grandma's attic anymore 'cause she's been sick. This is gonna be great! It's a miracle!"

Jean Grey did not disagree.

◈

"REVEREND CLANCY?" said Terrance, with a winsome amalgamation of timidity and determination. "Can I ask you a question?"

The evening had fallen, and was clear and unseasonably cool, and Clancy was surprised but not unpleased to see the young vulture, this late in the day, as he was usually with his brother and sister at their roost a ways into the woods. "Well certainly, Terrance! Ask me anything!"

"Thank you," said the young vulture. "Reverend, I've been wondering... well, I've been thinking that... maybe something's wrong with me. And I... I don't know who to talk to about it."

Clancy's fur bristled with anxiety, and he made himself silently recite the Lord's Prayer, which for him had an intermittent calming effect. He wouldn't dream of denying the young vulture an opportunity to confide in him with whatever was troubling him, but Clancy wasn't sure he would know what to say. He responded with what was perhaps palpably ersatz enthusiasm.

"Well, Terrance, I want you to know, you can always come to me whenever you want to talk. That's what I'm here for, that is my job as a pastor, to be a listening ear for my flock and to give them all the support and counsel that I can. And you know, anything you say to me is just between you and me unless you tell me otherwise. That's called the seal of the confessional, and I take that real seriously. And I promise you, no matter what you tell me, I won't judge you, because as the bible says, judge not, lest ye be judged, and lord knows, I know I'm not perfect! So don't worry about a thing. What do you think is wrong?"

Terrance glanced at the composter, in the fumes of which they stood.

"Oh! Lord!" Clancy cried. "What in the world am I thinking? Here you want to have a private conversation, and we're right in front of a whole colony of worms. Let's go on over by the birdbath. I promise you, Terrance, I'm not always this muddleheaded..." And so saying, Clancy loped across the churchyard to the birdbath, which stood like a Grecian monument in the pale dusky moonlight.

"That's better" said Clancy. Assuming a relaxed but pastoral attitude, he stood on all fours and looked up at the larger creature. "What's on your heart, Terrance?"

Terrance felt better at this distance from the composter.

The birdbath, which held no water at this time but only a dry crust within its bowl, seemed comfortingly inanimate, a trustworthy bystander to what was bound to be a difficult conversation. "Reverend—" He decided it would be easier, rather than try to articulate all of his ambivalent feeling about all the changes in his life, to present the rodent with a concrete pastoral problem. "What are you supposed to do when someone you love isn't happy, and isn't being very nice to someone else that you love?"

Clancy did feel a wash of relief. Though he hoped never to shy away from a parishioner's existential questions, he felt himself to be on far more solid ground with interpersonal issues. "That's a real good question, Terrance," he said. "But I don't think there's just one answer to it. I think every single situation is different. Do you feel like telling me more about what's happening?"

"It's Tiffany," the young vulture said. "Reverend, she's just been awful. She says she hates it here, and that she wants to go back to the swamp and stay with our father, and she says that our mother doesn't pay enough attention to us, and she really— she won't even speak to Bertram and Pru—, I mean, Sudie Mae. She just sits around the roost and won't even eat with the rest of us. Mother says that she misses the swamp, and that she just needs time, but sometimes I don't think Mother really knows Tiffany. Mother was away for a long time." And Terrance here hung his head dolefully. "Tiffany can be a lot like Father," he said. "A whole lot."

After a moment, he looked up at Clancy, who was making a conscious effort not to betray his own concern regarding Tiffany. For Bertram had not been unforthcoming about the tensions between Sudie Mae and Donna and Donna's daughter. "That Tiffany is a real stinker," Bertram had confided. "Tell you the truth, Reverend, I wish she'd go on back to the swamp, if she likes it so much better there. But that would break Donna's heart, I know. I guess we just have to put up with her..."

But, as with any coping mechanism, the acceptance of Tiffany's hostility was taking a toll, especially, it seemed upon her older brother. "I just want everyone to be happy," said Terrance to Clancy. "And Tiffany thinks she'd be happier back with Father, and maybe she would be, but I don't think things would be the same. And... I just think she could be happy *here*, if she just would try. Todd likes being here, and so do I! But Tiffany misses Father..." And once again Terrance's head drooped on his featherless neck.

"Do you miss him?" said Clancy with a gentleness that seemed to come from above.

Terrance seemed to shrink a little with shame. "A little... I guess... but not like Tiffany. He always liked her best, I think... until Prudie came along."

It took Clancy a moment to remember that Prudie and Sudie Mae were in fact consubstantial. "Well," he said, "I know it's hard... when the ones you love aren't... getting along. I know how you feel, Terrance, because as a reverend, it's my job to make sure that everyone in the church is a peace with one another, and that's not always easy. Folks feel different ways about different things, just like you and Tiffany feel different about your daddy. But that doesn't mean you aren't brother and sister, and that you don't love one another deep down. And I know that when you're happy with something, and someone you love is not happy about it, it can make you feel—" Clancy paused, to choose the right word among so many—

"Like a bad person," Terrance supplied.

"Yes." Clancy felt himself not a little impressed by the young vulture's perspicacity. "You're a sharp fellow, Terrance. I was just saying to your mama the other Sunday, you sure do pick up things quick. I think you have real leadership qualities, Terrance. I sure do."

Terrance flushed with pleasure, from the top of his crepey scalp to his scaly feet.

Clancy sensed the young creature's gratitude, and this made

him feel less inadequate to the thorny pastoral dynamics of the situation. "You know, Terrance, I think that we all have to be patient with Tiffany, until she can straighten out her feelings, but in the meantime, it might be a good idea just to try and get her out of her shell. And you know, ever since you all have been with us, I've just been feeling like something's missing, and thanks to you coming and sharing with me, why, I think I know what it is! We just don't have enough for you young folks to do! And that just might be the answer. Terrance, what would you say if I told you that I thought it might be good for St. Aloysius Jr. to have a Youth Group, and that you might be a real good Youth Leader?"

The young vulture's bald head lifted, and his red-rimmed eyes widened. "Me?" he croaked.

"Amen!" Clancy confirmed. "Of course! Why not! You've done a real good job being usher, just about everyone in the congregation has mentioned it to me, and I can tell that even though Tiffany isn't real happy right now, she knows you're her big brother, and she looks up to you. And what with Ometa's young'uns getting bigger every day, and so many new squirrel families in the neighborhood, well, I just think it's time we were more intentional about engaging our youth. What do you say, Terrance? Would you be interested?"

Terrance felt as if he could rise up above the treetops without flapping his wings once. "Do you really think I could do that, Reverend?"

"I sure do."

Terrance had to press his talons into the dusty soil around the birdbath, so suddenly unbound by gravity did he feel. For the moment, at least, his own sense of unease around his sister's turmoil was blessedly forgotten.

"Praise the Lord!" he said.

❧

IT WAS DECIDED, between the reverend rat and the young vulture, to keep the new initiative between themselves until Clancy could make a formal announcement regarding it at the next Sunday service. "But you'll probably want to go ahead and make sure it's all right with your mama," Clancy allowed.

"Oh, she won't mind," said Terrance. He knew that he was the least of Donna's worries.

And so that Sunday, following the communion service, at the usual time set aside for brief announcements, Clancy assumed his position on the lid of the composter/al-tar/lectern/pulpit and raised a forepaw to signal that he desired all gathered to pay special attention to what he was about to say. "Friends," he began, "I guess you all have figured out that over the past few weeks or so, our little community has really all of a sudden grown up by leaps and bounds! We've gotten a lot of new members, and I praise the Lord for that! The spirit of St. Aloysius Jr. is really moving! I don't believe we've seen so much growth in such a short time since the church first started! But it means, of course, that there's a lot for me to do. I need to make more time to be available for more ministry, and that means... I'm going to need some help! Now, I know that each and every one of you here supports the ministry of St. Aloysius Jr. in your own special ways, whether it's by singing in our choir, or visiting and comforting one another when someone is sick or upset, and some of you have even pitched in and helped with preaching from time to time! But I know that all of y'all have your own lives and your own families to take care of, and every one of us has only so much time to give. And that's why I'm real happy to let you all know that the Lord has raised up from among us a young fellow that we all know, who has a real gift for leadership, and a heart for young creatures, because he's still a young creature himself. And on account of his gifts and his skills, and his willingness to take a leading role, I want us all to congratulate Terrance here, on being called to accept the posi-tion of the very first minister of the St. Aloysius Jr. Church of

All God's Creatures Great and Small Youth Group. Terrance, come on up and say a few words, won't you?"

Terrance, who had been standing between his mother and his little brother Todd throughout the announcement, looked self-consciously left and right, and, with his entire featherless neck and scalp flushing, he made his way to the composter and leaped up on the lid to perch next to the rat. From there he could see, standing near but apart from the rest of the family, Tiffany, who never failed to make a show of her reluctance to attend these services, and yet never stayed back at the roost. He tried to meet her gaze. He knew that there was very little chance that Tiffany would willingly take part in any group, youth or otherwise at the church, but he wanted to somehow communicate to her in this moment that he hoped she would. But Tiffany's gaze would not be met.

"Thanks, Reverend," Terrance said, setting aside his unease. "I still can't believe that I'm really going to be a Youth Leader. I'm just happy to have the chance to help out, and I want everyone to know that I'm going to do my best to be a good friend and a good minister to all of the young creatures of the church. And I'd like to invite any of the young folks here who are interested to join me during fellowship hour over at the playground. I just want to take this time to get to know everyone better, and we can talk about what kind of Youth Group we want to be. And... well... I guess that's all. I'll just go over to the playground now, and whoever feels like it, just come on over when you're ready."

And with that, Terrance stood and flapped his wings, and flew across the churchyard to the playground, and perched on one corner of the sandbox that had been empty of sand for innumerable years, and waited for his ministry to begin.

❧

IT DIDN'T TAKE MORE than a few minutes, though it felt to Terrance, sitting there by himself, like a lifetime indeed, waiting while those among the congregants who were parents either encouraged or cajoled their young and adolescent to take advantage of this new opportunity for specialized fellowship. First to make their way to the playground were about a dozen young squirrels. These were notorious for their rambunctiousness, and in fact, before Terrance could even greet them and ask them to introduce themselves, they began chittering amongst themselves and chasing one another frenetically up and down and all around the dilapidated jungle gym.

These were followed not long afterward by all eight of Ometa the opossum's latest brood, and while they were by nature and by their mother's example pretty high-spirited they were also far more disciplined by their no-nonsense mother than the squirrels, and they plopped themselves as a group before Terrance and introduced themselves, which was a relief to the young vulture. Lessie, who was not one to countenance disrespect, hollered up to the squirrels to calm down and get off the swing set and act like they had some sense, to which they responded by chittering crossly back at her. But after a few more seconds of defiant activity, they complained and settled into relative collectedness beside the eight opossums.

As all this was occurring, Olaf, the youngest of the buck deer Magnus's three offspring trotted over. Gracefully bending his delicate legs, he settled sphinxlike before Terrance with a pleasant, wide-eyed expression. Coiled loosely around his downy left antler was a slim pink earthworm, who introduced himself as Igly, one of the composter's innumerable inhabitants, who were of course all descended from Hertz.

"Wow!" exclaimed a gratified Terrance as he surveyed the group. "This is great! This is a good turnout, isn't it! I guess we better—" A shadow in the distance caught his eye, and, looking up, he was astonished to see, proceeding towards the playground on foot, the figures of his sister and brother—Tiffany and Todd! Never in a million lifetimes would he have expected Tiffany to join the Youth Ministry, and yet here she came, and seemingly of her own free will. He could not help but feel more than a little apprehensive. He hadn't counted on Tiffany.

There was nothing to do, however, but acknowledge her and Todd, and so he did, and his apprehension faded—a bit—when Tiffany settled herself beside the young deer with his accompanying worm, and stiffly returned the greeting of the group.

"So!" said Terrance. "Here we are!" He looked across the churchyard just to make sure there were no more latecomers, and spread his wings nervously. "I guess the first thing we ought to do..." he said, "is decide what we *want* to do! Does anyone have any ideas?"

There was a long silence. Terrance felt his entire scalp burn and he just knew he must be purple with self-consciousness. *You dummy,* he said to himself, *a leader is supposed to lead.* He tightened the grip of his talons on the splintery wood of the sandbox and asked himself what the reverend would do.

"Well..." he said. "Why don't we all get to know each other? Maybe we should introduce ourselves. Who'd like to start us off?"

There was nothing but silence, even from the squirrels. Terrance couldn't stop himself from looking across the playground to where his sister sat, regarding him with an unnervingly unwavering gaze.

"Well..." he said. "I guess I'll start. I guess you all already heard, back at the church, that my name is Terrance, and I'm a vulture, and my mom Donna has been a member of St. Aloysius Jr. for a while. I'm really happy that the Reverend asked me to start up a youth group. I think it'll be a great way for us to contribute to the mission of the church, and I look forward to working with all of you. I'm hoping that we can come up with some fun things to do and that we'll learn a lot about Jesus and God and the Bible, too. I guess that's really all there is about me.... Who'd like to go next?"

Silence. Terrance wanted to fly away. *Some leader*! a dismissive voice within him muttered, and as a hot flush of shame suffused his entire form, Terrance felt exactly as if he were back in the swamp, being a disappointment to his father once more. *Just pick someone!* he ordered himself, but he suddenly realized that he couldn't remember the name of any of the nonvulture creatures to save his life. Desperate, he looked over the group to where his siblings sat regarding him. "Tiffany?" he said.

"I'm not in this group," said Tiffany tartly. "I'm just here because my mother made me bring my little brother. I think this whole thing is stupid, and the church is stupid, too. It's just a bunch of stories and songs about humans. Who cares about humans anyway?"

Terrance's heart sank. And the hot flush that was turning his head and neck a vivid shade of burgundy deepened and filled his vision so that he was seeing red. Here he was, having been given a chance by the rector to make a difference, and his mean, bratty sister was going to ruin everything. *That's my girl!* he heard his father say.

"Humans *are* pretty scary," came the low, yet gentle voice of the young deer. "They just do whatever they want. They cut down all of the trees where we used to live, to put one of their roads through. My brother Hans can't stand them..."

"Neither can my great-great-great-great grandpa Hertz," said the worm around the deer's antler. "He says humans just make a mess and only care about themselves. He says its worms who keep the world going. We keep the soil alive, and without the soil, there wouldn't be anything."

"And they don't watch where they're going, in those big smelly boxes they move around in," chittered one of the squirrels. "They ran over my cousin Timmy!"

Terrance felt the skin of his scalp begin to cool slightly. He was sure his sister had not intended to facilitate a meaningful discussion, but that seemed to be what was occurring. He seized the opportunity to guide the discussion in a less negative direction. "I hear what you all are saying," he began, "but..." He searched his mind and came up empty, for, having lived most of his life so deep in the swamp, his experiences and observations of the human world were all too new.

It was Ometa's little Lessie, always outspoken, who managed to articulate Terrance's reluctance to condemn. "My mama says that deep down we're all the same. The humans just do what they think they have to do to keep themselves alive, and that's no different from anybody else. She says the only reason we all get along with each other is because of the rat reverend; she says before he come along it wasn't nothing strange about possums and squirrels and deer and worms and buzzards and whatnot just keeping to themselves. She says humans are more scared of us than we are of them."

A mutter coursed through the gathering, the spirit and tone of which was one of intermingled disbelief and intrigue.

"I think Miss Opossum is right," Terrance made bold to say. "I—"

"Name's Lessie," Lessie interrupted.

"Lessie. Thanks, Lessie. I think you and your mom are right. I think deep down we're all the same, and that we should give the humans a chance. I think that the first thing we should do... as a Youth Group... is reach out to them and ask them to join us. What do you all think?"

"Not me!" chittered one squirrel after another. "They're too big!"

"Count me out!" said Igly. "My great-great-great-grandpa would flip out!"

"I don't think that's a good idea," said Olaf. "My brother told me he used to peek into those houses they live in late at night, and some of the things he saw them doing..." His mournfully beautiful eyes shone with distress. "They can be terrible. At least, once they're full grown..."

"But that's it!" Terrance heard himself exclaim. "It's the grown ones who are causing problems, it sounds like! Maybe they're not so bad when they're young! Maybe all we need is to let them know we want to get to know them! We'll ask them to join our Youth Group!"

For Terrance, at that moment, the morning, already bright and sunny and relatively brisk, seemed to take on an additional glory, as if illuminated from heaven above. Of course! Here was something the youth could accomplish, that their elders, hardened and or intimidated by the passage of time into an intractable suspicion of the race of two-legged, cloth-enclosed, aloof fellow creatures. Even the reverend rat himself, as deeply spiritual as he was, avoided detection even by those humans like Grace and the legendary Reverend DeBassompierre whom he had come through observation to admire, and simply took it for granted that even the best of the humans could not handle the truth that they were not the only creatures made in the image of God.

*That can't be right,* Terrance realized. He recalled, from just the other day, his own observation of the young human mowing down the grass in front of the church, so young, so carefree, so possessed of an inexplicable inner serenity. He felt sure that a creature with such qualities would never willingly destroy habitats. Humans simply needed to know that they were loved. Then they would behave more thoughtfully.

And it was the mission of the St. Aloysius Jr. Church of ALL Creatures Great and Small to manifest that love.

"Friends..." Terrance said, in quite conscious imitation of the Rat Reverend Clancy, "I think it's time we wrapped up the meeting. The humans are about to leave the building... but I think this has been a great first meeting. I think it might be good to meet next time during the evening... when we'll have more time to... meet. How about... let's see... Thursday, about sundown? Right back here at the sandbox? Is everybody free?"

Again, a mutter, chitter, grunt, etc. of general assent.

"Great! I guess I'll see you all then. And if you happen to run into another young creature you'd like to bring along, feel free! Just like in the church, in our Youth Group, all are welcome!"

And with that, Terrance spread his wings and took off, feeling light as a spring breeze.

꧁꧂

BACK AT THE roost that evening after a supper of dead coyote scavenged by the ever-obliging Bertram, Tiffany, for the first time since leaving the swamp, initiated a conversation with her eldest brother. "You have really swallowed all this crap, haven't you?" she said. "You're as bad as Mother. All of this Jesus and God and church business. I would have expected it of Todd... He's too little to know any better. But you—" She made a retching sound.

"Tiffany..." Terrance did not know what to say. Certainly, he did not feel that he had figuratively swallowed anything, much less the figurative crap his sister was equating to the faith of the church, but he rather welcomed this opportunity to at least dialogue with his sister, who had been so hostile and distant. Now it seems she was being hostile and close, which was at least a beginning.

"Don't Tiffany me!" said Tiffany. "I don't want to hear it. I know what you think of me. You think I'm not being fair to Mother or Bertram or that gross "Prudie" or Sudie Mae or whatever her stupid name is. Well, I don't care. We don't belong here, and if you don't realize that, that's your problem. Maybe Father doesn't care about us anymore, but I don't know why that makes you think these crazy creatures around here do. They're just dumb, and I can't believe you can't see that."

"Don't you think I miss Father too?" Terrance felt, as he hoped his sister could not sense, the ambiguity, if not the sheer insincerity of that statement. But he wasn't about to say anything that could be used against him. "I just want to make the best of things. I don't think these creatures are dumb! Why do you? If Mother likes them, why shouldn't we?"

"Mother used to like Father." Tiffany's riposte was quick and sharp. "And now look at them. Mother may not be as bad as Father wanted us to think, but she's not perfect. No one is."

"I know that," said Bertram. "But you have to give everyone a chance. Otherwise, you'll be all alone. Why don't you go talk to Reverend Clancy about how you feel? He really is nice, and he doesn't mind listening."

"Well, I don't want to listen to any rat tell me what to think and what to do. Can't you see that he just wants everyone around here to listen to him and do what he says? I've never seen anyone so in love with himself!"

It did not escape Terrance—indeed it struck him like lightening from heaven—that his sister, in disparaging the reverend, could well have been describing their own estranged father. She seemed to have some inkling of this herself, for she flushed a deep burgundy, and spat. "You're a fool!" she said. "And don't think I'm coming to any damn youth group meeting. I'd rather drop dead."

"Then do it!" Terrance could not help himself from croaking as Tiffany leaped off the branch with a sudden spread of her wings. Of course, even as the words left his beak he regretted losing his temper. That's not what Reverend Clancy would have done, he reprimanded himself, and he resolved to apologize to Tiffany the first chance she gave him.

⚘

"Jesus Christ! What the hell is all that God-awful racket!" complained Hertz, poking himself out of one of the ventilation slots in the casing of his composter. "It's been going on since sundown! How is anybody around here supposed to get any sleep!"

Indeed, the noise issuing from the interior of the church

building was something to hear...voluble, dissonant, and extremely inorganic. It sounded, at least to Clancy's ears, like he imagined the pandemonium of hell to sound. But he knew, from overhearing the new reverend's conversation with Tommy, that it was supposed to be music. Tommy's 'post-hardcore emo experimental band,' The Vomiters, was practicing in the Sanctuary.

"I know it's kind of loud right now, Hertz, but I think it'll be over soon. It's just Tommy and some of his friends. They're practicing in the Sanctuary."

"Practicing what!" demanded the irate worm. "Torture?!"

"Now Hertz," said Clancy. "Don't be ugly. It's music. It's just not the kind of music we're used to hearing... but that's okay. Tommy and his friends are young, and they have different ways of expressing themselves."

"Well, they don't have to express themselves so loud," Hertz grumbled. "And so late. You'd think they'd have more consideration. But I forgot... they're humans. No one matters to them but themselves." And so saying, he withdrew back into the warm muck of his composter, before sticking his tip back out into the evening to deliver himself of one final observation that he knew would get the rodent's goat. "I just hope that bear doesn't go up there and tear them to pieces when they wake him up..."

"Oh! Lord!" Clancy cried, for he had not thought of that. Without another word, he jumped up and scrambled around the cornerstone of the church and squeezed himself through the gnawed-out gap in the crawlspace door down into the cellar, to be on paw to placate the sleeping giant should the cacophony from above indeed arouse him.

The worm and the rat having thus suddenly departed from the scene of the usual impromptu evening gathering at the composter, young Terrance found himself alone in the churchyard. He'd been debating with himself whether or not to discuss with the reverend his plan to offer membership in the Youth

Group to a young human, but now it was too late. He'd have to bring it up another time. The rat reverend had other fish to fry right now. For a few moments Terrance took this opportunity of unexpected solitude to contemplate the stars and meditate upon the beauty of nature, but indeed, what with all the noise coming from within the church building, it was kind of difficult to concentrate and attain a state of inner peace. He spread his wings and prepared to take off for the woods and home, but then, as if on cue, the music came to a stop. Terrance relaxed. Maybe the reverend would come back out now, and they could discuss outreach strategy.

And so he remained and waited, enjoying now the silence and the dusky landscape and the warm scent of compost. After a while he heard, at first faintly but becoming nearer, the rather reedy, sibilant sound of human voices, and he spread his wings once more. What in the world! From around the side of the church building opposite Clancy's crawlspace door, four young humans walked towards him and arranged themselves on the unsteady jungle gym in the playground! Terrance's beak fell open with astonishment. What an unexpected opportunity! How uncanny! If he had known just a bit more at that moment about monotheistic metaphysics, he might have considered it to be providential! For, leading the way and settling himself upon one of the swings of the jungle gym swing set was the young human whom he'd observed mowing the front lawn just a few afternoons ago. That would be Tommy! And, following close behind was a tall, thin to the point of being gangly young human with hair so pale and thin as to be invisible, a large, beaklike nose and skin mottled with severe acne. This unfortunate looking individual settled himself upon the swing beside Tommy and then, bringing up the rear, came a young human, short and stocky with a mop of thick brown curly hair, pushing before himself a contraption that looked like a chair with two large wheels at the rear and two smaller wheels at the fore. Perched within this rolling seat was a human whose most striking characteristic was the fact that his arms and legs were rudimentary, that is to say, the limbs were not developed in proportion to the rest of his body. The stocky fellow rolled him just to the left of the swing upon which Tommy sat, and then walked over to lean against the ladder to the monkey bars. There he reached into one of the front pockets of his trousers and brought out a small white cylinder, that looked rather like a stiffened worm. Then he brought out a translucent looking rectangle, pressed the top of it, and this produced a small flickering flame. He held the cylinder to his lips, with the flame at the other end, inhaled, and after a moment, released from his mouth a voluminous and pungent cloud of smoke, the smell of which, when it reached Terrance's nostrils, reminded him not a little of skunk. He then passed the little cylinder, with its tip now smoldering, to the tall, gangly, pimply fellow, who passed it to Tommy, who repeated the inhalation and the exhalation of cloud, and then held it to the lips of the fellow in the wheeled chair, who followed suit. Thrice this procedure repeated, and then the stocky fellow pinched out the smoldering tip with a grimace, and placed it back in his front pocket.

Terrance watched them, himself well concealed behind the composter and within the shadow of the church building. It seemed to him that the young men were partaking in some form of communion, for the passing of the smoldering little paper cylinder reminded him of the way that those animals in the St. Aloysius Jr. congregation who had prehensile forelimbs passed among themselves the plastic twist off bottlecap filled with consecrated water that served as the animal church's chalice. "Gosh!" he said to himself. "They sure are religious!"

"This is pretty good shit," said Tommy after some moments had passed. "I'm already baked as a biscuit." The simile seemed to strike him as highly amusing, as he then emitted a cascade of high-pitched giggles which shook him so that he had to clutch the chains of the swing with both hands to keep his balance.

"Got it from my mom's bf," said the stocky fellow. "He

always has a dime bag in the garage he thinks we don't know how to find." He blinked and nudged the tall, gangly fellow. "What's up, Luid? You going straight edge on us?"

"Taking a break," said the human named Luid. "I want to be clear when I sing."

"But we're done with practice," said the limbless fellow in the rolling chair.

Luid shrugged, communicating somehow a melancholy wisdom, which caused the young vulture to regard him with fresh curiosity. There was something about this gangly human, with his large nose, negligible hair, slim neck, receding chin, deep-set eyes and ravaged complexion that the young vulture found relatable.

Still peering at the young human gathering from behind the composter, camouflaged by the dark of night and the shadow of the building, Terrance listened as the rather motley crew of human musicians went on to discuss what they referred to as their band practice, and the logistics of what seemed to be a unique concatenation of differing abilities and sensibilities. The fellow in the wheeled chair, it became clear, was responsible for contributing keyboard instrumentation to the music, and on account of his disability composed his melodies mentally and dictated them into what he referred to as a software program. Apparently this method of instrumentation presented challenges relating to timing, and the sturdy fellow in the striped sweater, who apparently played the drums, was advocating for a slower tempo. While Terrance could make very little sense of much of what was being discussed, he found himself admiring of and wistful for the effortless camaraderie they shared, which seemed to encompass at once contention and cooperation. This, Terrance said to himself, was what the Youth Group ought to be... everyone working together because and in spite of significant differences and perspectives. The conversation went on for some time, with the fellow in the chair, whose name was Arthur, eventually agreeing to at least consider modifying his pace, when Terrance noted that Tommy seemed to be dozing even as he sat upright on the swing, and the fellow named Luid began to yawn. Additionally, the languid maritime evening air had gradually acquired a slight chill, and Terrance felt the featherless flesh of his head tingle.

*It's now or never,* Terrance heard a voice within his consciousness calmly but firmly proclaim. *We are all here together for a reason. If I don't say something now, I might not ever get another chance. I wish I could have talked with Reverend Clancy first... but I know he'll understand.*

Resolved, the bashful young vulture made the decisive step from behind the concealing safely of the composter and faced the humans just a few yards away. But they did not immediately register his unveiled presence. Never had he imagined that he would ever be a part of, much less initiate, a conversation as momentous and unprecedented as the one he was about to undertake. He felt as he imagined a flightless creature must feel if it found itself at the edge of a precipice. He could turn back, or he could take what was perhaps the greatest leap of faith in the history of the universe. Holding his head up high, Terrance stepped forward.

"Hi, guys."

His vocalization, which to his own ears sounded perfectly clear and comprehensible, went totally unheeded. He could not help but feel some degree of relief. He hadn't given any thought to his approach and the manner in which he might introduce himself. Perhaps "Hi, Guys" was too blasé. Then again, he didn't want to come across as too formal. He wanted to make a friendly first impression. That was paramount. He paused, still somewhat shrouded in the shadows of the night, and tried to come up with the perfect words with which to begin a conversation of such momentousness. However, nothing else came to mind. *I guess it's as good as anything,* Terrance reassured himself, and so the young vulture once again summoned up all of his courage and forward marched until he stood in the not insignificant illumination of a nearly full moon and a canopy of stars and presented himself to that gathering of young men.

It was Tommy who noticed him first, and his reaction was explosive. "Ack!" he screamed. Then, "Jesus Christ! What the hell is that!"

"Hi, guys…" Terrance said again, a bit less surely, and indeed it seemed that his words were swallowed up by the general alarm that his presence seemed to have caused. Tommy had drawn his legs up and was now standing upon the uneven swing and was wide-eyed and slack-jawed with what could only be terror. The face of the stocky fellow in the striped sweater was pale beneath his bushy brown hair and he seemed to brandish the wheelchair, and the equally terrified looking young man within it, like a shield. From each of these young humans vocalizations expressive of fear and perplexity and what could only be understood as disgust came rapid-fire so that Terrance could hardly discern who was saying what.

"Holy shit!"

"What the fuck!"

"It stinks!"

"Get away!"

"Gah!"

"Hi, guys…" Terrance tried again, summoning all of his hard-won courage. Maybe, he told himself, he should have let them know right off that he came in peace. He should have kept in mind how nervous humans could be. "I'm sorry if I startled you… I just wanted to come and say hi, and I was wondering if you all would be interested in getting involved with an inter-species Youth Group that we've started here at St. Aloysius Jr. Church of Urban Wildlife and All God's Creatures Great and Small. We're gonna meet right here in the church playground every Thursday evening, and we'd love to have you all join us, and any friends you might want to bring along. We think that if everyone could just come together and get to know each other, we wouldn't be scared and we could all work together to make the world a better place. What do you all think?"

It was as of his words, at once preconceived and inspired and to his own ears, at least, perfectly clear and reasonable signified nothing to the increasingly blanched and noncomprehending faces before him. The vulture's heart sank to his bowels. *They don't understand,* he admitted to himself. *They can only understand themselves.*

He shut his beak, and so as to signal non-aggression, took a step backwards in an attempt to at least reassure them that they had nothing to fear or dread from his presence. But it was as if he had advanced, judging from the effect his motion had; Tommy leaned back, still precariously perched on the swing like a caged bird. "Ack! Get Arthur inside!" he shouted to the stocky fellow who still brandished the fellow in the wheeled chair. "Quick! It's attacking!"

"Calm down." This rather incongruently mellow voice of reason emerged from the gangly young man with the ravaged skin. Terrance turned his attention to him, and saw with some relief, that he, at least, had remained in basically the same spot, position and attitude, leaning against the jungle gym ladder, his hands in the pockets of his shorts. "It's just a vulture. Vultures don't attack. They scavenge."

"That's right," said Terrance, hope rising in his feathered breast as his heart lifted from the turmoil of his bowels. "Thank you! I'm a vulture, and I'm nonviolent, and I can promise you that all of the members of our Youth Group and of our whole entire church have nothing but love for humans. Even if we don't always understand you."

"Luid!" screeched Tommy. "Get back! It's coming for you!"

The fellow named Luid rolled his pale blue eyes. "Jesus, Tommy, I *told* you... vultures don't attack. They scavenge. It probably..." Luid regarded Terrance with an expression of eager, if morbid resignation. "I think it just senses... corruption..."

And he cast his gaze meaningfully towards the cross atop the ornamental belfry of the church building.

Terrance's heart sank again. This one didn't understand him either. He just wasn't afraid.

The young vulture tried once again... though he knew it was futile.

"Well, I thought we could be friends," he said. "But I guess it's not going to happen." And, stepping back, he spread his wings and took off, leaving the young humans to their projections and their willful ignorance.

He was reminded of what the reverend had advised him regarding his sister Tiffany...that he should try to be patient, and wait for her to see the error of her ways. *Okay*, he said to the reverend within, but he couldn't help but wonder, as he flew home under the stars, why God couldn't make these lost souls face the fact that their attitude was ruining everything?